Tempt the PLAYBOY

NATASHA MADISON

Editor Emily Lawrence
Formatter CP Smith

To A.C. who changed my life with one word!

Tempt the PLAYBOY

CHAPTER ONE

Kaleigh

Beep. Beep. Beep. The sound coming from my sister's room makes me turn over and check the time. "Five-thirty," I groan into my pillow where I cuddle back into the heat of my cocoon. The first thing I did when I moved in with my sister was have blackout curtains installed. Oh, and a lock on the door. I like to sleep naked, so having my ten-year-old nephew and six-year-old niece walk in while I'm sleeping is not something we want repeated. I close my eyes, but it's only six more minutes till I hear the beep again. I pull the covers over my head and think about how my life has changed in the last six months.

I was a single girl enjoying her life. I was finally my own boss thanks to having my own yoga and Pilates studio. Something I'd worked my ass off for since I was eighteen years old. Fuck, I was pushing yoga when it wasn't even a popular thing. I still lived at home, which was how I could afford the down payment on the studio. Everything was smooth sailing, till I got that dreaded phone call from my sister, who was hysterically crying from her car.

Cheated on me. Those were the only words I could remember hearing, the only words that mattered. Her spineless weasel of a husband had cheated on her. And if that wasn't enough, he had banged their ten-year-old son, Gabe's, teacher and tutor. He obviously payed her for more than just her tutoring. So I grabbed everything of his that I could, brought it down the stairs, and tossed it on the front lawn.

Lauren pulled up to the curb right when I started walking to the back. I came from the side of the house with the gasoline container in my hand. I poured it all over his clothes, walked over to Lauren, and handed her the packet of matches.

"Let's burn this motherfucker down."

We sat there on the lawn watching it all burn, till one of the neighbors called the fire department, who rushed out, three full trucks, lights blaring in the night, an EMT, and one police cruiser. We watched the flames rising up from the pile of everything that he owned before the whole mess was drenched in water.

Needless to say when the scumbag showed up some time later, the fire department had just finished putting out the last of the fire. His clothes were now turned into ash. The only things that had survived were some of his golf clubs.

While he pulled his hair with his hands he started yelling, "This is the final straw. Lauren, she is not to go near my children."

I sat there on the stoop of the house they'd built a home in while my sister sat there next to me. Her eyes blinked and she looked far away.

"You slept with Carmen." Was the only thing Lauren finally said. "That was the final straw."

"Pencil dick." It just came out, and his head whipped to me. "You heard me." I raised myself from my sitting position. "She gave you two children, not one, dick weed, two." I pointed my finger at him. "Kept the fucking house clean while you went to wet your dick. Take a look around." I motioned with my hands. "You lost it. Buckle up, cowboy, we're coming for the farm."

His eyes pinched together, taking in my threat. "What does that even mean?" he asked, looking from me to Lauren.

She stood up, walking over to us to stand by my side.

"It means she's going after everything, dipwad. Now why don't you take that sorry excuse for a two pack and bounce." I looked over at Lauren. "I told you we should have gone to the gun range and learned how to shoot." I grabbed her hand, turned, and brought her inside the house.

Once the door was closed behind us, she sat on the couch. "He fucked someone else," she whispered silently. "Sex was max one minute most times."

I sat next to her, my arm going around her shoulder. "Oh, honey, that was the first sign you should have left his ass sooner."

Her head fell on my shoulder.

"I mean, his feet stink like cheese."

She nodded her head to agree.

"His penis is meh."

She kept nodding.

"He didn't even go down on you. In a year." I forced her to look at me. "He's not worth your tears. Okay, maybe a couple of tears because he did give you the best two kids on the planet, but other than that, when was the last time he was actually here?"

Her head tilted to the side as she tried to think.

"Exactly, he was here, but he wasn't here, and frankly you guys fucking deserve better."

"I do deserve better." Her voice came out in a whisper. "Where are the kids?" She looked around.

"Dad came to get them," I informed her. "They'll be back tomorrow. Because tonight"—I headed to the fridge and opened the freezer, taking out the bottle of Grey Goose she always put away—"we purge him from your system." I took a couple of shot glasses out of the cabinet. "Or at least till you pass out." I poured the first shot. "To assholes and the skanks who fuck 'em."

She grabbed the shot and downed it, then winced. "Burns." She slammed the glass down again as I poured another shot. "To women without stains on their shirts and their hair perfect."

I raised a brow in question but took the shot anyway and poured another one.

"To husbands who leave the toilet seat up and finally manscape for another woman."

"Oh, honey." I placed my glass on the table. "Did he actually have a bush?"

Tears welled up in her eyes. "That should have been my first clue, right?"

"It should have been the first clue to run for the hills, but who are we to judge." I picked up the glass. "To bigger dicks and manscaped pubes."

She clicked my shot glass and downed her third shot in a row.

"I think I'm going to be sick." She ran from the room. That was the beginning of let's destroy Jake. She dusted herself off all right, started doing yoga with me and spin classes. All her frustration was put into what I called revenge body.

A knock on the door makes my head pop up. "Auntie Kay, can you do a fishtail bwaid for me?" my niece, Rachel, says from the other side of the door. "Pwease. Momma is trying on dresses."

I roll out of bed and grab my robe before unlocking the door. I open it and she runs in and plops down on my king-size bed. It's a small room that fits just my bed and a dresser, but has a huge closet, so I'm okay. The bedding looks like I sleep on a cloud and that's because I sleep with two down comforters.

"So what type of braid do you want?" I ask her, sitting behind her on my bed.

"One like Awielle."

I continue to comb her hair, making her a short mermaid braid. "Okay, sweet pea, go get dressed before your mom yells again with a warning." I kiss the top of her head, watching her bounce out of the room. I dress after she closes the door, then head downstairs to get myself a coffee. Stopping at the door, I bring in the newspaper that was thrown on the doormat.

I'm sitting on a stool reading the paper while my sister runs around yelling out the time limits. Today is the first day at her new job. She's going back to work. She took a job as a temp, not what she was looking for, but it's better than nothing. I know she's a nervous wreck because she's been nonstop pacing without even realizing it.

I'm in my yoga pants trying to enjoy my second cup of coffee, my loose sweater falling off one shoulder. I'm not wearing a bra, because, well, frankly I'm not in the mood for it. My perfect size B cups are not going anywhere. "How do you remember this stuff?" I ask her while she starts putting the breakfast plates into the sink.

"It's magic. Once you become a parent, you'll get a brain," she tells me with a smirk.

"Then what happened to Jake?" I smile back while taking a sip of my now almost cold coffee.

"Okay, I take that back. Once you become *a mother*, you get a brain.

I mean, I don't think all men are dicks. Look at Dad," she tells me while she puts the milk back in the fridge and picks up the cereal box, putting it back into the cupboard. Her phone alarm sounds again. Another thing, my sister is OCD with being late. "Two minutes, guys!" She even has different alarm sounds.

"Aren't you going to be late?" she asks me while she grabs the lunch boxes and walks to the door with the kids.

I fold the paper in half. "Nope, I have a client at ten-thirty. We are doing yoga in the park today. Become one with the earth and all that." I finish it off with Namaste hands while she walks out with the kids to go to the bus stop.

I check my phone to see what else my day has in store for me. It's not like I can't afford to be in my own place; it's because this is where I belong for now. I take in the house and how it's changed since that fateful day eight months ago.

I snap back to the present when I hear the bus honk its horn. I walk to the living room where I move the coffee table to the side and start with my stretching moves. Lauren walks back in, admitting that she's nervous.

"You are going to go in there and kill it. And if you don't"—I shrug my shoulders—"then you don't. What's the worst that can happen? You fall face first in your boss's crotch?"

She glares at me, throwing her hands in the air.

"Don't forget, the kids are off the bus at two forty-five. Did you set an alarm?" she asks me.

"Yup, on my internal clock." I roll my eyes at her. "Stop stressing. It's going to be fine. You are going to be late if you don't leave now." I usher her out the door. "Don't forget to play nice and make friends. Friends who are nice and hot and have big dicks!" I scream after her as she gets into her car and closes the door.

Mrs. Flounder, the next door neighbor, gives me the thumbs-up, clearly in agreement with me.

I wave at her while she backs her car up, honking once when she drives forward.

"It's a beautiful day, isn't it?" Mrs. Flounder asks me from her side of the yard.

"It sure is." I nod, agreeing with her. "You know what would be better? Being chased by the hot UPS guy who keeps coming around. I bet you he has a huge package in that truck of his."

Mrs. Flounder throws her head back and laughs. "Honey, if I was a little bit younger I'd definitely find out what type of services he offers." She winks at me.

"That's what I'm talking about." I point at her. "I've got to get ready. Have a great day, Mrs. F." I wave at her, going back inside and getting ready for the day.

CHAPTER TWO

Noah

My feet pound the pavement as I finish off my ten-mile run. It's something I usually do in the mornings, that's if there isn't anyone in my bed. I usually burn off more calories than running. I get home just as my neighbor and best friend, Austin, is rushing out of his apartment building.

"Hey." I stop and jog in place to not cramp up.

"I'm fucking late. Why didn't you call me?" He checks his watch while he waits for his valet driver to get there with his Porsche.

I shake my head. "I just figured you'd be busy. Didn't you have a date last night?"

Austin and I have been best friends since we were in kindergarten. Our parents were both criminal lawyers, so we were always with our nannies. Of course, no one could top Austin's nanny, Barbara, while I kept getting different nannies every week. Until I was old enough to fire them myself and hire whoever I wanted. By the ripe old age of fifteen, I had gone through thirty nannies, and at that point, I was hiring them to teach me everything they knew about sex. And let's just say I was their prized student. That was until my parents found me fucking my last nanny bent over the pool table while she was wearing my mother's shoes. We still laugh about it today; well, at least he does. I usually just sit there and groan.

"Nah, I was swamped at the office. I got to go. My new temp starts today," he tells me, putting his Ray-Bans on.

"Dear God, how many is this now?" I ask him, knowing full well he must be on at least his tenth. "You need to chill out and just go with the flow."

"Look who's talking. You're on your twentieth of the year," he informs me, making me smile.

"Yes, but mine didn't leave because I was an asshole."

"You had sex with most of them and then didn't even blink an eye."

"Hey, no strings, it's my policy. I'm a lone wolf," I tell him, smiling. "Anyway, I have to go. The partners are having a meeting today. Something about a sexual harassment suit, and guess what, it wasn't even me. Boom, motherfucker." I make an explosion with my hands, running backward till I turn around and continue my run to my house. I live in a great neighborhood, an up and coming, chic, modern one, where all the houses are three stories high. I notice the house next to me just went on the market. I grab my phone and snap a picture and send it to Austin.

Would you be my neighbor? I press send, running up the stairs two at a time, entering my code into the lock.

He texts me back right away,

Yes, I need to get out of my place.

Then call the girl. If she's hot, I'll come with you to visit. Maybe she can come over, give me an estimate.

I just hit a bus.

Holy shit. Are you okay?

It's the last text that we have. I wait a second till I don't see the three dots with the bubbles. I whip off my shirt, which is drenched from my run. Thirty minutes later, I'm knotting the blue tie that goes with the blue custom Italian suit. Shrugging on the jacket, I run my hands through my hair, grabbing my phone and keys and heading out to my new Mercedes convertible, black with a deep red interior. I take off toward my law office. You see, I learned from my parents that criminal law is more work than I care to put in, so I'm a corporate lawyer. Nice, easy, simple, or at least most of it is.

I pull up to our law firm, Coco and Associates, sliding into my reserved parking spot. The law firm was started some forty years ago by the founder Leonard Coco. He started the firm with just himself. He did family law, but now we handle it all from family law to criminal law, to immigration law, to environmental law. I was lucky enough to sign on as partner last year. I make my way to our fortieth floor office. I walk past the new receptionist, who is young, blond, and looks really willing, just my type. I greet her with a side smile and a wink.

"Good morning, gorgeous." Her smile shows me that by Saturday her legs will be wrapped around my neck.

Walking to Harvey Rhinaldi's office, one of the partners, I smile at his secretary. "Good morning, Ruth, you are looking fine this morning." The office door is open, so I just walk in. "Harvey, you must have the best looking girl in the office." I face Ruth, then return my gaze to him while he picks up his cup of coffee. He has been the top family law attorney of the city.

"You know she's ninety, right?" He puts down his cup while I sit across from him.

I fix my tie. "She's not ninety, she's top seventy. Okay, maybe seventy-five, but—"

"You're insane. It's a good thing that we're good friends because one of these days, you're going to spread that seed of yours and I'll have to defend you in front of the judge by confirming that you're actually human."

"Hey." I point at him. "I like to shoot my seed, I just do it in plastic, or her mouth." I shrug. "And can we not curse me with this whole having a child, please?" The frame on his desk shows he's happily married with three point five kids. "Besides, it's my duty to make sure all women are taken care of. I think I took an oath somewhere."

"Oh, I know all about the oath. Trust me, but after a while it gets old. You'll see you'll meet that one girl and she's going to grab you by the fucking balls and never let go."

"I really fucking hope she grabs me by the balls daily. Fuck that, in the morning and the night." I wink at him. "Anyway, I have Luca starting today. I'm fucking excited. He graduated top of his class from Harvard Law. He's going to be a great addition to my team."

"We have that sexual harassment conference that's mandatory right after lunch." He eyes me.

"Oh, is it going to be given by Hannah?" I ask him. "I would so bang her. She's so hot."

"You know she's head of Human Resources, right? That she has you flagged as the biggest liability of this firm. You know that she hired your latest PA and the first thing on her list was male."

"I don't know why I was the only one singled out." I check my phone that has buzzed in my inside pocket.

"You fucked your last twenty secretaries. Sometimes at work." He points out to me, leaning back in his chair. "And a couple of the interns, some data processors, and let's not forget a mother or two."

The text that comes in is from Austin.

I'm going to need a stiff drink after work.

"Now," I say, putting the phone back in my pocket, "if you can excuse me, I have a merger or two to get to." I get up, looking down at his caseload. "And you have people to divorce and alimony to screw people over with." Another reason why I'll never get married. This whole 'I love you forever, or till someone else comes along and then guess what, I want half of everything' isn't that appealing to me. Not now, not ever.

I round the corner to my office, stopping at my assistant's desk. It was once the home of Cassandra, who stood six one and had legs up to her armpits, as well as the perfect size C implants I've ever seen. I mean, let's not forget she had no idea what she was doing unless it was under my desk. Fuck, could she maneuver her mouth like the best prosecutor in town. Now there sits a guy old enough to be Ruth's husband with glasses as thick as Coke bottles. "Morning, Alfred," I say, gathering up my messages.

"Sir, my name is Aaron. I've told you numerous times."

I smile at him. "And I told you I'm batman and you're my confidant." I wink at him, going into my office and trying to read his chicken scratch. I pick up the phone, calling Hannah, who answers after two rings. "Hannah darling." I smile.

"Noah King, to what do I owe the pleasure?" It comes out almost harsher than it should.

"We need to talk about my assistant and the fact that he can't write nor can he use a computer." I flip through my messages again. "I mean, I think one message said to call Dr. Chen."

"Noah, we've gone over this. You can't have any women. The last one was the final straw and you know it."

"Okay, fine, but can I have a man who can at least surf the web and type with both hands?" I stare out through my window at Alfred as he puts his face almost into the computer.

"Fine, but I expect you at the seminar we set up this afternoon." It's the last thing she says before she hangs up on me.

I open my own computer and go through all my emails as well as some mergers that we need to get fixed up.

At noon, I find myself getting off the elevator at Austin's company. I turn the corner, getting an eyeful of the nicest ass I've seen. Well, today, that is. "Holy mother of God," I say loudly.

The woman goes to straighten herself up but knocks her head on the desk. The bang echoes in the vast office space.

"Oh my God, are you okay?" I rush behind her as I try to help her up. "I'm so sorry. I didn't mean to scare you."

I'm holding her hand while her other hand is rubbing the back of her head. "It's okay. You startled me," she starts to say and then looks at me.

"What the hell is going on here?" The roar comes from behind her.

She pushes away from me and looks over at Austin. He stands there with his hands on his hips, the vein in his neck twitching.

"It's my fault, Austin," I tell him, while I drop her hand. "I came in and was surprised to see her. I startled her, and she knocked her head under the desk. I was just helping her up," I tell him as I walk around the desk, right up to Austin, where I slap him on the shoulder. "I was wondering if you wanted to get lunch."

I look at Austin, who hasn't taken his eyes off this woman. "No, I'm eating in. I have to go over the Grey Stone Park file. Lauren, can you get me lunch? Go to the deli at the corner; we have an account there. Just tell them it's for me. They know what I like."

She puts her hand on her hip, glaring at him.

"Please," Austin hisses out.

"Fine." She grabs her bag and walks out.

We both watch Lauren walk away, her ass swinging from side to side with each step. Austin is so intent on watching her, he doesn't even notice when I push him aside and walk into his office.

I throw myself on the couch he has in his office, while he opens the shades to see out into the office space.

"Jesus Christ, who was that sex kitten in heels? I nearly had a heart attack when I walked up to find her bending over," I ask him, looking in the direction of her desk.

"My new stay-away-from-her assistant," he grumbles as he sits down on the other side of the couch.

I throw my head back and laugh. "Oh, what happened to the 'don't fuck where you eat, Noah' speech that you always give me?" When we were in college he would never ever fuck anyone he was in the same class with, never slept with a girl who was in his work-study. He stayed away from anyone in his circle. Which was great for me, because I took them all.

"She's crazy," he says. "I hit her car this morning, and then she shows up in the office. I thought she was fucking stalking me."

That just pushes me over the edge, and I can't stop laughing, crouching to the side. "You hit her car and then thought she was following you? Holy shit. Were you an asshole to her?" I ask this question because he can be an asshole of sorts.

He smirks at me. "She named me Asshat in her phone." That set us both off.

"You know you're fucked, right?" I finally stop laughing and throw my hand over the back of the couch. "When you saw me touch her, I thought you would charge at me like one of those bulls running toward the red sheet."

"She's nothing more than a crazy chick with a tight ass. Who will get me coffee daily."

"Oh, really?" Her voice cuts through the air. My eyes go from Austin to Lauren, who stands there with a couple of bags, and my man looks like he's catching flies. "Well, then, I'm happy I could assist you in your day," she snorts, coming in and dumping the bags on the table in front of us. "I also got something for your friend," she huffs and then walks away. This time slamming the door on her way out.

"Oh fuck, you are in so much fucking trouble. Dude, she is going to fucking string you up by the balls. Remember that chick you played in college? The one you promised to bring home during spring break? She turned around and cancelled all your tickets. Then she put that ad all over Craigslist. 'Lonely man searching another lonely man,'" I remind him.

"She was fucking crazy! I had to change my number four times.

Four! Then I had to start wearing beanies so she wouldn't recognize me." He shakes his head, while I laugh so hard I fall over. He looks over at me. "It was fucking May! I had to take three showers a day. I had no idea the head could sweat so much."

I finally stop laughing and look in the bags that Lauren just dumped on the table in front of us. "If I were you, I'd enjoy this. It's probably going to be the last meal she hasn't had the time to spit in."

We spend the next thirty minutes eating our lunch while shooting the shit about everything else.

"Are you going out this weekend with Deborah?" I ask him.

"Not sure what my weekend plans are. What do you have planned?"

I take out my phone, scrolling down the list of names. "Andrea, that is who I plan to do. I met her at Starbucks yesterday. She has the longest legs I've ever seen. I plan to have them wrapped around my neck, and not in a wrestling move, either." I raise my eyebrows. "If you know what I mean."

I get up, putting the garbage in the bag. "This has been a hoot, but sadly, I must run."

I get up and walk out, going straight to Lauren's desk. She is busy typing something, so she only turns her head. "Thank you so much for lunch, Lauren. You were a lifesaver." I walk away, leaving her with a wink. Just to piss him off even more.

By the time I get to my office the sexual harassment bullshit is underway. I slide in the back and sit next to Harvey. "Did I miss much?" I ask him.

"They just showed a picture of you and what to stay away from."

I smile at the PowerPoint Cassandra is going over. Listening to what she's saying.

"If at any time, anyone corners you and makes you feel uncomfortable"—she looks around at the people in the room—"whether by touching or with sexual innuendo, it's your right to come and say something."

I lean over, keeping my voice low. "If you corner someone and what you say and do is making her uncomfortable, you aren't doing it right." I can't continue because Cassandra calls my name.

"Is there anything you'd like to add to that, Mr. King?"

"I'm just wondering if we're going to have a dress code restriction.

I wouldn't want to offend anyone if I"—I shrug my shoulders—"wear my kilt one day and it isn't long enough."

"You're Scottish?" one of the interns asks.

I smirk at her, almost tempted to ask her if she wants to see under my kilt, but Cassandra interrupts again.

"If at any time you have a complaint about what someone else is wearing, please send me an email with the description of the outfit in question."

"Or lack thereof," I interrupt.

Some interns roll their eyes while the other half try to catch my eye.

The rest of the seminar or conference or whatever the fuck you want to call it goes by with me laughing at all the 'situations' she talks about. They're mostly stuff I've done. Don't get me wrong. I'm not one to throw myself at a woman, or make her uncomfortable. But if I connect with her and she connects with my cock, who am I to say no to that.

By the time I get home and unwind, I fall asleep to SportsCenter.

CHAPTER THREE

Kaleigh

I finished doing outside yoga by eleven forty-five. If my client wasn't so sweaty and hairy, I might have been tempted to do the plow pose with him, but I just can't handle back hair.

So instead I stopped by Starbucks to get myself a soy Frappuccino as I made my way to my yoga studio. Opening the glass door, the seashell wind charm zings. There's a reception desk as soon as you walk in to the right. On the walk in block letters form the word Namaste. When you walk around the corner you enter what we call the 'chill out room', painted all white. White and tan cloth chairs align one wall while there's a low canvas brown couch against the other wall. In the middle is a low white wooden table with ivory candles. To the left of the room are the men's and women's locker rooms. Straight ahead is the door that leads to the 'Zen room'.

The room is darker than the chill room. The walls are painted a dark chocolate brown. A square black box hangs suspended in the middle of the room. White chiffon curtains hang and are tied together all the way around. In the center is a round dim light and crystal beads are hanging to the floor. Around the room are six love seats, all with big plush cushions you can lie on, tiny tree lights scattered all over the room. In the middle is a rug set out for stretching if needed. The music coming out of the room is gentle charms, with flutes in the background. Just the sound makes the stress leave your shoulders. I check to see if there are people in there. During the day, there are many people who pop in to just sit down and block out the everyday hustle we all live in. It's also a no phone zone. I know it's a shocking concept, but it's the way I roll.

When I close the door and walk past the locker rooms, I check into the yoga studio that's on the other side. I open the door to see Stephanie is in the middle of her hot yoga session. The room is huge, with one wall being floor-to-ceiling windows overlooking the garden I have outside. The natural light coming in bounces off the wall that has the mirror all across it. There are about twenty people in this class. Hot yoga is a vigorous form of yoga performed in a studio that's heated to one hundred and five degrees and has a humidity of forty percent. The formal name for hot yoga is "Bikram yoga." It's the biggest craze right now. People usually just dress in sports bras and shorts. Anything else would be too much. On one wall hangs a picture that says, "You are one yoga class away from a good mood." While on the wall where the door is hangs "Yoga Every Day."

I know she's at the end of her class since they're doing the stretching part. I close the door, going back to the reception desk where Kathy is now sitting.

"Hey, girl," she greets me with a smile.

"Hi there, sunshine. Can you add Mr. Bison to the same time next week?"

She takes care of everything that needs scheduling in here and also does the Pilates class we host on the weekends.

"You have a private group session starting in twenty minutes with three moms. Then I have to cancel the Pilates class on Saturday. My parents are coming in and I can't get out of it."

I look at the clothing rack we've set up, organizing it by color. "Don't cancel it. I can do it." I smile over at her. "I'll bring Rachel in. She loves walking around shouting at people to just breathe."

"Oh, that's even better." She continues posting about things on our Facebook page and putting a silly picture of me on the Instagram page. I run out of the studio at two-thirty, making it home at the same time as the bus pulls up.

Rachel is the first one to bounce off the bus. "You almost forgot us." She skips over, her big backpack over her head. Her arms barely make it around my waist. My hand cups her head while I lean down to kiss her.

"I was waiting for you in the car." I pretend.

"Sure, Aunt Kay." Gabe, my nephew, comes up the driveway bouncing his soccer ball. "I saw you swerve in right before the bus stopped."

"Hush it, kid, or I'll make you eat tofu raw." I dare him while he makes a grimace with his face. I'm a full-fledged Vegan. The kids, however, are not, and let's not even start with Lauren.

"Why don't we go in and wash our hands, grab a snack, and go do some poses in the backyard?" I lean down, picking up Rachel. "Whatcha say, Rachie, want to learn downward dog?"

She throws her hands up in the air. "Yes, I want to do the dog."

I laugh at the same time that Gabe does. "Don't say that out loud."

We go inside where I make them wash their hands and cut up some apples and cheese. I tried to pass them the vegan cheese, but they caught on and made me cut the normal cheddar one.

"I think I'm going to try a new recipe for dinner tonight to surprise your mom." I turn to the fridge where I spot the three bottles of wine I bought yesterday, and it's a good thing I got a text from her today saying that she needed it. "So what do you guys think about cauliflower?" I turn, nodding my head. "Yum, right."

Rachel holds her nose. "Yucky."

I pull up my phone, taking out a recipe. "Go start your homework and when I finish we'll go outside."

They both push away from the counter, going to the kitchen table where they take out their stuff.

I take out the cauliflower, wash it, and cut it in little pieces, mixing some spices together and drizzling them with oil. I wash my hands and set the oven. "Okay, rugrats, we have thirty-five minutes before I have to take it out. Let's go outside and soak up the sun."

"I want to do the dog, please." Rachel runs to me with her yoga mat.

"Let's go do downward dog, okay?" I walk outside, closing the door behind us.

Gabe runs out with his soccer ball, throwing it on the grass and practicing with it.

"Okay, Rachel, let's start." I go through about five or six exercises, then we lie on the grass together while we watch the clouds float by, trying to decide what they look like.

"I'm going to get water," Gabe says as he opens the door. "Auntie Kay, there's something smoking," he says with panic.

"Shit, the cauliflower." I get up and run inside. The smell of char hits me right away. "Oh my God, oh my God." I grab the oven mitt, opening the oven.

"Mom's here," Gabe says, running to the front door.

She walks in the door just as the smoke detector goes off. "Oh, dear Christ, Kay, what the hell are you doing?" She grabs a broom out of the closet and positions herself beneath the smoke detector, using the broom to fan the smoke away. "Jesus, Jesus, Jesus," she chants while looking over at the kitchen in time to see me pulling a tray of charred, smoking cauliflower out of the oven.

"Oh my God, oh my God, oh my God! I'm so sorry! We went outside to do some kid yoga, and I totally forgot." I try explaining while I walk with the pan to the sink, turning on the water and soaking the smoking remains of what was once cauliflower. The sizzling sound of water hitting a hot metal pan fills the quiet room, along with a burnt, smelly, steamy smoke that has the potential to set off the now silent smoke detector again.

"Oh, Auntie Kay, what are we going to eat now?" Rachel asks. She would have been the only one of us to attempt to eat one of my creations.

I slap my hands together. "Oh! I have some tofu we can cut up and—" Before I can even finish that sentence, Gabe and Lauren both yell a combined firm yet panicky, "No!" I glare at both of them.

"Okay, I'm going to change. Gabe, start your homework. Rachel, go start studying your spelling words. You"—Lauren points at me—"clean up this mess. I'll find something to throw together for pasta."

I groan. "I don't have any gluten-free pasta here." I walk up to the fridge while Lauren goes upstairs to change out of her 'work clothes.' When she comes back downstairs I am putting things in the dishwasher. "Oh, good news," I inform her. "I found some rice, so I'll throw whatever sauce you make on there. Yumm-O."

She shakes her head, laughing at me as she starts prepping the veggies to go into whatever she is making. I go to the table where I study words with Rachel.

"Kay, set the table," she calls out to me.

I walk over to see that she has done some pasta primavera and it looks delish, but I see the container of Parmesan cheese next to her. "I can't eat that. You put cheese in it," I complain to her.

"It's okay," she whispers to me. "I won't turn you into the vegan police. We'll pretend it never happened." She serves up some pasta onto plates for the kids.

I open the freezer, squealing when I find a frozen meal. "Score. Look! Tofu ravioli! Saved!" I do a little dance on my way over to the microwave, raising my hands in the air and shaking my ass as I pop it in. "Oh yeah, oh yeah, oh yeah!" I continue dancing till the microwave beeps.

I pull it out, peeling off the filmy plastic cover, and wave it under Lauren's nose. "Smells so good, right?"

She nods, but I know she is totally lying. Throughout the meal, the kids tell her about their day. Rachel tells me that today someone threw up in class because someone else farted. Apparently, this is hilarious to her, since she is in stitches about it as she retells the story.

As soon as everyone finishes eating I round up all the dirty dishes looking at my sister, seeing her tired eyes. "I'll clean up. You go give the kid a bath and do homework."

I rinse and put all the dishes in the dishwasher while I clean up the kitchen and it almost looks like I didn't burn anything today. Well, almost. The smell is still lingering. When I see Lauren go upstairs I take out a couple of candles, lighting them around the room, then dim the lights and put on some light jazz music.

When Lauren comes back downstairs, a full glass of a crisp, perfectly chilled white wine is waiting for her. "Aww, if you weren't my sister—and I were into chicks—I'd make you my woman." She grabs her glass and curls up on the couch with her feet under her.

"So, tell me about this boss of yours?" I prompt her as I sip my own wine.

"Oh, where do I start?" She closes her eyes. It's like she is in a trance.

"Good-looking?" I ask, curious as to what has my sister going tick-tock like a bomb.

She nods her head and finishes off her glass of wine in one long gulp. She picks up the bottle, pulling the cork out with a pop, and pours herself another glass. "Too good-looking."

"Fit or chunky?" I ask. I usually start off with little questions till we tackle the big things like penis size, full package size, does he hang left or right? Can you see it or is it flat?

"Fit," she answers, thinking, then taking another gulp till it's half drained. "Very fit." She looks around before leaning into me and whispering, "I think he has a six pack." I try to not laugh out loud while she drains the rest of her glass.

"Hair color? Eye color?" I fill up her glass again. To most people it's just wine, to my sister it's like a truth serum.

"Brown and hazel-green with gold specks." She drinks a little more.

"Facial hair? Would you get a burn from his beard or not?"

She looks up and blushes a bit. I don't say anything. Instead, I hide my smile with my wine glass. "Depends on the time of the day. He was clean-shaven this morning, but he had a good five o'clock shadow going by three o'clock." Her head falls back on the couch, while she closes her eyes like she is thinking of him.

Sitting up straight, I look at her and finally see something I haven't seen since pencil dick fucked her over. "You like him?"

Her eyes snap open as she turns to me, denying it, but I know that look. "No! No, I don't. Absolutely not. I don't like him at all."

She giggles as she takes another sip. "He hit my freaking car, Kay, and then the asshat asked me if I was drunk." She tries to plead her case. "Drunk at *fucking* eight a.m."

It's that final sentence that I know she thinks of him more than she cares to admit, even to herself. "He's gotten under your skin! There hasn't been anyone who's pushed you this far. Well, there was Pacey from Dawson's Creek…" We all know how that turned out. She called the television station and tried to have the show cancelled and banned. We won't even mention the petition she tried to start on Facebook.

"Hey!" She points at me. "Joey went sailing with him all summer! Just because Dawson is there and crying, she thinks she should be with Pacey. He was always her choice." She now pours herself another glass, spilling it.

"Do you think he manscapes?" I ask while I put my glass down on the table.

"I have no idea, but I would guess it's probably manscaped. I mean, who doesn't manscape these days?" She looks over and wonders.

I am not here nor there. It's a choice really. Just because I like to be well groomed doesn't mean everyone feels the same. "Some like to be free and let things be natural; there is nothing wrong with that. Don't judge. Well, unless you have to suck his dick, then by all means, you put your foot down. You don't need to be choking on long pubic hair. In fact, if you think it isn't, then just run. Run fast, like he's waving a bomb in front of you." I use my hands to mimic an explosion.

"Shoes?"

"Nice. Black ones." She looks at me, my eyes opening wide. "And clean. Very nice." Her pet peeve when your shoes are scuffed. She won't even mow the fucking lawn in scuffed shoes.

"Teeth? Straight? Crooked? White? Stained? Stinky breath?"

"I don't know." She looks confused.

"Big hands?"

"Oh yeah, so big." She opens her hands wide to make me see how big, but she shakes them a bit. "This big." She motions with her hands, making big circles. So from what I got he has hands just like the toy green hulk hands that Gabe has.

"You think he has a big dick?"

She stops moving. "He would have to. You can't be that good-looking and have a small penis. Actually, maybe that's why he's such an asshole! His penis is small. He has small penis syndrome." She looks at me, waiting for my input. "I mean, why else would he be smoking hot and an asshole, unless"—she giggles—"unless it's so big it hurts when he walks." She puts her hand over her mouth and laughs out loud, as if she is keeping the biggest secret ever. "I can't sleep with him. He's my boss and besides, he doesn't even like me."

She rises from the couch, picking up her glass of wine and spilling whatever was left in it on the floor. "I need a dog, so if I spill something, he can lick it up."

I watch her and silently laugh at her. Having a dog that drools and pees all over the floor would send her into the mental ward.

"You think we can get a dog and train him to bite my boss?"

"Yes, I think you just need to bring a picture and a sweater with you to training school so they can use his scent. They'll train the dog to attack your boss as soon as he gets close." I nod my head, agreeing with her.

Her mouth forms an O. "Oooh, we need to look into that." The next thing I know she is walking toward the stairs, going upstairs, while I follow her. She stumbles over the last step and falls on the bed face first.

She opens her eyes, blinking at me, the tears forming at her lower lid. "You think he doesn't like me because I'm old? Or ugly? Or is it because I'm fat?"

I lean over and stroke her cheek. "You are not old. You are the opposite of ugly, and you are definitely not fat. He acts like he doesn't like you because he probably likes you too much. Remember Ricky in the third grade who chased you with a frog because he loved you? This is just the adult version." I make a mental note to find this fucker and slice his tires. If he fucks with her, that is.

"No way would he go for someone like me. He did say I had a tight ass, though. That means he was looking at it, right?"

I tuck a strand of hair behind her ear. "He was definitely checking you out." She closes her eyes while I continue talking, "Why wouldn't he check you out? You're hot, smart, and you have a tight body and a great smile. Your whole face lights up when you smile. You don't do that enough. Now if it makes you feel better, I think tomorrow we will make beef vegan soup, minus the beef obviously, but I wonder what we can use to make it brown. I should Google that." I don't say another word because her snoring fills the room. I stare at her, hoping that her boss just relaxes before she goes crazy.

CHAPTER FOUR

Kaleigh

I didn't pray hard enough because for the next two weeks it was downhill, with her slipping him Dulcolax and him giving her a porn virus on her computer. She went fucking nuts on that one. No matter how many breathing techniques we tried to center her. But the more she thought about him, the more the vein in her neck started to tick. Till she did the unthinkable. She put itching powder in his pants, as a joke, of course. How was she supposed to know he would end up in the hospital? It was all too much for me, so finally on Saturday night I left her and went to let my hair loose. I had way too much fun, so much fun I snuck out at eight while he lay face down. His surfer lanky body was exactly that.

I unlock the door, hoping to sneak in so they don't see me in last night's outfit, but there she is in the middle of the kitchen enjoying a nice hot cup of java.

"Oh, the walk of shame. Nice. Very nice."

I sit at the counter, hoping she takes pity on me, but of course she's an evil bitch ever since she started with her boss.

"What's a walk of shame?" Rachel asks, and she looks over at me with her eyes as big as saucers.

"It's when you are still wearing last night's clothes," I disclose to her and then I whisper to Lauren, "After they were on the floor of the hot guy whose cock you rode all night." And then I throw my fist, pumping.

Lauren smacks my arm and picks up Rachel. "You get to wear the pretty dress today. Are you excited?" she asks while I rub the sting away from my arm.

"So excited! We get to go get our hair fixed?" She throws up her hands, mimicking me.

I smile at Lauren, mouthing to her, "She's going to be just like me."

Lauren glares at me, probably adding me to her list of enemies. "Now when are people expected for the anniversary party?" I ask as the doorbell rings, and she lets in the caterers. We go upstairs to get dressed so we can leave the caterers to do their thing while we get pampered. I jump in the shower quickly and make it out just in time to slide on a summer tube dress. Closing my bedroom door behind me, I come face to face with Lauren.

"I hate you. How can you shower and be dressed in five minutes and still look like it took you an hour to get ready?"

"Good genes. Wait till you see my outfit for later." I wink at her, bouncing down the stairs to the front door.

Even Gabe comes along for the fun that is all things hair and makeup. Well, not fun for him, but he pretends. Once we get home, we all rush upstairs to change with only twenty minutes to spare.

I hurry into my room and pull out my pink sundress that I bought for this occasion. I pull out the same color bra. My mother should be happy. It's tight on top and flares up a bit at the waist, with pleats to my knees. It's chiffon so every time I walk it swooshes around my knees. I pull out my cream heel shoes that tie around the ankle, going down to a T at the toes. I look out just as I see something in the backyard that shouldn't be there. "Is that a penis balloon? "Umm, Lauren? I think you should see this," I yell at the same time the doorbell rings. I walk to the back door and take in the scene before me. "Jesus." I don't have time to say anything before the door opens and my parents walk in followed by their friends and Lauren finally comes down the stairs. I try to signal her with my hand, but she is too busy being a good hostess. I grab a glass of champagne that is set up on the counter, downing it in one gulp and grabbing another glass right away. The caterer is smiling at me. "Not now."

"Happy Anniversary, Mom and Dad." Lauren greets them with a hug.

"Thank you, dear," my mom says, hugging her in return.

"Please, everyone, come in. I had the backyard set up for our brunch." She points the way to the backyard.

"I think you need to see outside before everyone else does," I say with my teeth clenched, which confuses Lauren because she tilts her head to the side.

"What are you talking about?" she asks me and then the doorbell rings again. Lauren answers it before I do. Big mistake, because the person on the other side of the door makes Lauren catch flies by opening and closing her mouth. Standing there is a guy holding a huge chocolate bouquet.

She gasps in shock when she sees that all of the chocolates are made of penises and the pail holding them is adorned with a huge pink bow. "I have a delivery for Lauren," he announces, looking at the clipboard in his hand.

"I…" she stutters while he pushes the pail into her hands. "I didn't order these." I look down and see that there are both white chocolate and milk chocolate ones, all on white sticks. She shakes her head, while he walks to his truck that is parked in the driveway and comes back with two more pails. "I don't want this," she finally says to him, but he's just a delivery guy, so he just smiles and leaves.

"Oh my God," I say from beside her. "Don't freak out." I look at her, seeing that she is starting to sweat, and her hands are starting to shake. Plus, I can hear her heart beating.

"Why would I freak out?" she asks right when my mother yells from outside. I try to stop her from walking in the back, but she

walks past the caterers, who are still preparing.

When she opens the door to the backyard, her eyes survey the scene as her mouth hangs open at what she sees.

She looks at the white tables she ordered that are all set up with the turquoise tablecloths that were also requested. The little glass vases are holding the white flowers in them just like she ordered in the center of each table. Except there are also bouquets of balloons—all white and turquoise, each one stamped with a penis.

Now, as if that isn't bad enough, there are also approximately fifty two-foot tall pink, penis-shaped helium balloons. The penis has a smile on the head and a blue bow around the shaft. They are all floating around the yard.

"Oh my God, oh my God!" she cries, looking over to see that there are penis straws in all the glasses. The table in the corner that she had set up for the cake is now filled with cupcakes with little penis cake toppers.

"Dear, what is this?" my mother asks her with a forced smile on her face.

My father is holding a glass of scotch, which he is sipping, mind you, through a penis straw.

"I didn't order this. They made a mistake." She looks around, making sure everyone hears her.

One of the servers walks by with the chocolate penises. Of course, my mother grabs one before she even realizes what it is.

"Grammy, why are you eating a chocolate willy?" Rachel asks. "Look, Momma! It's just like Gabe's willy!" She grabs a balloon and runs over with it.

I look over at the guests, who are all snickering at this point. "Surprise!" I yell, trying to diffuse whatever fuck up this is. I also make a note to warn whoever did this, because it looks like I'll be digging a grave tonight. "You guys are in for a treat!"

Mom's best friend, Sarah, comes up to me. "I love it. It's very liberating. And fun." She giggles as she takes a sip of her drink through her own penis straw.

Lauren looks like she is about to have an epic meltdown, and we didn't even serve the meal yet. We hear a knock on the side gate and in walk, or should I say saunter, two men I have never seen before in my life.

They both look like they just stepped off the pages of a GQ Magazine. One is dressed in blue jeans and a linen button-down shirt rolled up at the sleeves. His silver Rolex is on his wrist, and his gold aviator glasses are on his face. A dusting of two days' worth of stubble gives him an edge.

"Oh, I'm sorry. I don't mean to crash your party," he says with a megawatt smile on his face.

The other guy who walked in with him has blond hair, long on top, but seems like he just brushed it back with his hands, so it falls on his forehead a bit. His blue eyes are the color of light blue with a darker blue around. A little scuff is on his chin, but nothing big. He's dressed in a white button-down shirt that is covered by a navy sweater, the cuffs and tail of the white shirt sneaking out. He has one of those beaded bracelets on one hand and his own black Rolex. His jeans are darker blue color jeans. One of the knees is torn. Tight-fitting, with the cuffs rolled up. White shoes finish off his look. My eyes automatically go to his package, and what a package it is. Nice and full, rounded. You know his dick has to be huge. Either that or he's stuffing that shit. The way he stands with his head high, shoulders square, it has to be all him. I don't know who he is, but he is checking out all the penises, his eyes bulging out of his head. He turns and looks at the other guy and covers his mouth with his hand. It is in this moment that I know my sister has been played.

"You." She points at the bearded one.

He walks up to Lauren, turning his smile at Mom. "You must be Lauren's sister," he says, kissing her hand.

She smiles and throws her head back and laughs.

"Oh, you silly boy. I'm Deidra, Lauren's mother. You can call me Dede," she invites while she smiles at him.

"You can call her nothing, because you're leaving. Now. And"—she turns to him—"how did you know where I live?"

"Lauren, stop being rude to the guests," my mother scolds while my father walks over and introduces himself.

"Hello, son, I'm Frank, Lauren's father."

"No," she says, shaking her head furiously. "He isn't a guest. This is my former boss." She looks at him, while my mouth now hangs open. "I quit. Done. Finished. Finito. I'm out," she snaps with her hands on her hips.

Fuck, this isn't good.

"Who is the other one?" I finally ask with a chin lift in the other guy's direction. I smirk at him while the guy gives me a sly smile. That's right, buddy, this is going to happen.

"That's Noah," she answers. "Gabe, can you go inside and get my car keys? Mr. Mackenzie is coming to get his dry cleaning."

I watch as Gabe runs inside to get the keys.

"Mom, can I have a willy chocolate?" Rachel tugs at her skirt while she asks me the question.

"No, you cannot have a willy chocolate. We are going to eat in a minute." She turns and storms inside.

"This is not good for anyone. You must be Asshat." I point to him. "You've poked the bear now." I don't say anything else since he turns and follows Lauren inside. I turn to Noah. "So, how you doing?" I say in my best Joey Tribbiani voice.

His voice comes out smooth. "It's looking up now. I'm really hoping it's going to look up more tonight." He winks at me, and my knees go weak, and I really wish I didn't wear that bra.

When I start to drag my eyes up and down, taking him all in while I lick my lips like a Cheshire cat, I hear Rachel yelling, "Daddy, look, a willy."

"Fuck, this just got interesting. The ex is here," I say, staring at the gate where Jake just walked in and is kissing Rachel's head.

CHAPTER FIVE

Noah

I wave goodbye to the blonde standing at her door wearing her pink kimono and nothing else as I am pulling away from the curb. I turn on the music, but it's not on long before I see a call coming in from Austin.

"Go for Ho," I say to him.

"Where are you at eight a.m. on a Sunday?" he asks me.

"That you even ask this makes me question how well you know me."

"Fuck off. You can go a Saturday without having sex and your dick won't fall off. You know this, right?"

Is he serious with this question?

"I don't even know who you are right now. I think the problem is that you haven't used your dick since Lauren fucked your balls up."

"My balls became the fucking size of watermelons. That shit was not funny."

I burst out laughing. "Dude, they were not pretty. I thought they'd explode and you'd have just your testicles left on the floor."

"You better have deleted those fucking pictures that I saw you take."

"Delete them? Fuck, it's my screen saver at work and on my phone. I might get a T-shirt made with that image."

"You're an asshole."

I smirk at his insult.

"I've been called much, much worse," I inform him. I mean, just last week I was called a cocksucker, which is totally not true, because I will not be sucking any cock at any time. *Ever.*

"Anyway, brunch, pick me up at noon," he demands.

"You live next door now. Can't you walk over?" He moved in within two weeks of seeing the house. It was so fast and came almost furnished, so he was in within a day.

"Fine, I'll walk over at noon. Be ready."

"Later, princess." I disconnect the call as soon as I arrive home, pulling my car into the garage. At noon he knocks on the door, opening it, and coming in before I have a chance to make it downstairs.

"Let's go. We'll take my car," he yells from downstairs.

I run my hand through my still damp hair before walking downstairs.

"You're so antsy today." I look at him as he bounces on the heels of his feet. I follow him out, getting inside and leaning my head back, closing my eyes.

When we show up in front of a house, that is when Austin fills me in.

"Where the fuck are we? I thought you said we were going to brunch." I look over at all the white picket fence houses.

"Yeah, pit stop first. I have to pick up my dry cleaning at Lauren's," he tells me, getting out of the car.

Once we make our way around her house, I ask him, "Why are we at her house?"

"She's having a brunch." He shrugs. "I may have sent her some penis decorations," he says to me before walking to the fence at the side of the house.

The first thing I see are all the balloons. Fuck, my hand goes to my mouth. "Holy shit, she is going to cut your dick off with dental floss," I say before he knocks on the gate and walks into the backyard.

Austin stops in his tracks, mid-step. I almost run into him when I see that it isn't just a small brunch, but there are about fifteen or so people scattered around the yard.

"Holy shit," I whisper, looking at Lauren. "Dude, I think she's going to cry."

Austin's eyes snap straight to Lauren.

But I'm not looking at Lauren anymore. In my eyesight is the blonde standing next to her. She's a knockout. Actually, that isn't even a good enough word for her. She is breathtaking. Her blond hair moves a bit with the wind. Her blue eyes are almost like the Caribbean ocean that you want to plunge into. I can't stop looking at her. I don't even hear what Lauren and Austin are talking about. Instead, I watch the woman, who finally looks over at me. I'm about to say something to her when I hear something about a chocolate willy.

"No, you cannot have a willy chocolate. We are going to eat in a minute." She turns and storms inside.

"This is not good for anyone. You must be Asshat." She points to him. "You've poked the bear now."

I don't say anything else since he turns and follows Lauren inside.

The blonde turns to me. "So, how you doing?" she says in her best Joey Tribbiani voice.

That she is trying to use the best line to ever be said I smirk thinking I might have found my soul mate. Okay, maybe my sex mate, for the night. "It's looking up now. I'm really hoping it's going to look up more tonight." I wink at her and smile.

When she starts to drag her eyes up and down my body while she licks her lips like I'm her next meal, my cock suddenly starts to stir, wanting out.

I hear Rachel yelling, "Daddy, look, a willy."

"Fuck, this just got interesting. The ex is here," she says, looking at the gate where a man just walked in and is kissing Rachel's head. "I better go save Austin and warn Lauren." She walks away.

I watch her ass sway from side to side. I look down at my hands. Yup, definitely a good fit. I run after her as she closes the back door.

She's about to knock on the door when we hear Lauren's voice go high.

"Didn't you get your revenge already? You penis-bombed my parents' anniversary party!"

I move behind the blonde and notice that her head goes up to my lips. My hands go directly to her hips. Her head turns to the side. "I want to hear what they are saying."

She just smiles at me and I'm feeling my hard cock against her back.

"Should I bend over so you can put your ear to the door?"

Fuck me, I think I just jazzed in my pants.

I pull her even closer to me. "You bend over and there will be one more penis added to this party." I'm about to lean forward and kiss her when I hear Austin finally yell back.

"You made my balls swell to the size of fucking grapefruits. I thought they were going to explode."

I laugh at that.

"They were fucking huge. I have the pictures to show. Lauren was a pain in his balls, that's for sure."

She leans into the front of my chest.

"I did no such thing." She tries to deny weakly. "But this, this... You pushed it too far."

"How about we call a truce?" Austin tries to plead. "I don't think I can take any more. I almost died, and my testicles almost exploded."

"Fine," she complies.

"Truce." I hear whispered.

"You think they're fucking in there?" We both lean into the door to hear.

"My sister wouldn't fuck with a party in her house."

"That's a shame. Is this a family trait?" I try goading her to see what line she will pass.

"I have no problem having sex with people around." She winks at me. "I mean, if he was really, really worth it."

This woman will be the death of me, or I might faint from all my blood going straight to my cock. Which is as hard as a marble statue.

She lifts her hand to knock on the door. "Hey, I don't mean to interrupt, but, um, Jake is here."

The door unlocks, swinging open with Lauren standing there with a pink tint to her cheeks and Austin has his hand rubbing his neck.

"What do you mean, Jake is here? Why is Jake here?" she asks with her voice rising with each question.

"Hi"—the woman pushes Lauren aside—"I'm Kaleigh, her favorite sister," she introduces herself.

"She's my *only* sister, and she will be homeless in a second if she doesn't get out of my way." Lauren's voice is angry.

I chuckle behind her. Lauren turns and points at me. "You, if I find out you helped him, it's going to be on," she hisses and leans in closer to me when she continues, "like Donkey Kong." And then she walks away.

"What the fuck does she mean, like Donkey Kong?" I turn to Kaleigh, looking for an answer.

"Oh, I was on that list only once"—she leans in closer to me—"and I begged and cried to get off of it." She looks at Austin then back at me. "It was like living in that movie *The Shining*, but worse."

I feel my face pale at that little tidbit of information.

I point at Austin. "If I get it like Donkey Kong, I'm going to put the pictures of your swollen, abnormally large testicles on a billboard in Times Square," I threaten him, while Kaleigh just watches us.

"Who the fuck is Jake?" Austin finally asks.

"Her ex. This should be fun," Kaleigh claims, walking away from us.

"You took a picture of my nuts?" he asks when Lauren storms out.

I shake my head at him. "No, I took a burst of shots of your nuts." Then I walk out, following Kaleigh. My dick leads the way to her. He hasn't even met her yet he's already on radar for her.

"What are you doing here?" I hear Lauren ask a guy who must be Jake.

While I take in the scene, I turn my head, catching one of the waiters passing around some canapés. I also grab champagne from another tray.

"What the fuck are you doing?" I hear Austin hiss at my side while he watches Lauren and her ex.

"I'm eating and drinking," I say, showing him my full hands. "I mean, this is a party. You did bring me to a party." I finish off the food. "You should try those mushroom things. They are really good," I say, finishing off the champagne and signaling the waiter for more. I grab another glass. "Did the ex leave?" I ask Austin as I drain my second glass.

"Yeah, he came to get the kids and forgot it was the party. Guy looks like a douche," Austin says.

Kaleigh informs Lauren that we are sitting at their table.

"They aren't staying," Lauren says before she turns around, heading inside.

"Oh, come now, Lauren. That would be rude," Dede chides. "You can sit at our table." She turns to Frank. "Let's go sit down, honey."

Once everyone is seated, I look around our table. It's Kaleigh, Frank, Dede, Lauren, Austin, and Josh, who I found out is a doctor and bears a striking resemblance to Newman from *Seinfeld*.

He sits next to Lauren, standing up when she gets to the table and pushing her chair in. She looks over at him and smiles. I watch all this take place and then see the tic in Austin's neck start to throb.

He grabs his glass of wine and downs it in one gulp. "Slow down there, slugger. We don't want you flying off on one of those penis balloons," I whisper in his ear while he glares at me.

"So," Josh starts, looking at Lauren. "I hear congratulations are in order. You're back in the work force now." He continues in that annoyingly nasal voice of his, "How does this weekend sound?" He blushes and looks down at his hands. What a putz.

"Oh, um, she can't do it this weekend," Kaleigh answers for Lauren. "She's having her bikini area waxed and styled," she explains, nodding her head.

"What?" He looks confused.

"Well"—Kaleigh leans in and whispers—"it's like the Amazon down there."

I spit water from my mouth, almost fucking choking while their mother puts her hand to her mouth and Lauren throws her fork down on the plate, the clatter hushing the whispers at our table.

"Kaleigh," she grates out, her jaw ticking.

"What?" she asks. "Was it a secret?" She shrugs. "So sorry." She brings her glass of wine to her mouth in an attempt to hide her smirk.

My eyes shoot to each of them like I'm watching a tennis match.

"Dear," Lauren's mother questions, "are you okay? Is this procedure normal?" She gives her daughter a look filled with concern.

"Mom—" Lauren starts before she is cut off by her father.

"Lauren, it's been a while since Jake left. Maybe if you"—he gestures with his hand in a circle and his finger sliding in and out—"you won't be so stressed."

She slams her hands on the table, the glasses clinking and rocking with the force of it. "I'm not having any hair removal procedures done, because it is not necessary. Can we please just—" This time, she is cut off by her mother.

"So, you've had sex since Jake?" Dede asks her, a smile on her face. "This is so good to hear." She claps her hands together then leans over and puts her hand on Lauren's. "I thought you had that glow about you."

"I'm going to the bathroom," Lauren excuses herself as she gets up and points to Kaleigh. "You"—she growls—"come with me."

"Oh," Kaleigh replies, completely unperturbed, "I'm good. I don't need to go. I'll just wait here. Keep the guests entertained."

"Not a word. Or else Donkey Kong," she promises before she storms off.

"So," Dede starts, turning to Austin. "How long have you two been dating?" She looks at him and then at the door Lauren just walked through.

Kaleigh laughs. "Oh, they aren't dating, Mom. He's her boss," she helpfully points out. "He sent all these penis balloons."

Frank looks over at Austin. "You sent all these balloons and ruined all her hard work?" he asks.

"Um, sir, if I could just explain." Before Austin can say anything else, Frank puts up his hand to stop him.

"I like you," he declares right before someone clinks their glass and the speeches start.

I put my hand around Kaleigh's chair while my thumb rubs her exposed shoulder. I lean in to whisper in her ear, "So since we are talking about bikini waxes and everything, will I need a machete?"

She puts her shoulder into my arm, fitting there perfectly. "No machete needed. You see, I have a very well-manicured lawn." She raises her eyebrows at me.

"We should have a picnic. I heard eating well-manicured lawns can fill up a person."

Her cheeks pinked.

"I've never eaten manicured lawn before, but I have eaten some pretty good sausages." She bites my ear, making me almost groan, but then Austin kicks my chair to get my attention.

My eyebrows shoot up when Austin says urgently, "Gotta go," then glances over at Lauren, who is coming straight for us like a bull and Austin is the one waving the red cape. "Now would be good."

He throws his napkin on the plate in front of him. "This has been fun," he murmurs, trying to escape.

"Running off so early, guys?" she sing-songs as she comes up behind us. The way she says it, even my balls are inverted.

"We intruded," Austin says. "Thank you for having us. Dede, Frank, I wish you many more years of happiness." We rush out on a wave, out the side gate.

"Run," Austin says the minute the gate closes behind us, and he doesn't have to tell me twice.

"What the fuck just happened? I didn't even get Kaleigh's number," I whine, getting in the car, not even buckling in before he races away.

"I may have had male strippers show up," he says, looking into his side-view mirror.

I turn my head, seeing about twelve men all getting into a big bus of sorts. "Yup, you've done pissed off the fucking Donkey Kong. She's going to rain down on you. I suggest you run, move, and don't look back." I buckle myself in. "Oh, and don't tell me where you're going because I'll fucking tell her." I grab my cock in my hands. "She's not getting next to my pride and joy."

"She'll be fine."

I laugh at him. "You think?" I shake my head. "You have no idea."

CHAPTER SIX

Kaleigh

I don't know what is going on, but one second I'm talking about eating sausages on my manicured lawn and the next Lauren is storming across the lawn and Austin and Noah are running away.

I get up. "What did I miss?" I look back and forth from the gate where it just slammed and to my sister.

"The entire cast of *Thunder From Down Under* just arrived." She looks around to see if the guests are okay.

I get up, raising my skirt a little bit to show off more leg. "Where? Are they inside? Shit, do I look okay?" I fluff my hair.

"Kaleigh," she whisper-hisses, "they aren't here anymore. I sent them away."

I groan and slam one hand on the table. "Why? Why would you do that?" I get up and run to the side gate to see if they're still in the driveway. "Buzz kill," I call her as I pick up Rachel. "Can you protect me from Mommy?" I whisper in her ear before blowing kisses in her neck while Lauren sits down and starts her meal of wine.

The rest of the afternoon goes by without any further penis-related incidents. All cupcakes have been consumed, minus the penis cake toppers that Lauren removed before serving them.

Once everyone has left, Lauren plops down into her chair and throws her feet up on the one Austin sat in. "That was fun, right?" I ask, grabbing a strawberry.

"You told people I had a strange excessive hair issue on my hoo-ha that required a complicated bikini wax and styling." She glares at me.

"I was trying to get Josh to imagine that you're a woman with a hairy bush so he doesn't ask you out again!" I drink from the wine glass I'm holding in my hand. "You're welcome." I smirk.

"What the hell are we going to do with all those penis balloons?"

She looks around. "Asshole," she grumbles under her breath.

"What's the story with Noah?" I try to ask casually, thinking back to the conversation we had. I would have let him plow my lawn.

"No idea. He's Austin's best friend from what I gathered," she tells me while looking at Rachel, who is running in circles with, unfortunately, a penis balloon in her hand. "Ten minutes to bath time!" she calls out, hoping she acknowledges her, but she just continues her one-girl—with a penis balloon—parade.

"Mom," we hear Gabe call from behind us. "Can I go to Jesse's house to kick the ball around?"

She checks her watch before answering. "Only for thirty minutes, okay?"

"So, what are you going to do to Austin for all of this?" I ask, pointing to the balloons.

"Nothing." She smirks. "We called a truce."

I sit up and put my glass down. "I know that smirk. I've been on the receiving end of that smirk!"

"I mean, we called truce today, right? We didn't call truce on Wednesday when he made me run back out for a fucking crisp kosher pickle, because the one that came with his sandwich was limp, right?" she asks me with a perplexed smile on her face. It's almost like you're looking into evil.

"What did you do now? From the pictures, his balls were almost the size of Gabe's soccer ball." I think back on Noah's phone that he took out when he got a text from someone. His lock screen was of swollen balls.

She slaps the table. "You saw pictures?" Her mouth is hanging open.

I nod. "I did. Not the actual frank, though, just the beans. But they were ginormous." I motion with my hands, forming them into huge round objects in the air. "Now, what did you do?"

"Nothing that will make any part of him swell. I will never, ever do something like that again." She shakes her head. "I may have shredded one of his parking tickets that had to be paid by yesterday so he could avoid his car getting booted," she confesses quietly, looking into the glass she picked up from the table.

"Holy shit. I hope you kept the photocopies, because you can't not pay that. He is going to know it was you," I warn her.

"I know, I know. I kept them, so just relax." She puts her hands on her hips and states defensively, "I'm going to pay them."

"When?" I ask her again, earning an eye roll from her.

"Next week," she replies. "Rach, bath time." She walks to the back door. "Don't you dare sit there and judge me, missy." She points at me. "By the way, the potatoes had butter in them. That's for the bikini wax," she says before she turns her back to me and walks inside with the sound of her curses filling my ears.

"Are you fucking insane? I'm vegan. That's fucking wrong." I shake my head, picking up a penis straw and throwing it at her, where it nose dives on the table.

I sit down, finishing the rest of my wine while the cleanup crew comes and starts taking down everything.

"Excuse me, ma'am," one of the men calls me. "Where do you want all the balloons?" he asks me.

I smile at him.

"In my sister's car." I point to the gate door. "The minibus in the front, just pile them in there." He smiles at me and nods, the balloons following him as he walks to the car, shoving most of them in there.

"Take that, Donkey Kong Bitch." I smile into the wine glass, finishing off the last drop.

I walk inside, closing the door, then walk upstairs right as Lauren comes out of the bathroom. "Are the guys still cleaning up?"

"Yeah, they are almost done." I smile at her, walking to my room and closing the door. I turn on one soft light in the room, undressing, tossing my dress into the basket. My phone buzzes and I pick it up as I lie on the bed and see I missed out on quite a bit.

There are messages from the studio about a change in the times. Then there is another one from an unknown number.

Hey, I hope I have the right person. Do you have a manicured

lawn?

I throw my head back, laughing at the message.

It depends on who is asking. How did you get my number?

I jump onto Facebook while I wait to see if he'll answer right away.

It's called stalking 101. I went on Lauren's Facebook, went to her friends list, found you. Clicked your page, and on your about section I saw your studio name. Clicked the studio and then boom, I got my prize.

I shake my head.

Wow, you put a lot of thought into this process. Well, I should make it worthwhile. I take a picture of my bare legs.

Holy shit, are we exchanging pictures already? This is fantastic news.

The picture is of him lying down, wearing a pair of basketball shorts, on the bed. The elastic rides very low, showing you he's a landscaper also. His chest perfect, his abs defined. He's not a muscle man, but it's the side abs that get me. Cut and lean. That is the best way I can describe him.

Thanks for that. It made it into my spank bank.

I got a lot more where that came from, but I don't give it away on the first night. Have dinner with me?

When?

Tomorrow.

I shrug my shoulders, thinking what the worse that can happen is.

Sure, where?

My place, your place, the fucking park. I don't care as long as you're sitting in front of me.

I giggle.

That's a good one. How about I meet you at your place say 6 p.m.

Perfect. What's your favorite thing to eat?

I smirk at myself while I answer him.

Cock. Lots and lots of cock. See you tomorrow, Noah. Send me your address.

974 Sherville Rd. Oh and that answer made this happen.

The picture that comes through is his shorts, hiding a very erect cock.

See you tomorrow, beautiful.

I turn on my side, watching the stars twinkle outside. Closing off my light, the lights from outside stream in. I yawn and slowly close my eyes and drift off to sleep, dreaming of blue oceans and eyes that make me get lost.

My night dreams are of the beach, chasing the waves, running, doing cartwheels in the sand. Sitting in the middle of the sand, taking in the beauty of the sun going down. My alarm wakes me with charm bells. Slowly at first, soft, going higher and higher till it's like a siren.

"Aunt Kay." I hear Rachel outside my door. "Mom said to get your bony hind downstairs and get the willy balloons out of the car."

I turn over, laughing while I throw the covers off, grabbing my robe and going to the door. I open the door and Rachel is still standing there. "You're in big trouble, missy."

She leans in, whispering as I pick her up, bringing her close to me, "She used her mom inside voice."

I lean back, my eyes going wide. "Oh, dear."

"Yes," she says, nodding, "she talks like this." She imitates Lauren talking with her teeth clenched.

"Oh, well, I better go get dressed and bring my behind downstairs." I kiss her neck. "Go brush your teeth while I get dressed." I put her down, watching her run into her bathroom.

I walk to my drawer, taking out my pink yoga capris with the matching bra. I head downstairs while Lauren gives the ten-minute warning.

I smile as I step into the kitchen. "Good morning, sunshine." I stop at the coffee machine.

"Did you put the penis balloons in my car?" She turns to ask me, stuffing papers into Rachel's backpack.

I bring the cup of coffee to my lips. "No." I shake my head, hiding my smile while I take a sip. "I didn't put them in your car." I'm not lying either. I myself didn't put them in her car.

"My whole car is filled with penis balloons."

I put the cup down as Lauren yells bus up the stairs. Rachel comes hopping into the room, grabbing her backpack, with Gabe right behind her. He grabs his bag from Lauren, kisses her cheek, then comes over to me and does the same.

"Have a kick-ass day," I tell him.

"I'm going to kick ass today," Rachel says, walking out the door.

"Watch your mouth," Lauren says and follows them outside to the bus.

I pick up my cup and watch them walk to the bus stop. The bus arrives right on time. I wave goodbye to them as Lauren returns.

"You okay to work today?" I ask her, knowing that somehow things between Austin and her aren't quite what they seem to be.

"I'm more than okay. I'll be fine now that we have all"—she waves her hand in the air—"that animosity out of the way."

I laugh at her. "Is that what you're calling it?" I hold the cup with both hands, taking another gulp.

She glares at me, opening her car door, one helium penis balloon floating up into the sky. We both watch the balloon float off. She opens the back door and the rest slowly float out. "Let them go, Lauren," I say loudly as Mrs. Flounder comes outside, her hair still in curlers, with a scarf around her head. "It's raining penises, Mrs. Flounder. They are raining down on us."

I raise my hand to the sky. She claps her hands together. "I would like to be rained down on." She winks at Lauren. "For a whole five minutes. That would be my dream."

I raise my cup to her. "Here's hoping."

"I don't have time for this," Lauren says, closing the back door, then climbing into the front seat. "Don't forget the kids."

"Aye aye, captain," I say, saluting her. "I have a date tonight." I wiggle my eyebrows. "A date I hope to become the pretzel."

She laughs as she pulls out of the driveway.

By the time I make it to the studio doing my routine and making it back home where I get the kids ready and settled, I have just enough time to throw on a dark blue summer dress. I pick up my purse from the bed, tossing the bra and panties that I am happily going without.

CHAPTER SEVEN

Noah

Sitting at my desk, the files are open all over it. I tap the desk when I hear the sound of Austin's ringtone.

"Yeah," I say after finding it under a file that's now littered all over the floor. "Shit."

"What the fuck was that text you sent me?" he asks, making me wonder what he's talking about.

I take the phone from my ear, turning the speaker on while I go through my text messages. There it is, the text I sent this morning.

What should I cook for someone who eats cock?

I laugh at the vagueness of it. "I think the question is pretty spot-on. I have a date tonight. When I asked her what she likes to eat she said cock. Obviously I've got enough cock to feed her, but should I put out an appetizer before the cock dish?" I smile, putting my feet on my desk.

"Where do you find these girls?" he asks, sighing loudly.

"Wouldn't you like to know, Swollen Nuts?" I laugh at him. "So what do you think I should put out? Should it be something that could be eaten off my dick?" I tap my chin with my finger, thinking.

"Like what, a fucking sushi roll? Buy the wrap and wrap your dick. You know other people actually have bigger problems."

"Oh, shit, did Lauren fuck you up like Donkey Kong?" I sit up, wondering how much more he can take before he snaps.

"No, we called a truce. It's all good," he whispers now. "So seriously, where do you meet these girls?"

"It's for me to know and you to find out. So whipped cream? Chocolate? What do you think?"

"I have to go," he says, hanging up the phone.

I toss it back on my desk and pick up the papers that have fallen on the floor. When I finally have them in order I get up, walking to my assistant's desk.

"Alfred, can you order me a platter of fruit, with chocolate and whipped cream? I'll swing by and pick them up at six." I watch him write it on the paper, his hand shaking. "Oh, and you can have tomorrow off. I'm in court all day." I walk toward HR where I knock on Cassandra's door before walking in.

"Hey, I'm not interrupting you, am I?" I ask her, pretending I care. I don't. I sit down in the chair in front of her desk.

"What can I do for you, Noah?" she asks, leaning forward on her desk.

"I need a new assistant," I say while she rolls her eyes. "I'm serious, Cassie, he just took a message I think Mickey Mouse called, because I can't read it. It looks like chicken feet."

She leans back, picks up the stack of papers in front of her, and taps it on the desk. "Noah, we have gone over this. You can't be trusted with female assistants. You slept with the last four out of five."

I laugh at her. "Actually, it was five out of five, but who is counting? And I didn't sleep with them here."

Her eyebrows shoot up.

"Okay, fine, I didn't sleep with them all here, while we were working, she was punched out."

"Noah, it was noon. And her husband came to have lunch with her."

I shake my head, thinking about it. "It wasn't my fault he showed up unannounced and she told me they were separated. She cried on my shoulder. What was I supposed to do?" I ask her. I make it a rule to not fuck with anyone who's married. I honestly thought she was getting divorced. She told me for a month that she was feeling down about the separation. "She lied to me and broke my trust also." I put my hand to my heart. "Now how am I to trust anyone else who tells me they're getting divorced? Should I ask for the filed papers? Should I look them up while in the bathroom?"

"This is serious, Noah. She could have come back and sued you. If you want, I can give you Norma. Leonard is going on vacation for a month. You can have her."

I throw my head back and blow out a huge breath. "Okay, fine, but can we start looking for a replacement? Someone who can take notes fast and be on the balls."

Her eyes go big.

"I meant ball. Sorry, on the ball."

"One more chance, Noah. After this I will no longer take your call or even answer your emails. Now go."

I slap my hands together in celebration.

"Don't make me regret it!"

She eyes me up and down as I get up.

"See, I didn't even try to check out the color of the bra you're wearing today. How is that for turning a new leaf?" I smile at her like a kid in kindergarten who just found out how to color inside the line. "See"—I point to myself—"I can do this." I salute her walking out the door, closing it behind me.

The next thing I do is go online. It's amazing how much shit comes out when you type what to eat with a side of dick. Some of those pictures have permanently scarred me.

By the time five-thirty rolls up, I close everything down for the night. Walking out, I ask Alfred, "What name is the fruit under?"

He peers up from his newspaper; I shake my head, thinking do they still print newspapers? "Name for what fruit?" His bushy eyebrows fold together.

"The fruit I asked you to order me for tonight?"

He shakes his head, taking off his glasses. "I must have forgotten to order them." He goes to pick up the phone, then looks up at me. "What did you want again?"

My jaw seals shut. "Nothing, absolutely nothing. I'm going to go now." I nod down to him. "Have a great night."

I walk away while he tells me the same. Dialing Austin, he answers after one ring.

"What do you want? Did you get your dick stuck in seaweed?" He laughs by himself.

"Very funny." I unlock the car, getting in. "Is Lauren still at the office?" I ask, starting the car while he is transferred to Bluetooth.

"Why the fuck would you ask me that?" he hisses out. "Is she the one you are feeding your dick to tonight?" The vein in his head must be ready to pop. "I swear to fucking Christ, you touch her and I'll cut off your fucking dick. I will make sure they won't even be able to attach it. I swear to fuck," he continues.

"Are you foaming at the mouth yet?" I ask him, smiling to myself. "You think I'd sleep with someone I know has you tied up in knots? I mean, honestly, how many times have you rubbed one off with Lauren's face?" I pull into a supermarket, hoping they have fucking platters and shit.

"I just don't want you to fuck my assistant and then she quits on me." He blows out a relieved breath. "And to answer your other question, what about Becca Sullivan, seventh grade? You knew I was going to ask her out, and I found you guys making out in the closet."

"That was a mistake." I stop the car. "I didn't actually think she'd suck my dick if I guessed her favorite number. Which, by the way, who chooses one as their favorite number?"

"Fuck you," he says. "What did you call for?"

"Where can I get fruit already cut up? With chocolate and whipped cream?"

"Edible Arrangements have those basket thingies that you can buy and they look like flowers and stuff."

I hit the steering wheel. "You're a genius. I gotta go find the closest one to me," I say, hanging up. I press the button for Siri to come on. Once she gives me the closest address, I make it there right before they are about to close.

Walking in, I head to the counter.

"Hello, how may I help you?" the woman who is named Tracy asks me.

"I'm looking for cut up fruit." I start out, checking out the different arrangements. "Like that one." I point to the biggest bouquet they have, with pineapple, cantaloupe, melon dew and most of all chocolate covered strawberries. "I'm going to take three like that, and do you have just chocolate covered strawberries in one basket?"

"You want three baskets?" she asks me, writing down the order.

"And we have boxes of the strawberries in the fridge over there." She points to the fridge behind me. "Your total will be five hundred and seventy three."

"For fruit?" I ask. "It's fruit."

"Yes, but it's cut up into a beautiful flower and shapes." She smiles at me, shaking her head.

"What if I just want it cut up, is that cheaper?" I ask, smiling at her.

"Sir, if price is an issue, perhaps you would like to downsize and get a more affordable basket."

I grab my wallet out of my jacket pocket. "That's fine," I say, pulling out my card. "How long will it take?"

"It should be ready in fifteen minutes," she says, going back into what I'm sure is the fruit dungeon.

I pull my phone out, seeing a text from Kaleigh.

We still on for tonight?

I smile as I answer her back.

You want me to serve my favorite dish, damn straight we are still on for tonight.

Perfect, she answers right away.

I should be home in about thirty minutes, so why don't you come by in an hour? Oh, and come with an appetite.

Oh, I plan on it. I'm famished.

My cock springs up to a semi attention, thinking about her lips on me.

"Here you go, sir," Tracy says, coming out with a bouquet that is so big I can't see her face.

"Holy shit," I say, taking it in. "Did you put all three in one?" I ask, grabbing it from her while she laughs.

"No. The other two are coming right up." She turns to go into the back. "Would you like to come back in and get the other two?" She points to the door.

I walk out, putting the basket in the back of the car, but it doesn't fit on the floor.

"No wonder it cost the price of a small island. I took all their fruit," I say as I set it on the backseat, placing the seat belt around it. The thought of me having to brake suddenly and then the fruit flying everywhere is much more than I care to clean up. By the time I pull out of the parking lot, I have three baskets all buckled up in the back. "Thank fuck I didn't buy a two-seater," I say to myself while I make my way home. It takes four trips to get everything into the house. "Fuck, the bag." I smack my head, thinking about the bag of chocolate sauce and whipped cream I picked up on the way home.

I walk into the living room. It's a total bachelor pad. The walls are painted white, with the big brown leather couches dressing up the room. A huge screen television is hanging on the wall right above the fireplace that I had installed after I bought the place. I place it on the table in the living room. "This looks like a place to serve dick, right?" I talk to the walls. I move the couches away from each other. I slap my hand and run to the closet in my office, grabbing a big black bag. "I knew there was a reason I bought this," I tell myself. Walking back into the living room, I make space in front of the fireplace where I take out a white fur rug. "Oh, yeah, I'd serve cock on this thing," I say, walking into the kitchen to the cupboard where I have the sex candles stored.

I'm a guy. I don't need candles in my house, at any time. So I take them out when I'm having sex. I have no idea why women love this shit, but I'm not one to ask questions.

I place the candles strategically around the room, then close the shades around the house. "No reason to give my neighbors another view of my dick," I say, checking my watch. Twenty minutes to spare.

I run upstairs, undressing and throwing my shit in the laundry basket in my walk-in closet. I fix my bed in my room, just in case we end up in here. The room is in a light gray, making the dark royal blue covers pop, or at least that is what my decorator said when she handed me the bill. She fucked me that day, figuratively. The dark brown oak bed frame is almost fit for a king. I smile at myself. Fuck that, I am a king.

Walking into my white marble bathroom, I turn the knob on the shower that is always set on the same temperature. The rain shower starts right away. I wash and make sure the cock is well groomed. I run my hand through my hair as soon as I walk out of the shower and towel dry myself off.

I grab my satin purple robe that's hanging behind the door. "No reason to dress up more than I need to be."

Making my way downstairs, I see she should be here any minute, so I light all the candles. Now everything fucking glows. I'm about to pick up the remote to put on some music when I hear the doorbell ring. I smile to myself, opening my robe and looking down at my dick. "Show time, buddy." I cup myself while I tie the sash again.

Opening the door, I take her in. Fuck, she's beautiful. She has nothing on her face, except lip gloss. No fake eyelashes, no caked on makeup, nothing but her natural glow. Her blue eyes shine bright.

"I didn't know I was having dinner with Hugh Hefner," she jokes as she steps in, her blue sundress swaying around her legs. "Had I known, I might have put my bunny outfit on!" She leans in and kisses my cheek. Natural, effortless, perfect. The scent of citrus hits me. I wrap my hand around her waist, bringing her closer to me, chest to chest. "Next time I expect nothing less," I tell her right before I bend to kiss her lips.

"I'll keep that in mind," she says while I release my hold on her and reach out to hold her hand as I close the door. It's a simple thing I've done a million times before, but it's like I have this electric current that has just run through me.

"I brought wine," she says, grabbing her bag and pulling out a bottle of white wine. "I mean, I went with fruity. I could have asked the girl what she recommended to go with dick, but"—she shrugs her shoulders—"I winged it."

"Fuck me," slips out of me. "I think I'm in love."

She throws her head back and laughs, her lean neck bare, nothing stopping me from leaning in and marking it.

CHAPTER EIGHT

Kaleigh

Pulling up to the address Noah gave me, I take in the houses on the street. Most of them look the same. I pull the mirror down to take one last look at myself. I fluff my still damp hair. Thanks to yoga in the park with the kids, I needed to shower right before coming here. I grab my bag, pulling out my lip gloss and applying a coat. The butterflies in my stomach are something I'm not really used to. Go in, do this, scratch the itch, leave. It's my motto.

"Calm down there, big boy, I'm here for dinner and a good time." I pull my hand from his once we get to the room with about a million candles. "You can burn down a house with this many candles." I walk into the room, taking in the massive fruit baskets that are placed on the table. "Holy shit, this is a lot of fruit."

"Oh, and I have chocolate also!" he says, running into what I assume is the kitchen. "And whipped cream." He comes back in with his hands full.

I smile at him. "That's sweet, but I'm vegan." I walk to him when I see his smile disappear. It's like I told him the tooth fairy doesn't exist. I grab him by his waist. "Besides. I like my cock straight up."

His hands drop the containers, both landing with a thud. "Fuck me," he says.

"Actually," I say as I reach between us for the sash, "I was hoping"—I pull on one piece while the silk falls from my hands—"that you'd be the one fucking me," I say, pushing his robe open. And fuck me is right. Holy fucking me.

If I could stand here and gape at him, I would, but I'm seducing him. I'm making this my bitch. But holy shit my mouth just lost all its feeling. My tongue's suddenly feeling like it's swelled up. Dry. So fucking dry. His chest is perfect, pecs a perfect shape, his abs defined but not too much, and his side abs…On. Fucking. Point. But nothing can prepare me for what I'm thinking is the most perfect cock in the world.

It's absofuckinglutely perfect. "Fuck me," I finally say.

"I'm happy I could accommodate you," he says, opening the robe more to give me a full view of it, not that I need it. I've mentally taken a picture of it.

Focus, Kaleigh, focus. Except the only thing I can seem to look at is his cock.

"Now that you've seen mine, how about I see yours?" His words pull me out of my trance.

"Is that right?" I ask him. "It's like show and tell then?"

"It's only fair."

"That I can do," I say, pulling the straps down my shoulders and watching the dress fall to the floor, pooling around my feet.

"You aren't wearing anything under your dress?" he hisses out.

"You aren't wearing anything under your robe?" I match his question.

"Yes, but—" He stops talking when I walk to him, going straight to my knees.

"Enough with this talk, I'm hungry." It's the last thing I say to him. The next thing I do is pull his cock head into my mouth. I moan as I taste his pre-cum on my tongue. I take him deeper into me now.

His robe hits the floor around his feet and my knees. Pulling my mouth away from him, my hands grip him, moving up and down. "I really like your cock." I smile at him.

His eyes close halfway, his hips thrusting into my hand.

"It's perfect," I tell him as I suck him into my mouth again. This time his hands are in my hair, pulling it away from my face. My eyes look up, watching him watch me. I swallow him, my hand matching the rhythm of my mouth. His cock is getting harder than it was before, bigger also. My mouth leaves him while my hand continues. My fingers can't even touch each other, his girth is that big. "I'm so going to fuck this," I tell him as I lean in, twirling my tongue around one of his balls. "I'm going to ride this like it's my last rodeo," I tell him, taking him all the way into my mouth, almost gagging.

His hands pull my hair, the pain shooting straight to my nipples that have been rubbing his legs. He holds my hair while his hips thrust into me, his cock going deeper, all the way down to the root. And I take him. "So fucking hot." He thrusts into me. "Taking my cock down your throat." His balls hit my chin. "I'm going to cum," he says, trying to pull out of my mouth, but my hands fly to his perfect ass, pushing him into me and keeping him rooted there while I swallow whatever he has to give me.

I don't let him go till he's done. His cock comes out of my mouth a second before he falls to his knees right in front of me.

"You've seriously rocked my world. My knees gave out," he says as he reaches out to me, grabbing the side of my neck with one hand. "Totally and fucking completely ruined me."

I smile while he pulls me to him.

"You brought me to my knees," he says right before his lips find mine.

I inhale one last breath before his tongue invades my mouth. I think my heart stops beating or it's beating so fast I can't tell. His second hand grabs the other side of my neck as his tongue invades my mouth. Our tongues dance with each other while I try to continue to bring him to his knees. Turning my head to the right to deepen the kiss, my hand roams up his chest, to around his neck, my fingers finding their way into his hair. My nipples ache, tight, with just a kiss.

His lips leave mine, kissing the side of my mouth. I'm breathless. "I thought I was going to shoot the minute your tongue touched my cock." He kisses underneath my jaw, tracing out with his tongue, his hands now dropping from my neck, rubbing my shoulders, going down my arms and finally cupping my breasts.

My head falls back, moaning out, while he rolls both nipples between his fingers. My breasts fit perfectly in his hands. His head bends as he takes one nipple into his mouth, sucking in so deep I almost lose it. I squeeze my legs together to get some friction.

"Not yet, not even close to yet," he tells me, paying attention to the other nipple.

"If you don't make me cum soon, I'm pushing you back on your porn rug and taking it," I hiss out, my body filling with goose bumps.

"Oh, I'm going to make you cum all right. Now lie back and show me that pussy." He doesn't have to ask me twice. I lie back, bend my knees to the side, and open myself to him.

He rubs his hands together before he leans down and pulls my legs back and blows on my clit. My hips thrust up in hopes of getting something. "Greedy," he says, finally licking me. My moan echoes off the walls.

He licks right up to my clit, but stops right before he reaches it, blowing instead of licking.

"Fuck," I hiss out. "Noah."

"It's coming back, girl. Patience," he tells me, letting go of my thigh, his fingers rubbing me up and down to get wet. His tongue joins his finger inside me while he adds another one. I roll my hips, my clit pulsing, waiting for a touch. He licks up again. This time he lets the tip of his tongue slowly graze it, his fingers pumping into me.

"I swear if you don't do something soon," I heave out. My hands come up to my breasts and I roll my nipples, making it almost worse since my whole core goes tight.

When he licks up again, this time his teeth slowly nudge it. I roll my head from side to side in frustration, my hand going down my stomach.

"If you touch yourself, I'll fuck you till you can't walk and I won't make you come the whole time." His voice is strong, and looking in his eyes, I know he isn't playing.

"Noah, please," I pant out. His fingers feel like they are all over me. My hips thrust on his fingers that are now pumping in and out of me fast. "My clit," I tell him, almost begging.

"So tight, squeezing me," he says and I'm so close to the edge I can taste it, almost reach it.

I reach out with my hand to grip it and just like that he pulls his fingers out of me. I groan out my frustration as he turns me to my stomach, lifting my hips, and slamming into me.

"First time I make you come it's on my cock." He slams in me again, gripping my hips so hard and tight my knees lift off the floor. "I'm not going to last. You're too tight," he says. "Play with your clit now," he adds, pounding into me.

The sound of flesh slapping together fills the room while my hand finally plays with my clit, rubbing it from side to side. I hear screaming, moaning, and finally a roar as I come. I don't know who is screaming or roaring more, me or Noah. But he doesn't let up, pounding into me until my pussy is pulsing over him, until I don't think I can breathe anymore. Until we both lie here, me on my stomach, him now on his back, my mouth dry, my eyes closed just a touch. I've never been fucked into almost unconsciousness, and fuck me if I want to go back for more.

"I can't move," I tell him. "I do yoga for a living. I'm in a constant state of relaxation all the time, but this…" I smile, facing him, his eyes slowly closing.

"I know," he says. "I just need a moment and we can go for round two. I just…" He looks over at me. "You drained me." He smiles at me.

I watch him, waiting for his breathing to even out. I roll myself up, grabbing my dress and quietly slipping it on. I walk around, blowing out all the candles before picking up my purse. I look down at him, the discarded condom right next to him. He's almost like one of those marble statues they have at the Louvre, perfectly sculpted except his penis is way nicer.

Turning around, I pick up my shoes, putting them in my purse. I walk to the door, opening it as quietly as I can and closing it softly. I make it to my car and home.

The house is dark as I unlock the door and walk upstairs. I see the light coming from under Lauren's door, but I walk straight to my room instead. The night replays in my head over and over and over again. Sleep finally takes me sometime after 3 a.m., right after I hear the first bing.

CHAPTER NINE

Noah

My eyes suddenly flutter open. The room is in darkness. My body feels like it's a damn gummy worm. I stretch my arms out to find Kaleigh, coming up empty. I rise up, my eyes adjusting to the darkness. I slowly climb to my feet. I walk to the kitchen to see if maybe she is there. After looking there and the bathroom on that floor, I make my way upstairs to my bedroom. Nothing. With my hands on my hips, I go see if maybe she is in the bathroom upstairs.

"There is no way she took off," I say to the room, because the truth is, deep down inside I know she bailed. I run back down the stairs, looking out to see that her car is long gone. Walking to the kitchen, I pick up my phone and send her a text.

Where are you?

I toss the phone on the counter, walking to the fridge, opening it up, and grabbing the orange juice. After drinking from the container, I close the light and make my way upstairs, slipping into bed. I look up at the ceiling as I remember the night. It was beyond my wildest dreams. I've had sex so many times I can't begin to count, but with Kaleigh it was like taking the roller coaster ride for the first time. The anticipation, your stomach dipping when it starts to climb, and then the scream when it finally plummets. Raising your hands in the air, letting the wind run through your hair. She knocked me on my ass. I swear. I couldn't feel my knees and it's a good thing that rug was there because I might have broken my kneecap. But why leave? I turn over, looking out the window. I mean, I've dipped and left before, sneaking out. Fuck, once I left my fucking shoes in the apartment and never went back. I don't have time to think of anything else because sleep comes to take me. Waking three hours later, I roll over, shutting off the alarm.

My morning routine is much the same: run, shower, shave, leave. Walking downstairs, I pick up the discarded condom, tossing it in the garbage can. I go back, picking up the chocolate and whipped cream, tossing them out also. I check my phone to see if I got any messages and nothing. My message was delivered, but nothing about it being read. I shake my head, grabbing the fruit baskets and buckling them in the car.

Once I arrive at the office, I get out and call over the parking assistant, asking him to have the three fruit baskets delivered to the floor. Once I toss him my keys, my phone beeps in my pocket. I pull it out and see it's from Kaleigh.

Had to get home. Had fun. Let's catch up soon!

Did she just blow me off? I throw my head back and laugh. This is going to be fun.

Yup, catching you is exactly what I look forward to doing. Have a great day, beautiful.

"Take that," I say out loud in the elevator while the three other people I don't know look over at me.

When I get to my floor I walk out and see Tara, the receptionist.

"Good morning, beautiful." I smile at her. "Pepe from downstairs will be delivering three fruit baskets for all of you as a thank you for all the hard work everyone does."

She crosses her hands on her desk, her smile lighting up. "Well, aren't you the sweetest," she purrs out.

"You know me." I wink at her, walking toward Harvey's office. I find him drinking his coffee while he reads something on the computer.

"I had the best night ever," I tell Harvey as I throw myself into a chair facing his desk.

"Do tell." He puts his cup down and turns to me. "We all live vicariously through you!"

"A gentleman never kisses and tells," I say, fixing my tie. My eyes shoot up to his when I hear him laughing. "What?"

"Um. You are no gentleman. You not only kiss and tell, you show pictures and give details. Details, we don't necessarily want." He leans back in his chair.

"Well, not with this one. All I'm saying is I think someone swept me off my feet. Literally." I'm about to continue when my phone rings and I see it's my client.

"Sal," I say into the phone, getting up and saluting Harvey while I walk out. "What's going on?"

"I found another club I want to buy." Sal is what you call a connoisseur of strippers and money. This will be his tenth club that he has bought in two years. He buys run-down clubs and brings them up to another level.

"How is this not a surprise?" I walk into my office. "Aren't you supposed to be on vacation?" I ask him, thinking of our last conversation we had last week.

"I am and then this fell into my lap." He laughs at his own joke. "I'm going to email you the specifics. Make it happen." He hangs up without giving me a chance to answer him.

I scroll to my phone book, getting the florist's number. I press call and then put it to my ear.

"Flowers Bloom in the Morning, Savannah speaking. How can I help you?" The owner's voice answers on the second ring.

"Savannah, Noah here."

"Oh, dear, what did you do now?" she asks me, knowing I only go to her in dire need.

"Actually, this time I'm the one who was wronged." I breathe out. "She took what she wanted and left me," I say, looking out the window at the sun, "like I was a piece of meat."

"You don't say," Savannah says like she is impressed.

"So I'd like to send her ten dozen roses. All pink. A dozen every hour." I look at my watch, seeing that it'll be way past closing time. "Actually, two dozen every hour."

"Hold on, let me get this straight," Savannah says. "She used you, you are the wronged party, and yet you're sending her flowers? Has hell frozen over?" She laughs out loud.

"Don't know what it is about her, but I want to let her know I'm still thinking about her." I smile, picturing her face when she gets the flowers.

"I have your credit card on file. I'll send them in a bit," she says, disconnecting as soon as I give her the address.

I place my phone down and start my day. I check my emails and messages, and by the time I look around, it's two hours later. I've gotten Sal's proposal all ready. I just pressed send on the email when my phone beeps next to me.

Oh my, thank you for the flowers, they are beautiful J

I smile, knowing that I got her.

Not as beautiful as you. Have dinner with me? Actual food.

Her reply comes right away.

Sorry. I have plans, maybe another time.

She has plans. What fucking plans?

See you later.

I get up, making my way out of the office. Walking past the receptionist, I tell her I'll be out most of the day. Once I get home, I go straight to my closet. What does one wear on a stake-out? Should I go full black or should I do camo?

Picking up my phone, I call the only person who would be able to answer all these question. John. My other best friend, Austin's business partner.

"Hey, what are you doing?" I ask once he picks up.

"Having lunch with Austin while he stares at Lauren's desk." He starts laughing at the groaning that is coming from Austin.

"You need to just ask her out and end this dry spell. Jesus, your dick must think you died at this point," I tell them as I toss clothes on my bed. "I have a serious matter," I finally say when I toss my old black Doc Martens that I bought in high school when I went as a punk rocker. "I need to go on a stake-out. Should I go all black or camo?"

"Why the fuck are you going on a stake-out?" Austin asks while John answers, "Green."

"So the girl I had dinner with, she took off on me," I say as I see if I have a dark duffel bag.

"Your dick scared her away?" Austin laughs as he fills John in on the conversation we had yesterday.

"It wasn't like that," I cut in. "She loved the D, but I fell asleep. I don't know what she did, but she fucking drained me." I put my hands on my hips.

"Why don't you just ask her out again, like a normal fucking human person?" John asks.

"I tried that, but she said she has plans tonight." I walk to the closet, taking out the binoculars I have there.

"Oh, shit," Austin cuts in. "You totally got Noah'd."

Then they both laugh.

"Ha-ha-ha, so funny," I say dryly. "Seriously, though, what should I wear?"

"You should wear a white straight jacket from Bellevue," John says, laughing. "What happens if she finds you and calls the cops on you?"

I shrug my shoulders. "I'm going to win her with my charm," I say. "So camo it is. Hurry up, I have to go Google map the place where she works."

Austin finally picks up the phone. "Noah, seriously, you can't do this, it's crazy."

"What would you do if you had the best sex of your life and she walked out on you? Would you let Lauren walk out of your life?"

"No," he hisses out. "Send us the info. We will meet you there."

"Squad," I say, hanging up the phone. I rush to my office where I pick up the Google earth map. I see there is a little park in front of her studio. "This can work." I print out the map and send a picture to both of them via text.

Austin answers right away. ***Be there at four. Don't go before.***

I look at the clock and see I have three hours to spare. I walk back into my room where I undress and shower. "Power nap," I tell myself. As soon as I finish the shower I set the alarm, making sure I'm up when John and Austin get there.

I toss and turn the whole time, sleep never coming for me. When I hear the doorbell at four o'clock, I know it's them. I run down the stairs, opening the door. They both stare at me with open mouths.

"Have you gone insane?" they ask me while they take in my appearance. I might have overdone it. I'm wearing black jeans, a black turtleneck, a black jacket, my black Doc Martens, and a black beanie.

"I need to blend in," I tell them. "Go change." I point upstairs to my room. "We leave in ten minutes. Let's go." I push them up the stairs.

They both go to my closet, coming out in jeans and green shirts.

"We need black under our eyes," I say, walking to the bathroom, taking out my shoe shine kit. I get up, smearing it under my eyes. "How does this look?" I ask the boys.

"Like you lost your fucking mind," John says. "Did she suck your brains out of your dick?"

"Don't talk about her like that." I point at John. "Now put some on, you look too polished."

I look at Austin. "You look fine with all those fucking bags under your eyes. You are just fine." I pick up the duffel bag, and clanging comes from it.

"What is in there?" John asks.

"It's our go-to bag," I say, walking out, going to the car.

They both get in the car, putting on their seat belts. "What exactly is a go-to bag?"

"A knife, an ax, a bottle opener, a crow bar, a hammer, flask oils, candles, matches, some string. Oh, and a bell."

I look at them from the side, their eyes blinking, their mouths opening and closing. "Are we going to kidnap her?" John says from the back. "Dani's going to fucking kill me."

I look at him through the rearview mirror and think that his wife, Dani, will kill me first then him.

Austin tries to talk but nothing comes out. "A bell?"

"Well, yeah, in case we have to alert each other we can ring the bell." My eyes roll. "Oh, look, parking right in the front."

"So we are undercover, but you'll park in front of her business?" John says, looking around once he gets out. The park behind us has kids running around, a couple of dogs barking. It's a family friendly area.

"Grab the bag for me," I tell him as I get out, crouching till I get behind the car and sit on the sidewalk. "Did anyone see me?"

"We need to contact fucking Bellevue," they say to me while they stand there out in the open. "And I'm not touching that fucking bag. Did you bring gloves?" they ask.

I smack my head. "Forgot the gloves on the counter." I grab them by the hands, yanking them down. "She might see you," I say right before a woman walks by us with her dog, holding on to her purse trying not to stare at us.

"Okay, let's move," I say, getting up on my feet, and duck, walking to the park. I sneak in between the bushes that line the street.

"I think I just touched dog shit," John says. "This is on another level even for you." He crawls behind me, followed by Austin.

"What's that smell?" Austin asks, dry heaving.

"It's shit and piss," John hisses out. "I'm a grown ass man and I'm crawling in a fucking park with a man who needs to be in a straitjacket."

"Okay, belly crawl is easier. Less people will stare."

"I can guarantee someone has already alerted the cops," Austin says breathlessly. "It's fucking broad daylight. We should have just waited in the car."

I stop crawling. "Why didn't you bring this up before?" I ask him, thinking that would have been a better and cleaner idea.

Austin looks like he is about to lunge for me, but a soccer ball comes in our direction, hitting John on the leg. A little girl walks over, about to scream for help.

"Can," she stutters, "can I have the ball back?" She runs to get the ball and then screams while she runs away from us.

"Okay, we are in position," I say, opening the bag and grabbing the binoculars, getting on my belly and peering through two shrubs to see the door to Kaleigh's studio straight ahead.

"What are we looking for?" John asks, trying to look through the hole in the shrubs.

"A blonde," I tell them, trying to spot her inside. All I see is someone sitting behind the desk.

"Do we even know if she's here?" Austin asks while smacking a bug that has landed on his forehead. "I really fucking hope there is no poison ivy. Scratch that. I hope there is and I hope you are the only one who rolled in it." He squeezes his head next to mine, trying to look out.

My head shoots up. "Where else would she be? I mean, people now work till five p.m."

"Are you saying I rolled in shit and we don't even know if the woman is here?" John says, standing up, his head going above the shrubs. Austin grabs his hand, yanking him down.

I'm about to say something when a car door has us all holding our breaths along with the beep from the locking of the door. Right in front of us. We look at each other, our eyes going wide.

The footsteps go away from us and I look out just in time to see Kaleigh running across the street to her studio, her long hippy skirt flowing through her legs.

"Are you fucking kidding me?" Austin says. "It's Lauren's sister. You have got to be kidding me."

"Oh, this isn't good at all. Her sister works for us. Can you imagine the law suit?" John shakes his head. "If we get away with this, I'm going to kick your ass."

"I'm always there for you guys, now focus. She said she couldn't see me tonight because she has plans."

"She probably sensed that you were about to go all Jack Nicholas on her and ran for the hills."

"Shush, she's coming out," I say as she walks out with two bouquets of roses in her hand. "Don't say anything," I whisper.

They both look at me as if they are going to kill me. We watch Kaleigh put the flowers in her car and then drive off. I put the binoculars back in the bag, rushing up. "Let's go follow her."

I'm getting up to run, but my foot had fallen asleep, so I fall on my knees while Austin and John grab me. We run through the shrubs, this time all getting in the car. I put the key in the ignition and am about to drive off when I see lights in my rearview mirror. Red and blue. "Shit just got real."

CHAPTER TEN

Kaleigh

"Inhale in," I say, bringing my arms up over my head. "Exhale out." My arms come down. "And again," I say, repeating the same movement. "One last time." I do my breathing, bringing my arms to my chest. "Namaste," I say, bowing my head. The class of twenty all say Namaste at the same time. I smile to everyone, getting up, bending over to roll up my yoga mat.

I watch as everyone does the same. Most of the women in the class are part of the PTA at school. I walk out of the room to the front and the pink roses stop me right away. "Who robbed the flower shop?" I ask, going over to smell them.

"No," Stephanie says, smiling, "The question is how good were you exactly?" She hands me the two cards. I look at her confused. I've never really gotten flowers before. I mean, my parents send me some on my birthday, but other than that not really.

I open the card, dragging the white card out.

Hope your day is as beautiful as you.

Noah

I shake my head, smiling to myself. "Well then?" Stephanie says. "Who is this mystery man?"

I shrug my shoulders. "Just someone I went on a date with." I turn my head, trying not to make eye contact with her. "It was nothing."

Her eyes close a bit, not saying a word.

"What?" I ask her.

She shakes her head, smirking at me. "Nothing."

I turn to walk away and slam into one of the men who just left my yoga class.

"Sorry, Kaleigh, I was texting and didn't see you," Richard says.

"It was my fault." I nod at him and walk to the relaxation room, taking out my phone and pulling up our text thread.

Thank you for the flowers. They are beautiful.

I press send and put my phone away, laying my head back on the back of the couch. My eyes close while I start my breathing, getting me back to center.

The music of the waves clears my mind, but instead of just happy thoughts all I can see is Noah and his blue eyes. His sculpted chest and his cock. Front and center. I've always been able to meditate. I've always blocked everything out, but for some reason I can't get him out of my mind.

I'm about to take my phone out and text him back. Tell him that I lied and I'm not busy tonight when Stephanie comes in. "You have another delivery." She smiles, giving me the card, but it says the same thing as the first one. I get up, going to the desk, the aroma of flowers hitting me right away. "Holy shit." I take in another four dozen that have arrived. "It's a good thing I'm leaving. Help me load the car, will you." I grab my keys and head out to my car, carrying two bouquets. "It's going to take us four trips," Stephanie says as she opens the door and places the flowers in the back.

It actually takes us three trips and a half. By the time I get into my car the smell of roses hits me right away. I open the windows to get some circulation before I faint from the smell.

Getting home, it takes me six trips to the car before I finally bring in the last of the roses. I tried to place them strategically as to not bring attention to them, but unless you're blind and have lost your sense of smell I can't hide this shit. I bring two bouquets upstairs, setting one in Lauren's room and one in mine. My phone beeps letting me know that the bus will be here any minute. I walk outside, sitting on one of the Adirondack chairs that Lauren set up. It doesn't take long before the yellow bus comes down the road, stopping right in front, letting the kids bounce off.

"Aunt Kay, Aunt Kay, I got an A on spelling." Rachel runs to me, her test in her hand, her backpack going up and down over her head.

"Did you, now? Let me see." I grab the paper. "You know what this means? Ice cream!" I throw my hands in the air while Rachel scrunches up her face. "What's that face?"

"Can we have normal people ice cream?" she asks with her head tilted to the side.

"My ice cream is normal people ice cream," I say, tapping her nose while Gabe comes up to us. "Gabe, didn't you like the vegan ice cream you tasted yesterday?" I ask him.

He shrugs his shoulders.

"See?" I get up, taking Rachel's hand. "But if you want I can get you the 'normal' ice cream," I say as she squeals with glee.

She unloads her school bag at the table, taking in a bouquet on the table, then another on the kitchen counter, and another in the living room. "Why do we have all this?" She points at all the flowers.

"Um, um." I try to come up with the words. "Who wants ice cream?" I throw my hands up, grabbing the cones and their 'normal' ice cream while I pretend she didn't ask me that question. It doesn't take much to make her veer off her question. Gabe doesn't even make a second glance at the flowers. Instead, he grabs a cone and shouts that he's going to the neighbor's house.

"Be back by five so your mom doesn't think I forgot about you!" I yell to the door slamming.

And he is in fact back by five as soon as Lauren rolls the minivan into the driveway.

Once she turns off the car, Rachel runs outside. "Momma, I get excellent in spelling. Aunty Kay gave me normal ice cream," she says, jumping into Lauren's arms.

"Did she, now, before dinner?" She kisses her nose, walking to the front door.

"Hey, Mom," Gabe says from the kitchen where he is drinking a tall glass of water, his hands almost black.

"Go wash your hands, dude," I tell him as he places the glass in the sink, running upstairs.

"Where did all these flowers come from?" Lauren asks, putting

Rachel down as my phone rings. "Saved by the bell." She smirks at me while I answer walking outside, seeing it's Stephanie on the phone.

"Hey," I say, sitting on the stoop.

"You got another six bouquets," she says into the phone. "I didn't think there was such a thing as too many flowers. I've changed my mind." She sneezes while I laugh.

"Okay, I'll come and get them now. Put one in the relaxation room as well as the women's changing area," I tell her as she continues sneezing. "You know there is a theory that if you sneeze eight times you orgasm. You just had an orgasm at work. Best. Boss. Ever." I laugh into the phone while she says fuck off and disconnects.

Walking back into the house, Lauren is already at the stove preparing what looks like chicken. "Are you eating with us tonight?" I look around at the flowers in the room.

"Not tonight. I have a date of sorts," I say, making a plan in my head. I go upstairs, changing into my blue tight jeans and baby pink linen top. The sleeves go tight around my wrist while the neckline falls off one shoulder. I grab my brown sandals to finish the outfit. I say bye as I grab my keys and head down to my studio.

I pull up to the curb across the street right in front of the park. The sound of children playing and dogs barking fills the afternoon. I run across the street, opening the door. "You were not kidding." I smile, taking in more roses.

"At this rate, we could open up our own flower shop," Stephanie says as she scratches her nose.

"Okay, let's get them loaded up. I'm going to bring some to the hospital and maybe church?" I grab a bouquet and rush to the car. It only takes two trips this time. I roll away from the curb, waving goodbye. I'm down the street when I see the red and blue lights in my mirror. I turn my music on louder, thinking of the plan I'm setting into motion.

I pull into my favorite Whole Foods store, picking up my phone.

So change of plans, are you still free tonight?

I send the text to Noah, waiting to see if he will answer.

I get out of the car, going into the store with a list in my head. Pepper, onions, vegan margarine, package of seitan, some garlic powder, oh, and the dairy free provolone. I throw in some fruit, but then put it back when I think of the fruit baskets he had yesterday. I walk around the grocery store aimlessly while I wait for him to text me back. I take my phone out again to check if he sent me anything. Still nothing. The message shows that it has been delivered.

I make a call to Lauren to ask her. She answers breathlessly after one ring, "Hello."

"Hey, so if you text someone and they don't text you back, what is the right etiquette?" I ask her vaguely.

"What do you mean, like you text someone and then they ignore you?"

"No." My voice comes out loud and then I lower it. "Or maybe. So I had a date yesterday. Today he sends me a million roses. When he asked to meet me, I said I had other plans. Well, then I changed my mind and texted him back and I haven't heard anything."

"How long has it been?"

"Seventeen minutes. Maybe. Give or take."

"Kay, he could be driving, in the bathroom, working out, cleaning."

"We really need to talk about the guys in your imaginary world who actually clean."

"Hey, if a man passes my vacuum I would blow him. No questions asked."

"I really have to wonder why you're still single." I laugh out. "So you think he's busy? Oh my God," I shriek out. "What if he's on a date with another woman?"

"Kay, calm down," she says calmly. "No one will send a million roses to a woman and then go out with another one."

"This is true, unless he had a back-up plan." I pick up a jar of vegan peanut butter, putting it in the basket. "Imagine I show up at his house to cook for him and there is another girl there."

"Wait a second. Back up. You're going to cook for him? You hardly know how to cook for yourself."

"Very funny. I'm making him vegan Philly cheesesteaks. He won't even know the difference." I smile at myself.

"Oh, he'll definitely know the difference, unless you're sitting there naked. Then maybe he might forget that chewy thing isn't actually steak."

I roll my eyes at her. "So I shouldn't text him again?" I ask, wondering if I should put everything back. "Or should I just scratch this plan and come home?"

"You like him?" She stops talking then continues before I can answer. "Holy shit. Hell froze over. Kaleigh actually likes a boy."

"Hardy Hard Har." I inhale. "I don't like a boy; he just makes me laugh and he's funny." I shrug my shoulders.

"Oh, this is going to be good. Did you try calling him?"

"What?"

"Like actually dialing his number, waiting for the phone to ring, then having him answer? It's an old-fashioned thing. Started in the 1800s."

"No one calls anyone anymore," I inform her.

"Shocking. Did you not just call me? Call him. I have to go. It's bath time." She hangs up on me.

I look down at the phone as soon as I see a text message come through.

I'm all free. How about you swing by in about thirty?

I smile at myself. "Call people my ass."

Perfect. I'll see you then! I'll bring dinner.

Oh, I like this even more.

No actual food. See you soon.

I smile, pulling up the text thread to Lauren.

He answered the text. See.

Her answer comes right away

All is right with the world now.

I roll my eyes, walking over to the cash register and checking out my purchases. I walk out with a bounce in my step and then stop. Holy shit, I might actually like this guy!

CHAPTER ELEVEN

Noah

"Let me handle this," I say to the guys as the police officer gets out of his car and walks over to my side of the car. I press the button to roll the window down.

"License and registration papers, please," he barks, his eyes hidden by his glasses that have a mirror lens.

I see myself in the glass and notice the black polish is smearing down to my cheeks. I have twigs stuck in my hat.

"What seems to be the problem?" I turn to get my wallet out of the middle console.

"We've had a couple of calls about some disturbances in the neighborhood," he says as he reads my name. Leaning in, he takes in Austin and John. "What is that smell?"

"Our dignity, along with some dog poop and I think urine, but I don't know if it's human or animal," John says from the backseat.

"Officer," I say, trying to cut in, "we might have been going undercover."

His eyebrows squeeze together, so I continue. "I was spying on a girl." I smile at him.

"Does she have a restraining order against you?" he asks, and Austin says from his side, "Not yet, but I'm sure it's coming."

I turn to glare at him, then turn back and smile at the officer. "I was just making sure she got my flowers."

"So you decided it was a good idea to hide in the bushes and scare innocent women and children." He leans in, looking from one to the other till his eyes finally come to me. "I'll be right back."

He goes back to his car while my phone beeps. A text from Kaleigh. My eyes open up.

So change of plans, are you still free tonight?

"Yes," I cheer out, "she has a change of plans and wants to meet tonight."

"If I get arrested, Dani is going to cut your balls off and then finish you off, so I don't think you should be celebrating," John says from the back.

"And whatever she doesn't finish I will," Austin says from his side. "You've done some crazy stuff over the years, but this one is right on top of everything. I want to scratch my face, but I'm afraid that the shit I rolled in will be all over my face. And I'm really hoping that the wetness on my knees is because the grass was wet."

"Nothing is going to happen. He is just checking to see if we have any priors and if there are any warrants out for my arrest."

"Are there?" John asks.

I turn in my seat. "I take offense to that. I'm a law abiding citizen."

"Who has a go-to bag to go and stalk a woman, in broad daylight. We all should be taken to Bellevue," Austin says.

"Hey, we were all there when your balls almost exploded. This is what friendship is," I state to them.

John shakes his head in the back, looking out of the window. We sit in silence for about ten minutes till the officer's car door stops me. I watch him come back in the mirror.

"Here are your papers." He shakes his head. "I'm letting you go with a warning. That warning is let this be the last time I meet you. The next time I'm hauling you guys down. Do I make myself clear?"

"Yes," we all say together. I watch him walk back and take off.

I answer Kaleigh as soon as he drives off.

I'm all free. How about you swing by in about thirty?

I smile when she says she is going to serve dinner. I don't bother going into it since I have thirty minutes to get cleaned up.

"She is going to be over in thirty minutes," I tell the guys, all excited.

"Oh, good," Austin says sarcastically. "I'm so happy this all worked out for you. Do me a favor and don't call me till next week," he tells me, his nose moving up and down. "My nose is so itchy."

"Just scratch it. What's the worst that can happen?" John says from the back. "What's a little more germs on your face?"

I laugh at them as thoughts of Kaleigh cooking for me run through my mind. Her naked with a tiny apron, her ass open for the taking. I might be smiling too big because Austin smacks my arm, bringing me out of my daze.

"I hate you right now," he says as soon as I turn into my driveway.

I scramble out of the car, running into the house.

"Jackass, you forgot your go-to bag," John says, walking in the house after me. "I'm grabbing my clothes and leaving. In case you're wondering, I'm throwing all these clothes out." He runs upstairs to my bedroom, coming down with his clothes in a ball.

Austin follows him. "I'm burning these," he says to me, walking out of the house.

"I don't give a shit. Thanks for today, boys," I say. "Fuck, it felt good, right? The whole hanging together and stuff." I shrug.

"Nothing about today felt good," Austin says, slamming the door closed.

I run upstairs, peeling the shirt from my body, the smell of urine hitting me right in the nose. I stop myself right before I throw it in the garbage along with the jeans and boxers.

I step under the shower, washing away the stench. I rinse the shampoo from my hair, grabbing some soap and scrubbing my face, washing away the black shoe shine. Finishing the shower in record time, I wrap the towel around my waist, walking to the sink to brush my teeth, but I stop in my tracks. The shoe shine is still on my face. Not dark black but a faded gray. What. The. Fuck. I open the water, grabbing some soap and rubbing at the dark gray lines. Nothing happens. I open Google right away to ask how to get rid of shoe shine stains.

Turpentine. What the actual fuck? I call Austin right away, but he sends me to voice mail. So I text him instead.

I have an urgent situation.

I don't care if you're in the middle of the street with a severed foot. Call 9-1-1

I need turpentine. Do you have any?

Why the fuck would I have turpentine on hand?

The shoe shine stained my face and now I have two gray lines under my eyes.

Good. It's karma.

Fuck you.

You wish.

I put my phone down. I don't have time to think about anything because the doorbell rings.

Fuck. I slip on a pair of basketball shorts and run downstairs to the door. I open the door and my breath actually stops. She isn't looking at the door, but instead I have her back and she turns around to look at me. It's almost like it's in slow motion. Her hair whips around, her smiling face coming into view.

"Hey." Her voice comes out while she looks at me from head to toe. "What happened to your face?" she asks, leaning in, rubbing her thumb over one of the stained parts.

"Um." I try thinking fast, nothing coming to mind. "We were playing football and I put on the black paint to hide the glare from the sun. Come in." I try changing the subject as I move away from the door to allow her to come in.

"Oh, fun, I love football," she says, coming in and kissing my cheek. "You must be the quarterback." She goes straight to the kitchen.

"Yeah, we don't really have positions." I shrug. "So what do you have in the bag?" I notice the big canvas bag she has on her shoulder.

"I brought stuff to make Philly cheesesteak. I hope you're hungry."

"That's my favorite sandwich ever." I smile at her. "How did you know?"

"Is it, really?" she asks and the happiness from her voice lights up the room.

"Yup." It really isn't. I tolerate it, but I'm not going to tell her. "What can I do to help?" I ask her.

"Nothing." She puts down her bag and starts taking the stuff out of her bag. "I'm just going to slice the veggies and stuff." She looks around. "I need a pan, I think," she says quietly. "You know what? I want to surprise you, so how about you go get some wine and stay in the living room till it's done?"

"Really?" I say to her. "You sure?"

"Yup, perfectly." She shoos me away. "Go relax on the couch."

I walk around the island to kiss her on the lips. "I'm glad you could make it." I wrap my arms around her waist, and she wraps her arms around my shoulders. I kiss her again. This time she molds herself to my body. "Really, really glad."

"I can feel that." She laughs, her lips still pressed to mine. "Now go relax," she tells me, opening cabinets to collect stuff she will need.

"Just let me know if you need anything," I tell her, making my way to the wine fridge. I notice that I have none. "I'm out of wine."

She looks up from drawers that she is opening and closing. "Why don't you go get some while I cook?"

"That sounds good. Is there anything else you need me to get?"

She shakes her head.

I run upstairs to grab a shirt and some shoes. When I get back into the kitchen, she has some jazz music flowing from her phone while she is cutting a red pepper. I walk to her, wrapping my arms around her waist from behind, kissing her neck. She leans her head away to give me access.

"Okay, call me if you need anything."

"I will," she sings out.

I walk to my car, getting in and opening the windows. Fuck, it stinks. "I need to get this shit washed," I tell myself. I make the first stop at the Home Depot store, buying some turpentine. Then hit up the wine store, walking out with a case of white and a case of red. Making my way home, I see that I've been out for about forty minutes. Grabbing the cases of wine one on top of the other, I carry them inside and I'm hit with the smell of char or burn.

When I make it into the kitchen, I see Kaleigh with her hair tied up, her sleeves pulled up, and the look of defeat on her face. "Honey, I'm home."

CHAPTER TWELVE

Kaleigh

The minute he shuts the door, I grab my phone to FaceTime Lauren. She answers on the second ring.

Her face comes into the screen. "What is on your face?" I ask, looking at her with a black mask.

"It's a mask to detox. What do you want?" She tries not to move her lips so the mask doesn't move.

"The recipe says to sauté the peppers and onions." I look back at the recipe that I printed before.

"Okay," she asks, not sure what the question is.

"What the fuck does that mean? Sauté. Is that code for something?"

"Jesus, you should have just got him pizza." She shakes her head. "It means put oil in a pan and then add the peppers and onions and have them cook. Stirring them often to make sure they don't burn. I would add some salt while they cook for flavor."

"Okay, I think I can do that." I nod, taking a silver frying pan out, pouring oil in the pan, and turning it on. Turning back, I ask her, "How do I know the oil is ready?"

"I'd wait about maybe a minute. It depends on the stove." She starts to press down on the mask. "Then I would take the veggies out and do the steak."

"Oh, shit, I have to cut the seitan." I grab it out of the bag. "Okay, I'll call you back if I need anything."

"Don't burn down his house." Is the last thing she says before I disconnect.

I tie my hair on top of my head and push my sleeves up.

I open the seitan, slicing it thinly, my head moving to the music. When I finish cutting it, I put the cutting board in the sink. When I turn around, I see that the pan where the oil is in is now brown and smoke is starting to fill the room. "Shit," I say, picking up the pot from the handle and turning the water on in the sink. The sounds of sizzle overpowers the music. "Fuck." I open the fan and run to open the windows in the kitchen along with the back door. I pray that the fire alarm doesn't go off. When I get back to the sink, I try to scrub the brown off the pan, but it's useless. I grab another pan. It looks the same as the other one, so I put it back on the stove. I take the burnt pan and place it in the back of his cabinet, burying it under a couple of other pans. "Never happened," I tell myself.

I get the oil out again, putting some in the bottom of the pan. "I'm not taking my eyes off this shit this time." I wait a minute, counting to sixty in my head. I put the onions and peppers in the pan and coat them in oil. Adding salt, I turn to change the music on my playlist. When some dance music comes on, I start moving my hips while I stir the peppers and onions. "Why don't I cook more often?" I ask myself.

I grab my phone and FaceTime Lauren again. I watch as it says connecting.

"Hey, are these ready?" I ask, turning the phone to the peppers and onions that are frying away.

"Almost. I would give it another minute or two."

"Okay. Thanks," I say, disconnecting again. I wait about a minute, grabbing a plate and placing them in it. When I have them all off, I put the pan back on the stove, adding the seitan. The sound of sizzle starts again. "Oh, shit," I say, trying to grab a fork to flip the pieces, but it's stuck to the pan. "What the fuck?" I try to pick them up, but the pieces are turning black so fast.

I call Lauren right away. "Why is the seitan sticking to the pan?"

"I have no idea."

"I scraped the peppers and onions out and then added the seitan like the recipe said."

"Did you add some more oil?"

"No, it didn't say to." I check the paper. "Okay, I'll add some now." I pour some oil into the pan, but I guess it was too hot because it smells right away of burn. I take the pot off the heat. "I added oil and it smells burnt."

"The pot was too hot," she tells me like it's something everyone should know. "You need to lower the heat while you cook the meat. Then just add the veggies again."

"Okay. Remind me to never cook this shit again," I tell her, tossing my phone on the counter, waiting for the pot to cool down, the oil being absorbed into the seitan. I lower the temperature on the stove and place the pan back on. When the seitan starts browning instead of blackening, I'm thinking I got this under control. I grab the bread, slicing it in half and placing it on the cookie sheet while I open the oven.

I look down at convention or bake. The sheet says bake, so I press that button and put the buns in. I add the peppers to the seitan and put it on simmer so it stays warm.

I go into the living room and light some of the candles from last night. I go to the table and see if there is anything I can set the table with. A beep sounds from the oven, so I go over and check on the bread. Opening the door, the smell of burning and smoke make my eyes burn. Grabbing a cloth, I take the cookie sheet out of the oven. I notice I pressed broil instead of bake. "Shit," I say, pressing the right button this time. Thankfully, the bag came with six buns.

Placing the buns in the oven, I set a timer for four minutes just to make sure. I grab the vegan provolone out of the bag, going to the oven and placing them into the buns so they can melt at the same time. Once the timer rings, I open the oven, taking out the buns with the melted cheese. I start putting the seitan at the bottom and placing the peppers and onions on the top. I place it back into the oven. I press the warm button to keep the sandwiches hot. Happy with my progress, I start cleaning up and come across the buns that are burnt. I hear the front door open and slam shut. Panic fills me as I take in the buns. I grab them up and toss them in the garbage and place the garbage on top of it.

"Honey, I'm home." I hear from behind me. I turn, trying to get the look of despair out of my eyes.

"Hey." I smile over at him. I should have gotten naked. This way he wouldn't notice the burnt bread. "Just in time. Supper is ready."

"Is it now?" he says, putting the cases on the counter and taking out a couple of bottles of white wine. "I'm told this is a vegan wine. I can't confirm that she didn't lie to me," he says, showing me the label which is in fact a vegan wine.

"Awww, aren't you sweet?" I grab a couple of wine glasses from the island that I found earlier. "Why don't you pour the wine, and I'll bring in the food?"

He comes closer to me. "I like seeing you here in my home. Cooking for me." He leans down, whispering the last part before he places a kiss on my lips. I'm about to go one step further by slipping my tongue into his mouth, but the beep from the oven lets me know that the warming is done.

He nods his head, opening a drawer and taking out a cork screw. I open the oven, grabbing a rag, and bringing the cookie sheet out. The hoagies look amazing if I do say so myself.

Placing a hoagie on one plate and then the other, I carry both plates to the dining room. The sun is starting to set and with no light on it's almost like it's dim.

I sit down and watch Noah uncork the wine, pouring my glass first, and then his own. Sitting down in front of me, he raises his glass.

"To the first of many home-cooked meals." He winks at me while I click my glass against his.

I take a sip of the wine, watching him lean over and pick up the hoagie, taking a bite. The bread crunches as he bites down. I reach for my own hoagie, cutting it in half.

"What's in this?" he asks at his second bite.

He wears a confused look on his face while he opens the hoagie to see what is in fact inside.

"Veggies and seitan," I say, grabbing a piece and biting down. Not too bad. It tastes a little like char from the burnt seitan, but it has that whole Philly steak vibe.

He grabs his wine, downing it.

"What the hell is seitan?" he asks. "Is there no steak in this Philly steak?"

I laugh at him, grabbing my wine and taking a sip to drown out the taste of burnt. "No, silly, it's seitan, which is a 'wheat beef'. It's a fake beef."

"Well, what happened to the real beef?"

I laugh at him. "I can't eat the real beef, so I improvised."

He takes another bite, peering inside the hoagie. "It's almost like foam texture, or sponge. It squeaks while I chew."

I shake my head, taking another bite, and he isn't wrong. It does squeak. "Maybe because I overcooked it." I take another bite. "Or burnt it."

"Babe, I really want to eat this, but…" He looks down, his hands going up. "But. But."

"But you won't be full?" I try to make an excuse for him.

"Yes, I won't be full. We should order pizza." He pushes off the table, going to get a menu from the drawer while I take a piece of seitan with my fork. Fuck, it's horrible. It tastes like burnt wood.

"What do you like on your pizza?" he asks, handing me the menu.

"I'm going to take the veggie one with no cheese and extra sauce." I smile at him. "You can get your own."

He picks up the phone, dialing the pizza guy. "Hey, I'll take a small veggie pizza, no cheese and extra sauce, and then I'll take a large meat lovers pizza extra sausage."

I laugh at his order.

He hangs up. "Should be here in thirty minutes. Want to go sit outside by the pool?"

I hadn't even noticed the pool, but now that it is dark outside the light from the pool illuminates the yard. I grab my glass of wine, following him outside. The whole backyard is free of grass. It's all bricks and cement. The pool sits in the middle of the yard. There is a wall of cement all around it, acting like a fence. But there are lights on the wall. Against the far wall to the back there is a ledge that is built in, filled with pillows and cushions. Two potted plants sit in the corner. Two loungers are on one side near the door and on the other side is a round lounger with a half cover over it.

"Where would you like to sit?" he asks, waiting for me to continue looking around.

"Let's go sit on the round one." I wink at him. "This way we can make out if we want." I smile at him while he grabs my hand, dragging me to it.

CHAPTER THIRTEEN

Noah

I walk her to the round lounger, waiting for her to crawl on. She places her wine glass on the side table next to the lounger and then sits down on it. I'm so happy this date didn't go to shit after I confessed that her cooking was horrible.

I sat down and looked at the hoagie. It looked good, but the minute I had bitten into it, it tasted like burnt feet. The 'steak' fucking squeaked with every bite. I had to swallow my whole wine glass to get the taste of it out of my mouth and even that wasn't enough. I couldn't stand to see her disappointment, so I took another bite. It was the bite that ended all bites. The taste was even worse with the second bite. It was grainy now, and the dryness of the bread made it almost like sand.

But now here we are sitting in the middle of my round lounger. I pick up my phone, turning on some jazz music. The sound fills the speakers outside.

She smiles at me. "Nice touch there, Casanova."

I lie down next to her, propping my back against the cushions, watching her kick off her brown sandals.

"So tell me," she starts. "Who is Noah?"

I laugh at her question, folding my hands on my stomach. The need to reach out and drag her even closer to me itches. "Just a simple guy, living a simple life." Even I laugh at that. "Okay, fine. My parents are both lawyers, so it was only normal I would follow into their path. It was actually implemented since I was old enough to remember that I was going to be a lawyer. They deal with criminal law. The stories they have told over the years, I knew right away I couldn't do it. So I went with the complete opposite, corporate law. What about you?" I say, reaching over to tuck a strand of blond hair that has fallen out of her pinned up hair. "Who is Kaleigh?"

Her head flies back as she laughs at that question. "Who is Kaleigh? That's a loaded question." She tilts her head. "I'm an aunt." She turns around, grabbing her wine glass. "I run my own yoga studio. Saved up all my babysitting money since I was thirteen." She laughs. "Okay, and my parents gave me the down payment, but I have paid them back in full." She drinks another sip.

"It's funny that you said you're an aunt first, a maternal instinct."

I pick up the bottle of wine that I brought with me, pouring her some more wine.

"Best thing to happen to me was becoming an aunt." She smiles when she talks about them. "I mean, minus the fact that their father deserves to have chaffing balls syndrome. Or like a constant case of hemorrhoids, bleeding and raw."

"Wow, that bad?" I ask, grabbing my own glass of wine.

"When you promise to love someone forever, it should be forever. It's not till someone pays more attention to me." She shrugs her shoulders. "It's why I will never get married. Why I will never put myself out there." Her smile gets softer. She puts her glass on the table and lays her head down on her arm. "There is no such thing as fairy tales, Noah, no Prince Charming." Her eyes close a little bit. Her eyelids seem so heavy.

I nod, palming her cheek in my hand. "Rest for a bit. I'll wake you when the pizza gets here," I tell her as she brings her knees up and lies in a fetal position.

I get up, walking to one of the benches that doubles as storage.

I take a cover out, going over to her and placing it over her. The doorbell rings, so I run inside to pay the delivery boy. Walking back to the oven, I place the pizza on the counter. I clean up the food on the table, picking up a plate and smelling it again. Grimacing, I toss it all in the garbage. I place a couple of pieces of pizza on each plate, bringing it outside. I walk to the lounger and I'm about to yell out that I'm back, but her eyes are still closed. I balance the plates, getting on the lounger with her. I try not to make too much movements so I don't disturb her. Once I sit with my back against the pillow, I fold the pizza, taking a bite. I moan out as soon as my tongue tastes the sauce, then the meat, then the cheese. Fuck, it's the best thing I think I've ever eaten. Okay, maybe not but after that squeaky fake meat, this is pretty fucking high up there.

After I finish eating my two slices, I go inside to grab my iPad. Might as well work. Bringing it to the lounger with me, I settle next to Kaleigh. Her hair is now fanning the pillow, so I take the iPad and take a picture of her. She looks like an angel, like a devilish angel. I smile, opening up my emails and reading through some contracts that need to be presented to Sal. I don't know how long I've been working when I hear stirring next to me.

"What time is it?" she asks, stretching her arms above her head, and her back arches.

"Almost ten p.m." I put my iPad on the side table, turning around to scoot down and grab her around her waist, bringing her closer to me. Her hands automatically wrap around me. "You missed pizza." I kiss her lips while she flings her leg up over my hip, my cock positioning right inside of her pussy. The heat radiates through my pants, my cock suddenly ready to party.

"I must have been more tired than I thought I was," she says, pressing into me. "Well, hello there, little man." She laughs out while my face dives into her neck.

"Little man?" My eyebrows pinch together. "I'll show you little man." I roll her on her back, her legs spreading and then locking at the ankles and resting in the middle of my back. "He's more than a little man. He's like a big blue whale penis." I lean down to kiss her, grinding into her as my tongue invades her mouth. My tongue takes control of this kiss.

Her hands go from around my neck, over my shoulders, down my arms, and up my chest before she breaks the kiss. "I really, really wish I didn't have a rule."

My arms hold me up. "What rule?"

"I don't sleep with the same person twice."

"Why in the hell would you make that rule?" I ask her.

"It's just easier for everyone and no one gets hurt. No shaded area.

And everyone is none the wiser and no ill feelings. It's like peace and love sort of, kind of, you know."

I shake my head. "But what if you really like the person after that one time? What if he's the best dick you ever had?" I wink at her. "In case you didn't understand the question, I'm the best dick you've ever had."

She laughs at me. "Even if it's the best dick I've ever had, I don't break the rule." She kisses underneath my chin. "And you really are the best dick I've ever had. Which now saddens me since you might have broken my vagina for all other penises out there."

"Then we should totally make our parts meet again." I grind into her. "My big, and I emphasize big man, would really love to come out and cuddle in you."

She giggles again and this time her stomach lets a big grumble.

"Well, then I guess this wooing will have to wait till you're fed." I roll off of her and my cock protests by jerking. "Maybe you're hangry and that is why you think we should fuck again."

She turns to roll off the lounger, sliding her hair back into a bun. "Yes, feed me." She picks up the glasses and bottle of almost empty wine, following me inside.

I take out her pizza, sliding it into the microwave. I grab her a fork and knife while she sits herself at the island. Placing the now hot pizza in front of her, I smile. "For you, milady."

She grabs a piece, folding it like me and eating it, totally ignoring the fork and knife. "This is really, really good," she says in between bites. "So much better than the steak sandwich, right?" she asks, grabbing her second slice.

"You can't call it a steak sandwich if there is no steak in it." I lean on the counter on my elbow. "And there was no fucking steak in that thing."

She takes a sip of water that I had placed down before I put the pizza there. "Okay, fine, the veggies sandwich then." She rolls her eyes as she continues eating.

"So how do I get you to break your rule?" I wonder how much she will stand on her vow.

"You can't." She shrugs her shoulders. "I won't put myself through that and I refuse to put the other person through that."

"So what if we just hang around as friends and if things progress then it's a win-win for both of us." I try not to sound desperate. I've never hung out with a woman in my life, but for another taste of her I'd be more than happy.

She looks at me with a perplexed face. "You want to hang out with me to see if I will change my rule?" She shakes her head, taking another bite of pizza. "You have lost your mind. Men and women can't be friends."

I stand up straight, folding my arms over my chest. "Why the hell not?" I ask her.

"Well," she starts saying, wiping her hands in a napkin, "women are from Mars, men are from Venus." She shrugs, picking up her glass of water like she just solved a case.

"What the fuck does that mean?"

"You can't possibly be friends with the opposite sex without the black and white becoming gray."

"So are you telling me that you aren't friends with any male people?"

She shakes her head. "No, I have many male friends. Most are gay and most are my friends' spouses. But I am not friends with males I've had sex with."

My hands shoot up. "Why the hell not? If you have a 'rule'"—I put my hand up into motion—"then why can't you close yourself off?"

She shrugs her shoulders. "I've never put myself in the position, so I can't answer that, but I can say that if you and I"—she points from me to her—"were friends, that black and white will turn to gray."

I smile at her. "You can't say no to my charm?"

"No, I'm saying that you won't just want a friendship with me. You will get jealous if I have another date. You will get jealous if we go out for coffee and then a 'friend'"—she uses quotations—"calls me or I meet another man."

"Bullshit. I think I can contain myself. I think you can't contain yourself. I think that once another woman looks at all this," I say, moving my hand up and down to motion my body, "you are going to do what girls do and that is to take out the claws and start laying claim."

She throws her head back and laughs. "You really think that highly of yourself." She continues, "How's this? Tomorrow I'm going to go to yoga with 'friends'. You should come," she says, getting off her chair, grabbing her plate, and going to put the plate in the sink.

I grab her around her waist, bringing her flush to me.

"Friends don't stick their penises in other friends' stomachs."

"My penis only gets up to salute really good, good friends," I say, letting her go. "Now let's prove your theory wrong, shall we?"

"All right," she counters, turning to grab her purse. "So I'll text you the address tomorrow and I guess I'll see you there."

"Wait," I say while she bounces down the steps to her car, "am I not picking you up?"

"That would be a date." She turns around again, walking to her car, unlocking the door.

"Wow, you don't think you can be in a car with me without it turning sexual?" I lean against the doorjamb, smiling. "Interesting."

"You're a funny guy, Noah." Is the last thing she says before she gets into the car and drives off.

I watch her lights till I can't see them anymore. Closing off all the lights around the house and making sure everything is locked up, I head to bed with a to-do list and a smile on my face.

My morning goes off without a hitch. I'm about to ask someone to get me lunch when Harvey comes in my office.

"I came to see if people were lying," he says, going over to sit on the couch.

I'm about to answer him when Austin walks in. "Asshole." He almost yells, looking over at Harvey. "Hey."

"Why am I an asshole now?" I ask, leaning back in my chair, my hands going to the armrests.

"Oh," he starts, "you're an asshole every single day, but now it's even bigger. He made John and I go on a stake-out for a girl yesterday."

"Really?" Harvey asks, all intrigued.

"It was during the day. In the sunlight. People called the cops because they thought we were pedophiles." He shakes his head. "I crawled through piss and shit for him. It took two showers to get the stench off of me. I actually think it was skunk piss," he finishes while Harvey laughs.

"Oh, please, you wouldn't be able to sit in the car if it was skunk."

"The office is buzzing about him also. He came in to work whistling." Harvey looks from Austin to me. "And he hasn't made one pass at any of the girls this morning." He nods his head.

"I'm sure I did," I say, trying to remember and realize that I haven't said an inappropriate thing all day. "Let me ask you," I finally speak up. "If someone would be doing goat yoga, would they wear a jock strap?"

They both stop talking and blink at me. Austin starts first, "Why the fuck would you be going to yoga, let alone goat yoga?"

"Kaleigh said she doesn't fuck the same guy twice. So, I convinced her that we can be friends," I say, folding my hands on my stomach.

"You've never been friends with a woman in your life," Austin and Harvey say at the same time.

"That's not true. I'm friends with Dani and Barbara. Oh, and…" I snap my fingers, trying to come up with more names.

"Number one," Austin starts, "you're friends with Dani because John would cut off your dick with a rusted saw if you even looked at her sideways, and that was before they were even married. And Barbara is ninety."

"Okay, can we not do this cross examination right now? Should I wear a jock or not?"

"So," Harvey starts, "you bang this girl. Stake her out, then when she tells you that she doesn't bang the same douchebag twice, you proceed to tell her that you only want to be friends with her, and she buys all this?" he asks with his eyebrows pinching together.

"Oh, God," I say, sitting up, now running my hand through my hair. "I can totally be friends with a girl." When they both shake their heads I continue, "I can. So what if she broke my dick? I can do this. How hard can it be?"

"So you are going to do goat yoga? What the fuck is that?" Harvey asks.

"I Googled it this morning. It's basically yoga and goats just walk around." I throw my hands up. "Free rein."

"Definitely wear a cup," Austin says, finally chiming in.

"That's what I thought also. Imagine if they come and bite my dick." I shake my head. "I would die."

"Yes, you should definitely cover the twig and berries," Harvey says.

"That's what I was thinking," I say, grabbing my crotch. "Keep everything in place and intact."

Harvey gets up, slapping Austin on the shoulder. "I should go. I need to order my wife jewelry or something to thank her." Then he looks at me. "For everything."

I laugh at him as he walks out. "You know that she is going to see through your bullshit, right?" Austin says. "You wouldn't know platonic if it hit you in the nuts and then kneed you in your face."

I tilt my head. "Dude, you have anger issues I think you should fuck out of your system." I get up. "Besides, maybe I don't want to fuck her either." I smile big. "I need to work on my game face."

"You are so fucked. Goats are the least of your problems." He shakes his head, walking out of the room.

"I'm fucked? You've been walking around with a boner for your assistant. That's even after she almost made your testicles explode!" I yell as he walks away, flipping me the bird in the air. "You don't have a yoga mat I can borrow by chance?"

He just shakes his head till he turns the corner.

I pick up my phone and text Kaleigh.

Where does one buy a yoga mat and clothes?

Her answer is almost instant.

I've got you covered. Show up fifteen minutes before so you can change.

Perfect. See you there, friend.

I smile, putting the phone down, making a list of things we could talk about. Things friends talk about. Weather, politics, scratch that, no one talks about politics. So far weather. I buzz for Norma to come into my office. Once she comes in, I ask her, "Norma, what do you discuss with your friends who are male?" I pick up my pen, waiting for her answer to take notes.

"You can discuss a bunch of things. Weather, travel, your day, favorite food, schools, kids, sports. The list goes on and on, sir."

I nod. "This is great. Thanks again, Norma." I smile at her as she walks out. She turns around right before leaving.

"This look is good on you," she says.

"What look is that?"

"Smitten," she says, walking out, leaving me smiling.

Shit, if this is what smitten feels like. I look down at my dick. "Sorry, dude. I'll take care of you as much as I can."

CHAPTER FOURTEEN

Kaleigh

"You did what?" Stephanie yells at me while slapping the desk next to her.

"I told him we could be friends. Jesus, it's not like I can't be friends with a man." I roll my eyes at her and pretend to check my nails so she doesn't see the bullshit in my eyes.

"The only male friends you have are gay. Or husbands of friends." She points at me accusingly. "You slept with him."

"I'm aware. My vagina is still a little tender, thank you very much." I glance around the studio.

"You never ever friend zone someone you did the dirty monkey with." She picks up her water, taking a long gulp. "He's that big?"

I roll my eyes again, not wanting to answer her questions. "Anyway, can you call Amelia and tell her to put him down and to bill me?"

"So let me get this straight, please, because I seem to be a tad confused. You meet this guy, hot guy, you have sex with him. Then he sends you a million roses. You blow him off." She looks at me and I don't say anything, so she continues, "Now he somehow cast a spell on you and you have given in to the cardinal rule that you will never be friends with people that have been inside you." She tilts her head. "Am I right?"

"First thing, I was introduced to him by my sister. I didn't go out to meet him. Second, women and men can be platonic friends. Apparently it's been done before, or so I've been told. And third, I admit that I have the same thoughts that you just outlined, but Noah wouldn't take no for an answer, so I just have to show him otherwise." I fold my hands across my chest.

"This is going to be better than watching *Bachelor in Paradise*." She slaps her hands together and rubs them.

I'm about to tell her that she's being ridiculous when I get a text from Noah, telling me he doesn't have a yoga mat or clothes. I laugh as I type my response, going to the rack of clothes hanging in the corner.

"Are you getting clothes for your friend who is a boy who you want to bounce on all night long?" she says, leaning over the counter to watch me grab a pair of loose shorts with matching tank top. "Why aren't you getting him the tight pair of shorts?" she yells while I glare at her. "You know the ones we all stand by and watch the men in, the ones who shows if they are packing?"

"Put an ad in the paper for a receptionist." I turn back around, grabbing him a blue yoga mat. "You're fired," I tell her, walking out, putting the stuff in my car and getting ready to go get the kids.

By the time I pull up to the yoga studio I see my friend Caroline, the owner of the studio, and Tammy, her partner. I grab the bag with Noah's clothes and both our mats, walking to them with a smile. "Hey." I kiss them both. "I'm so excited about tonight. Are the goats here already?" I ask them, searching for Noah.

"Yeah," Tammy says, grabbing my hand. "Come inside and see we have about thirty of them and they are babies also." I get dragged into the studio. It's not as big as mine; it's just one large room with a mirrored wall. There are some people setting up while the thirty goats get familiar with the room. The goats are all spaced out, some jumping on each other, some lying down. There are about ten to fifteen people already in the room. I see a couple of familiar people from my studio, so I smile and wave as I place the yoga mats down. I'm unrolling my mat and I'm about to sit on mine and start to stretch when Karen comes over.

"Hey," she says while I bend over to wrap my hands around my ankles, stretching out my hamstrings.

I come back up. "Hey, are you excited about the class?" I ask her, smiling.

Karen is known as a yoga cougar. She lies on her mat, checking out her prey before she pounces on them.

"I can't wait to see how it really is. See how the goats actually react." She is about to go on when the door opens, making the bell over the door ring. We both look over at Noah, who is now standing at the door. The sun coming in all around him makes him look like an angel. The smirk he gives me makes my panties melt and he hasn't even said anything. "Holy shit," Karen says quietly but stops talking when she sees Noah walking over to me.

"Hi." I raise my hand to wave at him, but he comes in, leaning down and kissing me on the cheek. "Glad you could make it."

"Wouldn't miss it for the world," he says, his voice smooth. I'm about to say something when Karen clears her throat. I see her moving from side to side with her hands behind her back. "Who do we have here?" she asks.

"Um, Karen"—I point to Noah—"this is my friend Noah. Noah, this is Karen." I point to her.

Noah reaches out to shake her hand that she brings in front of her.

"Oh, nice hard grip you have there," she says and I about groan out and make gagging noises.

"I have your change of clothes," I tell him, handing him the canvas bag that I put the clothes in. "There is a bathroom through there." I point to the door in the corner of the room. "Class starts in five minutes," I tell him when he nods and makes his way to the bathroom.

"Holy mother of god," Karen says, watching him walk away, "who is that fine glass of cold milk after a nice rice chocolate cake?"

"Oh, that's Noah." My eyes rove around in search of anyone else I can leave her with before she starts asking more question.

"Is he single?"

"He is, from what I know." I'm about to continue when the door opens and Stephanie comes in, walking straight to me.

"Hey, glad I'm not late. What's up, Karen?" she greets us both.

"Steph, do you know Noah? Does he take classes at the studio? Relaxation room? Anything?" Karen asks while Stephanie unrolls her mat next to mine.

"I have no idea. He's a friend of Kaleigh's," she says, bending to pet the goat that is trying to lick her feet.

"I'm going to totally go for it. You don't mind, do you, Kaleigh?" she asks, looking for Noah to come back.

"No, not at all, but I should mention." I look around to see if anyone is listening. "He suffers from IBS. You know, Irritable Bowel Syndrome."

Stephanie is giggling with a goat in front of her mouth to hide it.

"Oh, they have pills for that," Karen says.

"He also suffers from ED," I blurt out, shocked at even myself.

Karen stares at me, her mouth open.

"Yes, if it wasn't enough for him to have ED, the minute his penis is erect he suffers diarrhea." I see Noah coming back into the room. "He doesn't like to talk about it," I whisper at Karen, who gives Noah a once-over and then walks away.

"Friends my ass," Stephanie says as Noah finds his place next to me in front of his mat. He smiles at me. "Is this my mat?" he asks while I nod.

"Hi," Stephanie says from her sitting position. "I'm Stephanie. I work with Kaleigh."

"Hi there," Noah says, going to lean over and stopping when a goat bites his calf, making him jump. "Fucker," he hisses.

"Okay, everyone, before we start I'm going to go over a few rules. The goats are free to come and go as they please. They are not toilet trained, so there is a chance that they might go wherever they please." Tammy, the instructor, starts talking. "Most know how to jump, so there may be times where you can be in a position and the goat will take advantage of it and jump on you. Please, please do not freak out. You can hurt yourself as well as the goat. If by chance the goat jumps on your back, please go into the table pose position."

Noah leans over, asking me, "What is that?"

"Now with that said, if at any time you don't feel safe or comfortable you just say the word and Caroline or myself will come and help get you centered again. Okay, let's get started. Everyone on your mat. Feet shoulder width apart. Now let's take a deep breath in and exhale."

Noah is mimicking what Tammy is doing and trying to shoo away a goat that is trying to nibble on his toes. The movement just makes the goat come back, the goat head landing straight into his upper thigh giving him almost a Charlie horse. He falls on one knee. This time two more goats come to him, thinking he's their personal toy. One tries to lick his nose while another one is biting his shorts in the back. Two goats jump over the one, trying to make out with him, one of them hitting him in the junk, making a loud knock.

"I knew the cup would come in handy." He smiles at me, making the goat's tongue slide into his mouth. He gently pushes the goat away from himself. "Dude, you didn't even buy me dinner," he says, getting back on his mat.

"We are going to start off easy with the Sukhasana, which is the

Easy Pose," she says, getting to her position on the floor, folding her legs over each other. She goes over the instruction on how to properly do the pose. A little brown goat comes up to me, jumping in the middle of my lap and then lying down, placing her head on my leg.

"Ouch."

I open my eyes, looking over at Noah, who is now scratching his back on the side.

"Fucker bit me, twice," he whispers to me.

I try not to laugh, but I giggle silently.

"How do I get him to be calm like that one?" He points to the goat that is now sleeping in my lap.

"It's the energy you give out. I'm more Zen. You're more rock and roll," I tell him, closing my eyes and starting my breathing again.

"Just concentrate on your breathing," Tammy says as she inhales and exhales. We stay in that position for about two minutes, her calm voice starting again. "We are going to head into Adho Mukha Svanasana, which is the Downward-Facing Dog Pose," she says, getting on her hands and knees.

I don't have to watch her to do the pose, but I open my eyes, taking in Noah, who tries to get into position on his hands and knees, but the goats are all over him, as if he is hoarding food in his body. He is about to get up to his toes when a goat goes to his ass. He nips his ass cheek, making Noah swing his hips a little, but the goat doesn't let up and now his friend is coming to join in the party. This time both of the goats go straight for his asshole.

Noah bucks the goat off hissing, "Fuck off."

I'm just watching it and laughing to myself as a goat jumps up on my back. I lower myself to my knees to make sure the goat doesn't fall. Another goat is going up to Stephanie's mat and just shits right next to her mat. Noah is still trying to get the goat out of his ass. He swings left, but the other goat gets right in where. The goat gets out, both of them basically eating his ass while he swings from side to side. His shorts are being pulled by their teeth from left to right.

"This is goat rape," he says loudly while a goat goes on his mat and lies under him. He looks up and tries to bite the shirt that is hanging. "Umm, excuse me, uncomfortable here," he says out loud, having Caroline get up and walk over to him, shooing the goats away with encouraging words.

"They really like you," she says as one comes trotting over again, almost charging as if he's a bull and Noah is waving the red flag. They are caught by Caroline just before they reach their prime target, which is Noah. Caroline stays next to Noah for the rest of the class to ward off all the goats who seem to be taken with him. He is actually even missing a piece of the hem of his shirt.

Tammy finally calls out the last pose of the night, which is the "Savasana" also known as the corpse. "Now this is known as the most challenging pose," she starts off saying as she gets into position on her back. "It's challenging because you lie there and free your mind of everything. However, your mind never really shuts up. I know many of you will be thinking about the email that you should have sent, or what you will eat for dinner." She continues as she places her hands at her sides. "Or maybe some of you are wondering what that smell is, but here is something to help keep the menial thoughts at bay. I want you to think of something that would make you smile."

I close my eyes, forcing my head to clear, for the thoughts to store away for the next three minutes. I focus on exactly what Tammy said. I think of something that makes me smile. I think of my niece and nephew, think of my family, no matter how neurotic they are. I smile, breathing in and out as a goat comes to sit next to me and another sits on top of me. I'm about to continue my happy thoughts when I hear Noah's voice.

"Fucker," he hisses out.

I peel my eyes open. He has three new goats around him. One is trying to eat his crotch, one is by his ear trying to chew the collar of his shirt, while another one just pounced on his stomach and then fell on the side and pounced back up again. Tammy finally declares the class over. Noah rolls to his knees and gets up, bending over to roll up his mat. I walk over to him.

"You anxious to leave?" I ask him, trying not to giggle at the scowl on his face.

"These goats are fucking aggressive and should be kept out in the wild. I have been bitten, nipped, licked, pounced on, and I swear to God that goat had his whole nose up my asshole."

I reach out, grabbing his arm, but pulling my arm back when Tammy's voice breaks through.

"I'm so sorry that this wasn't as relaxing for you as for the rest of us. It just seems that they were drawn to you and your energy."

Noah nods his head, handing me his mat so he can roll up mine. When he finishes that, he grabs the mat I'm holding as well as the one he just rolled up and grabs the bag. "Thank you for your class," he says, walking outside barefoot.

I say a quick bye to them all, watching Stephanie smirk on the side as I follow Noah outside. I find him at the side of the building putting on his shoes.

"That has got to be the worst yoga class ever." He ties his running shoes then stands up. "How much do I owe you for the clothes and stuff?" He grabs the bag, getting his wallet out, opening it to grab some cash.

I put my hand on his, stopping him from taking anything out.

"Trust me, it was on me." I smile at him. "From one friend to another." I wink at him.

"Really, then can this friend buy you a drink? Or better yet a bite to eat? I'm starving," he says. "I know a great little Italian place around the corner."

I think for a minute that this could be bad news. I shouldn't actually go and eat with him. I am seriously playing with fire and right when I'm going to say no thank you I notice Karen lick her lips at him. Almost like a cat waiting to catch the bird about to fly over. "I would love to have a friendly dinner. Is it close enough that we can walk?" I ask him.

"Yes." He nods, pointing down the street in the direction of the restaurant. "I'll lead the way, friend."

We walk first to Noah's car where he puts the yoga mats and the bag in the trunk. As soon as he closes the trunk and locks the doors, his hand goes to my lower back as he ushers me in the right direction. When we make it to this little bistro, I notice that the inside is very small and they only have two tables outside.

"Hey, Mr. Noah." A short bald man comes up to him, his arms open wide to give him a hug. Noah leans down to accept it. "What is that smell?" He backs away, his nose scrunching up.

"Giuseppe, it's goat spit and probably shit." He turns his head to smell his own shirt. He leans in to smell me, his nose lightly touching my neck, making my body almost shiver. "You don't smell of goats."

"You sitta outside." He nods to the table. "Yeah, okay. I getta de bread."

He pulls out a chair and sits first, making me grab the seat in front of him.

"Come here often, Mr. Noah?" I ask, sitting back in my chair, folding my legs and leaning back.

"Only when I want the finest Italian cooking in the city. 'Mi Amore' is just like eating in Italy. He has everything flown in." He's about to say something else when the bus boy comes outside to pour some water in our glasses.

I lean in, saying "thank you," picking up my water, and almost finishing it off in one gulp.

Noah just nods at the boy.

Giuseppe comes back outside, grabbing the boy around the shoulder. "Noah, you meeta Giovanni. He's my nipote."

"I'm his grandson." Giovanni smiles at us, walking back inside.

Giuseppe claps his hands together. "So whatta you going to eat thisa time?" he asks us.

"Is there a menu?" I ask him while Giuseppe just smiles at me.

"Bellisima, you tella me whatta you want to eat and I make it for you."

"I'll have the osso buco with the pasta on the side," Noah says, drinking his water.

"Is that meat?" I ask him while he nods. "I don't eat meat." I look at Giuseppe. "I'm vegan."

Giuseppe gives me a confused look then looks at Noah for help.

"Um," he says, trying to explain what a vegan is. "Just vegetables," he finally says.

"Also no butter, cheese." When I see that he isn't getting it, I smile at him. "I'll take the salad with just olive oil and balsamic. And all the vegetables that you want to throw in it."

He slaps his hands together. "I doa you the best salad in the place." And he turns around, walking inside.

"Your smile totally threw him off of his game." He smiles at me, bringing his glass to his lips.

I shrug my shoulders as if I didn't know what I was doing. We both look at each other, each of us trying to find out what the next play will be and who will make it.

When Giuseppe comes back outside with bread and butter, he shocks me by adding a plate and putting a bit of olive oil and balsamic vinegar, moving it in the plate. "For you, bellissima."

"Grazie." I surprise both of them with my Italian word. "It's the only word I know along with si and ciao."

He throws his head back and laughs. "Noah, this isa good one. Si?"

"We are only friends," he tells him, the words making my heart flutter a bit, a pang coming.

"Aha, like me and my Maria?" He throws his hands up. "We go to a school together back in Italy." He starts his story. "Then I comma to America and she writes me letters."

I sit up, leaning and placing my elbows on the table as I take in his story.

"Then my mamma she calla me and tell me Maria is getting married. My heart it stopped." He places his hand on his heart. "I went back and told her you come with me to America." He ends the story on a smile.

"So she came with you to America?" I ask him, anxiously awaiting the rest of his story.

He shakes his head. "Ah, that Maria she never a do what I say." He puts his hands together like he's praying. "Dio mi, I fall in love with testa dure." His head is making the knocking on motion.

"She tells me, Giuseppe, I wanta babies. I tella her I give you all the babies you want. She wants tre." He shows us the number three. "I give her five."

"So she came to America with you. She left Italy for you." The thought of leaving everything that I know hurts my heart.

"She said no. I said yes. Then I go to her fadher and I say I want Maria to come with me to America. He said okay, so she comes. She notta happy." His hands go to his head. "Madonna, was she arrabiata. She refused to talk to me for a week. Now I think best week of my life, because now she never shuts up."

We both laugh out while we see this small little thing come outside with her hands on her hips, her dark brown hair tied at the nape of her neck in a bun, a white apron around her neck with what looks like tomato sauce all over it. "Giuseppe, come and get the plates," she says loudly. All he does is nod and follow her back in.

"See," Noah tells me. "You can be friends with the opposite sex."

I shake my head at him. "He basically did whatever he wanted."

"Same thing." He shrugs. "He knew in the end that she was what he wanted and didn't take no for an answer."

I don't say anything else because Giuseppe and Giovanni come back out with our food. They place the salad in front of me, a mix of greens, with onions, peppers, olives, celery, cucumbers, zucchinis, shredded carrots, and little pieces of broccoli. "This looks amazing, Giuseppe," I say, but what hits me the most is the aroma from Noah's dish. The pasta is tossed in what seems to be just a plain tomato sauce. My mouth waters, but what I don't see is Giuseppe place a plate next to my salad.

"This Maria make for you. She checked da Google with Giovanni."

I look down.

"It's mellenzanie, eggplant. She cooked it in oil, no butter and then she put da sauce on top." He brings his fingers to his mouth. "Deliscio."

"Thank you so much for going to all this trouble," I say, smiling at him, eager to taste it.

He bows and then walks away. I don't watch Noah. I just pick up my fork, cutting the tender eggplant, grabbing a piece with my fork, and bringing it to my mouth. The flavors hit my tongue all at the same time, making me close my eyes and moan. The tanginess of the sauce, with the sweetness of the eggplant…I open my eyes, still chewing. Noah's eyes are almost bulging out of his sockets, his hands gripping his fork and knife while his jaw clenches tight.

"You okay?" I ask him once I swallow.

"How about you never pull that sound again while we are eating? Or drinking, or ever." All this is said between clenched teeth.

I laugh at him, cutting another piece. "I'll try my best, but I make no promises. This is the best thing I've ever eaten, *ever*." Even the salad, which is tossed with a lemon, balsamic dressing is light, fresh, and amazing. “How is your dish?” I ask, watching him swirl the pasta on his plate, taking a big bite of it.

“It’s the second best thing I’ve eaten.” He smirks at me then winks. “Ever.” His voice is smooth.

My body stills. My breasts perk up as if they’re ready to participate in a saluting contest. My mouth goes dry and it’s a good thing because I have nothing to say, no comeback, nothing. Just a dry mouth, clammy hands, and a beating fucking heart. I was so fucking right. You cannot be friends with someone you’ve been with, but the thought of not seeing him anymore bothers me more than I care to say.

CHAPTER FIFTEEN

Noah

As soon as she tasted her meal, she threw her head back and moaned. Whatever fucking power I had was gone, poof, vanished. That and the fact that all my blood traveled south, my cock fighting the constriction of my shorts. I couldn't do anything except grab onto my fork and knife with all my might instead of flipping the table over and devouring her.

The minute I walked into the fucking yoga class I knew I made several mistakes. One, the smell was really horrible like I was in the middle of a barnyard. The second was her smile. Her smile stopped me in my tracks and then finally those fucking yoga pants. Jesus, good thing I had a jock on, which didn't make me show the world what I had to offer. Now here I am in the same state. This woman gets me going every single time.

This whole being friends is complete bullshit. There is no way that she doesn't want me as much as I want her. I can see it in her eyes, see it in the way her body responds to me. I'm about to lean in and take her hand in mine when Giovanni comes back out.

"Nonno wants to know if you want more food?"

Kaleigh smiles up at him. "I couldn't eat another bite."

He nods at her while he takes her plates. I place my fork and knife down.

He clears the plates, leaving us all alone.

"See." I grab my water. "We can have dinner together as friends." I wink at her.

"Yeah, yeah, yeah," she says, rolling her eyes.

Giuseppe comes out with a plate of fruit. Some watermelon, grapes, cantaloupe, and a couple of figs.

"Hmmm. I love fruit," she says, picking up a piece of watermelon, biting it, and it's almost as if it's happening in slow motion. Her teeth bite into the watermelon, the juice leaking out the side her mouth. She licks her lower plump lip, my eyes following the movement.

"Noah."

I shake my head.

"Where you go?" Giuseppe asks, laughing.

"Just thinking about my busy day tomorrow." I grab a couple of grapes, tossing them into my mouth.

"You worka too hard. The whole country same thing. In Italy you have to slow down and enjoy life. La Vita Bella."

The good life he says and I just nod at him. I pay the bill or at least I try, but since we are friends, Kaleigh chipped in.

Getting up from the table, Giuseppe comes over, kissing Kaleigh on both cheeks. "You come back, yeah?"

She smiles and nods. The walk back to the cars is quiet. The only sounds are the occasional cars along with the crickets. I follow her to her car, our hands grazing each other.

She opens her door, turning around as she stands outside. "Thank you so much for coming and for dinner."

I lean in closer to her. Her breath hitches softly. "There is nowhere else I would have rather been."

She stands straight. "Even with the goat rape?" She laughs, leaning in.

"Even with the goat rape." I move forward just a touch more. "Want to hear a secret?" I ask her and she doesn't answer, but I see her throat move as she swallows and nods. "If this were a date, I would end this differently," I whisper to her.

Her eyes blink. She folds her lips then licks them. "Like what?" she asks, her voice so soft it's almost like she didn't say anything.

"Like"—I lick my own lips now—"I would hold your hand walking here. I'd open the door for you to get in, but before you get in I would lean in and taste your lips. I would kiss you gently at first." I smile, thinking about it. "Then I would slowly lick your lips to have them open just a tad before I slide my tongue into your mouth. Our tongues feverish for each other. Tangled, wet, eager. The need to be in each other's skin would make us forget where we are and who is watching. Because in the end it's just going to be me and you." I lean in, my lips almost touching hers, but instead I move to the side, kissing her cheek. "But I don't want to ruin the friendship we have." I step away from her, raise my head, and walk away. Take that. I smile at myself.

"Oh, Noah." She finally speaks out. "If we weren't just friends, I would have gotten down on my knees." She shrugs her shoulders. "Have a great night, friend." And she gets into her car and drives away, leaving me in the middle of the street, cursing out. Noah - 0, Kaleigh - 1.

I make it home with my cock still up and begging for relief. The cold shower and jacking him off did nothing for him. I crawl into bed, the smell of goat still lingering. My phone bings with a message. I notice it's a picture from Kaleigh.

This was on the yoga page. Thought you would like it for your screensaver ;)

The picture is of me on my knees with a goat's face up my ass. I zoom it in and see Kaleigh giggling behind me. You don't have to zoom in to see my ass cheek clenching.

Thanks for this, but I think I'll stick to Austin's swollen balls.

Oh, that's a good one.

I stare at my phone, wondering how to play this. I'm supposed to be friends with this girl. Yet all I want to say is get your ass over here now. Just the thought has my cock stirring into action. Lifting the cover, I say out loud, "Simmer down. I just took care of you." I shake my head. I'm going crazy. This chick has me talking to my dick and the worst part is I'm expecting it to talk back to me.

I finally decide to write back.

Night.

That's what a friend would do, right? I turn off the light and end up tossing and turning most of the night. I drag my ass the next day. Gone is the quirky free loving guy. In his place is a grouchy, unused cock. When the hot new red-haired receptionist smiles at me the only thing that happens is a grunt. A fucking grunt.

"Whoa, who pissed in your corn flakes?" Harvey asks from behind me. He had gotten off the other elevator.

"I'm just cranky." I run my hand through my hair.

"You sound like an old married man. You're single, with no ties at all. You should be standing up shouting 'I'm the king of the world.'" He smiles, continuing, "This morning I woke up with the biggest case of blue balls. I haven't had sex this whole month."

I stand here gawking at him. "The whole month? That's like thirty days, sometimes thirty-one."

"Yup, the most action my dick has gotten this month was my daughter kneeing me in the balls." He shakes his head. "The baby is teething and keeping us up all night. If I'm honest, I'm just so tired that my dick probably wouldn't even get up."

My hand goes over my mouth. "Thirty days? Do you?" I motion with my hand the jerking off motion.

"Thirty days, if not more. Who the fuck is counting?"

"Are you sure it can still work?" I point at his crotch as we stand in front of his office.

"It works just fine." He laughs, taking a sip of his coffee. "Now stop being a cranky bastard and go get some pussy, for all our sakes." He turns to walk into his office.

I go into my office, sitting at my desk, staring into the sky when my phone beeps.

Are you sore this morning?

The text from Kaleigh has me smiling. Grump is gone with five words.

If only you knew. I answer back while I cup my cock.

It's probably because you kept tensing up with the goats.

Goats have nothing to do with this pain.

Bhahahah really??? So what ails you?

I'm seriously addicted to this woman and I can't get her out of my mind.

Noah!! she answers back right away

What? I reply back.

We are supposed to be friends.

Friends can't discuss other friends' love lives?

Oh, she replies. ***I thought.***

You thought I was talking about you? That I was talking about us? Well…

Is all she says before there is a knock on my door. Looking up, I see it's Norma. "We have all the paperwork drawn up for Sal's newest venture." She comes in, placing the file on my desk. "The owners are leaving at four p.m. this afternoon for vacation and would like this settled before then."

I place my phone down. "Then let's buckle down and get this contract in order," I say, taking off my jacket and rolling up my sleeves. "It's go time."

I don't know how long I'm at it, but when the phone rings and buzzes near my hand my head snaps up. I see Austin's dick greet me. I laugh to myself each time. It's still funny.

"Yeah," I say, putting the phone to my ear and circling something that needs to be changed.

"I need you to come and bring me to the impound lot!" Austin yells, but I can barely hear him. Some music is playing in the background. "Shut the fuck up!" he yells.

"Dude, where are you? Are you at the Disney store?" I ask him, looking at my watch, seeing it's almost two p.m.

"I'm in Lauren's school bus. She didn't pay my tickets and now my car has been impounded."

"See Donkey Kong."

"I don't have the time nor the patience to deal with you today. Just come and pick me up." He blows out a long breath. "This fucking song."

"What is that?" I ask him.

"Who the fuck knows? The CD is stuck inside and this chick is so fucking angry yet she wants to let it go," he says, his voice rising higher when she belts out Let it Go at the top of her lungs.

"Okay, I'll swing by at four so we can get to the yard before it closes."

He doesn't even say bye. He just disconnects with a string of curse words. I press the button on my desk phone, asking Norma to have a sandwich delivered. She walks in right away with a brown paper bag.

"This was delivered two hours ago by a tall blonde," she says, coming to the desk and putting it in front of me.

"What?" I get up, going to the door. "Why didn't you let me know?"

She smiles at me. "She left it with Samantha, the new receptionist."

She walks to me, tapping my shoulder. "She left a note on the bag." She walks off while I run back to my desk and see the bag.

Hope you have a baa day! And she drew a sheep. I toss my head back and laugh, opening it up. I find another note. *I usually don't buy meat, but I liked holding your meat! Bhahah.*

I sit down and take out the hoagie she left. It's got every single meat you can think of and it's the best sandwich I've ever eaten.

I send her a quick text.

Thanks for holding my meat.

I wait for her to answer but nothing comes through. By the time I finish eating and finalize the file for Sal, I get to Austin's office with almost no time to spare. Walking down the hall, I notice that most of the people have already left. Must be a quiet day. When I walk into his office, he's sitting behind his desk with his head in his hands, looking down at his phone.

"Whoa, dude, who killed your dog?" I ask as I throw myself into the chair in front of his desk.

"I fucked up," he confesses, looking up and then looking back down at his phone.

"Nothing new there. What happened now?"

"I may have told Lauren that if she weren't so uptight and she loosened up a little, that maybe her husband wouldn't have left her and she would still be married." He doesn't even finish getting the words out before I'm pulling out my phone. "What the fuck are you doing?"

"I'm making sure I clear my schedule for your funeral," I joke with him, but it only earns me a glare from him.

"Fuck off, asshole. Let's go get my car, and then I'll pass by her house. She has no choice but to answer the door, right?" he asks me as we walk out to the elevator.

I see Barbara come out of her office and head straight for us. Her mouth is pressed together in a tight line. Austin cuts off whatever she's going to say by holding up his hand and stating, "Not now, Barbara." He presses the elevator button.

"I think my balls just crawled back into my body, and that look wasn't even directed at me," I murmur from beside him as we watch Barbara turn and storm away. "If I were you, I wouldn't drink or eat anything that anyone else, especially someone who is a female or an employee here, offers you," I advise him as I follow him into the elevator.

We make it down to the impound lot, where I leave Austin to fill out all the forms and show all his documents in order to get his car out.

I walk to a seat where I take my phone out and see I have about fifteen texts from Kaleigh.

I can't be friends with you anymore. Your best friend is an asshat.

If he's an asshat, you're an asshat.

They usually only hang around together.

Like herding asshats.

I can't believe I held meat for you!!!

Isn't it ironic????

Why do you have to be a good-looking asshat?

I lied. You aren't good-looking, you're ugly.

I hope you get goat herpes.

I'm going to take lessons in Donkey Kong.

It's ironic… Rain on your wedding day.

Jesus, fuck me. They are listening to Alanis Morissette. "Maybe you should give her the night to calm down."

"No, I can't. I need to see her." He shakes his head, the look of dread filling his face. "I need to at least tell her I'm sorry." He pushes past me, getting into his car and taking off. I jog to mine and follow him there. Once he parks, I get out before he can open his door.

"As your friend, I'm going to try to talk you out of this."

He shakes his head, ignoring me. He gets out of the car and walks to her door.

"This is a really, really bad idea. Women who are pissed can do evil things. I mean, she wasn't even that pissed at you when she almost made your balls explode."

"I have to see her," he says and then knocks on the door. When I hear the locks click open, a smile starts to creep across his face. It's quickly replaced with a frown when we both see that it's Kaleigh who opens the door—with what appears to be a machete in her hand. Okay, so maybe not a real machete, but it sure as hell is a knife that looks like it can easily debone a chicken and probably take off a man's—hopefully not this man's—hand. She comes outside, closing the door behind her as the sound of Alanis Morissette is playing in the background.

"You have some nerve showing your face here," she spits out at him.

Turning to glare at me, it's then I notice she's a bit drunk.

"Is Lauren home?"

I look at him with a confused look on my face. Obviously she's here. Her car is here.

"She is," she confirms as she sways a little.

I look a little closer and can tell she's totally blitzed. Tipsy was an hour ago.

"Whoa, there, little lady." I wrap an arm around her shoulders to avoid the knife to my dick.

"I need to talk to her," Austin says, but all I can do is take in the fact that she's in my arms, she's soft, she's perfect, and she's also still holding that fucking knife.

"Not going to happen. Not now, not ever." She continues, "You fucked up bad." She is now pointing the knife at Austin, and her voice is rising. "Really, really bad."

"Babe, can we put the knife down?" I plead with a smile, and she smiles at me while bashfully giggling. I really fucking like drunk Kaleigh. She pushes her body more into me. We stand here staring at each other.

"Can I please just talk to Lauren for two minutes? Then I'll leave, I promise," he practically begs.

She stands up tall and pushes herself away from me. "Nope," she replies and then turns around, grabbing the door handle and talking to us over her shoulder. "If you're not gone in two minutes, I'm calling the cops and telling them you're stalking me."

He scoffs at that, and she glares at him.

"And show them the inappropriate dick pics you sent me."

Austin turns to look at me.

I put both hands up. "I may have showed them to her and she might have forwarded a couple of them to herself."

"Can you please tell her that I was here and ask her to call me? Please, Kaleigh?" He gets in right before she slams the door in our face and flips the locks with loud clicking sounds.

He hangs his head, while I pat him on the back.

"She'll call." I try to assure him, but unless hell freezes over… "Or send someone to kill you. I mean, she did say Donkey Kong."

He shrugs my hand off of him and walks back to his car, while I turn to look at the house and wonder what would happen if I go back and ring the doorbell again. I'm about to take that step right before I hear girls chanting "Ironic" at full volume.

"Yup, tomorrow is another day!"

CHAPTER SIXTEEN

Kaleigh

The minute the sun peeks through the curtains it lands on my face. I try blinking my eyes and swallowing, but I must have swallowed a pack of cotton balls, because I can't produce spit. I turn around and land on the floor. "Fuck." I'm not even in my bed. I'm on the couch. I look over at Lauren, who is sleeping in a curled ball. "Jesus," I say as I take in the room. There are about six empty wine bottles, some pizza in a take-out box, and an empty bottle of vodka with three shot glasses. "Shit." When I try to stand my head just turns over and over, so I sit on my ass, turning on my knees and crawling to the bathroom. "I really hope I can get up and not have to pee myself," I say to the walls, but I hear a groan coming from behind me.

"Oh, God," I say to the toilet when I try to get up on it. I close my eyes, breathing out of my mouth, trying not to barf and to stop the room from spinning. After I finish, I walk hunched back over to the couch. "I think a cat died in my mouth."

Lauren sits up and then falls back down.

"I'm never drinking again."

"I second that," Lauren says from her side of the couch, raising her hand in the air. "Shit, where is Barbara?" she asks and I take in the destruction of what used to be her tidy living room. "I'm in the kitchen making you girls the hangover special."

My stomach growls loud. "Is there a vegan option?" I ask as the smell of bacon fills the room.

She walks out of the kitchen, fresh and revived, which is the complete opposite of how we look. "I made two separate breakfasts. For the non-vegan, which is Lauren and myself, we have scrambled eggs, bacon, sausage, and some hash browns."

Lauren still hasn't moved. She just groans I think in appreciation.

"For the vegan, I fried some of the fake bacon, which I'm pretty sure is rubber, and some vegan eggs, which look like I can't even tell you. Is it even healthy?" she asks.

I just nod. "I need toast."

Barbara goes back in the kitchen while I lie on the couch, watching the wall, "Did I strip last night?" I ask.

"Yes, but Barbara threw a sheet over you for your dignity."

Lauren has her eyes closed.

I feel the couch vibrate, so I move my hand around it, coming up empty, till it buzzes again and I feel it next to my feet. I grab it in between my feet, bringing it up to my face. I press the home button, showing me Facebook notifications as well as Instagram and then texts from Noah. I close my eyes, trying to remember. Opening them, I enter my password before going to my messages. I see four from him.

You're cuddly when you're drunk.

I am not an asshat and there is no herd.

Please be my friend.

You're sexy AF when you use weapons, just not around my dick.

I scroll up to see our conversation and gasp when I see that I sent him about a million texts. Okay, maybe not a million, but at least ten. "You are a horrible wing woman!" I shout at Lauren, who raises the hand she has over her eyes up to look at me.

"What the fuck are you talking about?" she asks, puzzled by my sudden outburst.

"Rule one of drinking, phones are placed in a locked drawer. Where is your phone?" I ask her.

"I have no idea. I think the last time I saw it you took a knife out." She places her hand on her face again. "I can't believe you pulled the knife out and the pizza guy came. I thought he was going to shit himself when you threw the door open and said, 'I will cut a bitch if you don't get the fuck away from this door.'"

My hands fly to my face. "Oh my God. I pulled it out when Austin showed up," I say while Barbara comes out of the kitchen with two plates, placing them right on the coffee table.

"I'm not defending him, but the knife was a tad too much," Barbara says, going into the kitchen and coming back with her own plate. "You texting him our picture was like kicking him in the nuts. I think he answered back traitor."

"I'm sorry. It's the wine, or was it the vodka?"

She waves her hand in the air. "Please, I've been called worse. Serves him right. He really fucked up this time."

"Can we change the subject?" Lauren says, rolling off the couch and sitting on the floor while she grabs her plate, eating it on her lap.

"Yes," Barbara and I both say at the same time while I eat the eggs. "They are so fluffy. How did you get them this way?" I ask her, grabbing some hash browns.

"Water," she says simply. "Usually I add milk, but I didn't know what was what, so I just added water."

We spend the rest of the meal just eating. The two of us are almost like zombies. We try to help Barbara clean up, but all we do is bring our plates into the kitchen.

"Barbara, don't worry about the mess. I'll get to it after I nap," Lauren says while I side hug her.

"I'm going to go and collapse in my bed. Barbara, you can party like a rock star and look like a lady the next day. You're my hero."

I turn and walk out of the room while they continue talking, walking/crawling upstairs. I pass Rachel's room as I go to mine. It's a good thing they spent the night at my parents or I would have to donate to their therapy fund. How many nieces and nephews can say that their aunt almost sliced open a pizza delivery man?

Once I get to my room, I fall face first into the bed like a starfish and drift off to a fitful sleep. By the time night rolls around I feel almost normal, almost. The kids have come back and are now in bed while I lie in mine. I took a shower finally, so I'm lying in my bed naked. A dim light fills the room, the television playing in the background, but my mind isn't processing anything that is happening. Instead, my mind keeps turning to Noah. Him showing up with Austin was a huge surprise. What wasn't a surprise was the way my body got pulled to him. How he put his arm around me and all I wanted was to throw down the knife and wrap all my limbs around him. His blue eyes, his beautiful lips. A knock at my door has my mind coming back.

"Come in," I say, putting the television on mute.

Lauren opens the door, peeking her head in.

"Hey, just checking in. How you feeling?" She opens the door, standing there in shorts and a tank top.

"I'm okay, back as new tomorrow, I think," I say, stretching. "You feeling better?" I ask her, knowing she has been beating herself up about the whole thing.

"I just need to move on. Find a boss I don't want to kill or at least a boss who won't push me over the edge into insanity."

"For what it's worth, he looked really sorry when he stopped—" Her hand flies up to stop me from saying anything. "Fine, subject dropped."

"I'm going to bed," she says, closing the door behind her. And I do just that, turning off the light and getting lost in my dreams.

The next morning I wake to a knock at the door, followed by a soft little voice.

"Auntie Kay, I'm going bye bye soon and we didn't smoochacles."

I giggle, stretching. "You may enter for some smoochacles," I shout while she opens the door, coming in.

Her blond pigtails bob up and down as she hops over to me. She climbs on the bed while I turn on my side, opening my arms for her to lie down next to me. She lays her head on my outstretched arm while my other arm snuggles her closer to me. "I gotta go see Daddy and Ms. Camilla," she says, her small arm wrapping around my neck.

"It's going to be fun and when you come back we can make some cookies," I say. "Now give me smooches before mom calls you down. I think I heard a car door slam."

She leans in, rubbing her nose with mine and then kissing me on the lips. I blow zerberts across her cheeks and then her neck, her giggles coming out while her little hands try to push me away.

"Now be a good girl and smile big when you see mom, okay?" I kiss her nose one more time before she turns over and slips off the bed.

"And when I come back we can do doggy style again, okay, Auntie Kay?"

"Downward Dog, honey," I tell her while she slams the door. I grab my robe, getting up, glancing at my phone. I have a couple of texts from Noah.

I'm not an Asshat.

Let me take you out and show you.

I don't answer him. Instead, I close my phone and go to the bathroom and finally make my way downstairs to see Lauren at the counter reading the paper. "Morning," I say as I go to the coffee machine, taking a sip of the black coffee. "You know what we need to do? Go out." I watch her eyes move up from the paper. "Get our freak on."

She eyes me, still not sold.

"Dance, Lauren, shake our pom-poms." I shake my body, pretending I'm dancing.

"I don't know, Kay," she says while I put my cup down.

"When is the last time we went out just to go out and dance?" I don't wait for her to answer. "I'm going to go and do some yoga, rid myself of the toxins that are probably still lingering in my body, then we will have a nap and get ready to paint the town." I put my empty cup in the sink. "Better take a nap, grandma, it's going to be a long night." I smile at the dib while she tells me to fuck off. Going upstairs, I put on my yoga pants and sports bra, picking up my mat on the way out. My phone is dropped into the bottom of the bag. My fingers are tempted to answer him back. "I need to get laid and get him out of my system," I say to myself as I walk to the park near the house and I finally rid myself of the toxins.

By the time I'm showered and shaved, I take in my outfit. "Yup, this makes a statement all right." It consists of a pair of white lace looser-fitting short shorts with a small, shiny black belt. I've paired it with a black tube top. I have omitted the bra because I don't actually need one. The whole outfit comes together with a seriously sexy pair of black open-toe, lace-up stiletto boots. "Yup, let's do this," I tell my reflection as I grab my small clutch, putting my phone in it. I walk out of my room, coming face to face with Lauren, who looks a little scared.

"Let's go get us some dick!" She raises her hands in the air, and I can't help but laugh. Before she can answer me, we hear a honk outside. "CAB'S HERE!" she yells in her best Jersey shore accent.

We get into the cab and I give him the address to the club we are going to. "Steph's roommate's boyfriend's cousin is the bouncer at this club and she put our name on the list." I take my phone out of my purse. "We need a selfie," I tell her, raising my hand in the air and making a duck face. I post it on Instagram with the caption 'what trouble will we bring tonight?'

"Don't post everything on social media, Kay. That is how people get killed."

"Okay there, mom." I put the phone back in my purse.

As soon as we pull up to the curb, we make it inside in record time thanks to my main guy Nico at the door. Not only does he lead us inside he has someone escort us to a table, or better yet a booth. The booths sit in a section that is a bit higher than the dance floor. You can get to this area by using the set of six stairs leading up here around the dance floor.

"On the house." He winks at us as we take in the bottle of Grey Goose chilling.

"Did you sleep with him?" Lauren asks me.

I watch his tight ass walk away. "Nope, not yet, but the night is very young," I say, picking up the bottle and pouring myself some with cranberry juice. I take my phone out and take another selfie, captioning this one with,

Who runs the world? Girls!

I drop my phone into my purse. "Lauren, you need to get laid. Get those cobwebs out of the way."

She glares at me, then turns around to see if anyone is around. "Can you shut up? People can hear you. On the down low, Kay."

"Okay," I whisper. "I won't tell anyone that your vagina is dusty. It'll be our little secret."

She takes a shot of vodka, glaring at me. "I hope the guy you go home with tonight has short penis syndrome."

I gasp out in shock. "Why would you say that? I haven't had sex since Noah. I need to get laid, super laid, so laid I forget about him."

She takes another shot of vodka.

"I would slow down there before you pass out on this couch." I point to the booth we are sitting in.

Two hours later, we are finally sitting down after dancing our asses off and I'm finally drinking my vodka and cranberry when the Drake song "One Dance" comes on. Lauren stands up, throwing her hair back, putting her hands in the air as she yells how much she loves this song.

She grabs me by the hand, and we run back out onto the packed dance floor.

I watch as Lauren sways her hips to the beat of the song, singing out loud with Drake. My eyes are focusing on the blue eyes that are watching me from the bar. The guy is coming to hold Lauren's hips and then Austin, the man on a mission to get to Lauren, shows up. It happens so fast I don't even see him tell the guy to fuck off while he pulls my sister by the hand, walking away, the crowd on the dance floor swallowing them up. I'm about to walk back to my booth when my back is pushed into a rock hard wall or actually chest. I don't even have to look to know it's Noah. His smell is all around me. One arm wraps around my waist and the other holds my hip as we sway to the beat. His head dips down to my ear. His breath comes out softly, his voice even softer.

"You can't run now, can you?" The words make the hair on my arms rise up, the goose bumps coming out. "I dare you." There is something about his tone that tells me this is going to end one way and one way only, me underneath him. Naked.

I push my ass into his cock. I turn my head, tilting it backward, my mouth opening to say something, but stopping the minute his head comes down to meet mine. His tongue invades mine. The taste of bourbon lingers on his tongue, my body awaking for him, my arm rising behind me to drag my hand into his hair, my body then turning into his arms while his hands grip my ass, squeezing and pushing me into him. My hands now around his neck, the kiss goes deeper, our bodies still now. We get knocked to the side, but it doesn't break us apart. It just makes us hold each other tighter. I'm so lost in the kiss, lost in him, lost in his touch, lost in his taste, lost in the need for him that I don't notice the songs changing.

"One question," he finally says when we come up for air. He starts kissing my cheek, chin, and neck. "Did you drive here?"

I move my neck to the side, giving him full access to me. "We took an Uber," I reply right away, my body almost shaking with need.

He grabs my hand, leading me to the table that Lauren and I were drinking at. He grabs my purse, nodding at the bouncer who is watching the booths. Our fingers entwine with each other's as if we always hold hands. We are outside the club with him holding his hand up to catch a cab, before I can register what is going on.

"I have to go back and tell Lauren," I say as the cab stops and he opens the door.

"She's taken care of. Now, Kaleigh, get in the car."

I let go of his hand and walk to the door, my hand grazing his hip and then cupping his cock. "I can't be your friend," I tell him before I bend to get into the cab.

"Good," he says, following me inside and shutting the door, giving the cab driver his address. The light from outside streams into the car, showing his blue eyes are dark and cloudy. "I was through being friends with you anyway." His voice comes out husky.

I turn my back to the door. "Is that so?" I ask him, not sure what this means, my heart hammering in my chest, my breath holding itself in. "And why is that?"

He looks at the cab driver then turns his head to smirk at me. "We are way past being friends. Because I'm about to do very dirty things to you, things that friends don't do with each other." He yanks me to his side, leaning down and nipping my lower lip. "Dirty, dirty things."

I'm almost ready to beg him in the middle of a cab, but the driver stops right in front of his house. I open the door, getting out while Noah pays the driver. He walks past me as I follow him up the stairs while he unlocks the door. He holds the door open for me. I step in but don't make it far because he walks in with me, slamming the door behind him. His hands go up to my neck, grabbing my hair and tugging me back, a moan escaping my lips. My back lands on his chest again. His hand leaves my hair, and he's suddenly all over me. One hand pulls down my top, my breast springing free, my nipples achy with need while his other hand slides into my shorts, his middle finger sliding between my folds, finding me wet with need. My head falls to his shoulder.

"Yeah, definitely not going to be your friend anymore."

CHAPTER SEVENTEEN

Noah

Maybe it's a good thing that this whole thing with Kaleigh has ended. I was losing my touch. I went out running today and I didn't wink at one single person, not a fucking one. I didn't even try to see if the woman in front of me was wearing a thong or not. I spent the next day taking another run and rubbing one off in the shower. I look at my hands before I get dressed to make sure I'm not developing calluses with the amount of time I've jacked off in the last four fucking days. I look down at my dick. "You need to get out of your funk, man, and wake up," I say right before I go to my closet, taking out my favorite pair of black jeans. I pair it with a button-down white shirt and throw a gray cardigan on top. I roll up the sleeves to my elbows, making the white shirt fold over. I grab my black boots, finishing the look while I slap on my black Rolex.

I order an Uber and text Austin to be outside in ten minutes. We nod at each other and get into the car, both of us in our own turmoil. We stop by a pub, grabbing some wings and beer while we watch the Yankees on the screen.

"Where do you want to go tonight?" he says while a commercial comes on.

I shrug my shoulders, grabbing the beer and taking a long pull. "I don't care as long as my dick gets some action." I almost groan, opening up my Instagram app, and there looking back at me is Kaleigh in what looks like sex on two sticks, which are her fucking legs. Jesus, my cock finally sees his target. And she tagged herself at Lights club.

"Let's hit up Lights Night Club," I say, closing off my phone and finishing up my beer. It's now or fucking never.

Shaking the doorman's hand, we make our way over to the corner bar. I've spent many nights closing this place down. This is one of the first clubs Austin and John put their names on.

I lean on the bar, motioning to the bartender with my finger. When he comes to us, I order a bourbon straight up because at that minute I scan the booths and see her. The woman who has broken my dick and put a spell on him. She stands next to Lauren, who is dancing with her hands in the air. I notice right away when Austin finally spots her. He stands straight, draining his bourbon also in one gulp, his eyes never leaving her. We both motion for another shot. We watch as the sisters make their way to the dance floor. I watch Kaleigh sway her hips left and right while one hand goes up and the other stays by her side. A baboon goes up to Lauren and it takes Austin less than a blink of an eye to pounce on her. I make my way through the crowd, standing right behind Kaleigh while Austin drags Lauren off. My hand itches to touch her.

Now here I am, my two fingers in her pussy, her head on my shoulder. She turns her head to suck on my neck, her ass grinding into me. "Wet." My fingers fuck her. "I hope you napped today," I say, pulling out and then pushing all the way to my knuckles. "Because by the time I finish with you, the sun will be coming up." My cock thrusts, ready to fucking pounce out. My hand feels constricted, so I pull it out of her shorts, bringing my fingers to my mouth and licking them clean. Her eyes open wide. Moving from behind her, I get in front of her, backing her up to the door. "All week, my cock wouldn't get up," I tell her as I cup her tits in my hands, rolling the nipples, then twisting them. Her legs open wider. "Only got up when I thought of your mouth, your tits, or that sweet tasting pussy." I lean down, biting her neck, my tongue coming out to lick the teeth marks that are now there.

"Yeah," she breathes out, her hands trying to grab my belt. "Let's see him so I can tell him I'm going to make it all better."

"Not yet," I tell her, my tongue licking one nipple, twirling it with the tip of my tongue. My hands are holding her hips as I look for a zipper. "You haven't come on my tongue yet." I finally find the hidden zipper in the back, unzipping it while she closes her legs, letting the shorts fall to her ankles. She steps one foot out of them, then opens her legs. "Glistening."

"Well, my pussy is here," she says, her hands coming up to grab her nipples as she rolls them herself. "Ready to come."

"Fuck," I hiss out, getting on my knees, blowing at her core. "You are more than ready." My tongue comes out, licking her up then blowing out on her, her head looking down at me. Our eyes lock. I take another lick, stopping right where her clit is, instead opening her lips and blowing at the pink little nub that is begging to be touched. "This"—I touch her clit with my index finger, moving it from side to side—"this right here, does this need to be kissed or bitten?" I ask, leaning in, kissing it then biting it. "So bitten it is," I say, biting it again, one hand leaving her nipples while she grabs my head, forcing her pussy onto my face. "You want to ride my tongue?" I say, my tongue coming out, sliding inside her with my fingers at the same time.

"Noah, if you don't shut up and start making me cum I might just knock you out and ride your face myself," she hisses out, her pussy slowly closing in on my tongue.

I laugh when she starts moving her hips and her hands come down to her pussy, rubbing her clit.

"Want to help me?" I ask her as my fingers mix with hers, but then my tongue comes out, getting tangled in the fingers. I lean back, watching this little minx trying to pleasure herself. I see her stick two fingers inside of herself, one hand still rolling her nipple, her eyes closed. I can tell she is close, her hands moving faster, her hips thrusting out while she opens her eyes and watches me. Two can play this game. I get up, standing in front of her, her hands slowing down.

She's leaning against the door with nothing on but her top that is bunched around her waist and her boots.

"You know what I really missed this week?" I ask her as I unbutton my jeans, the zipper slowly coming down, the sound echoing in the room. My cock springs free, the tip with pre-cum already oozing from it. So hard. "Sinking my cock into you." I squeeze the base of my cock, trying to relieve the pressure. "Having you come on my cock." I move my hand up and down, mimicking her. "Having you squeeze my cum from me."

Her hands move faster, so fast her eyes land on my hands that are jacking my cock, the head almost purple it's so hard.

"I'm going to come. Are you close?" I say, closing my eyes and tossing my head back. I don't have time to jack myself one more time because she is bent over, her mouth landing straight on my cock.

Ass in the air, legs spread, mouth on my cock, her hand in her pussy, taking what she wants and not shy about it. She takes me to the back of her throat and moans out her orgasm, the vibration making me cum down her throat. She swallows me, all of me. Never stopping till I stop thrusting my hips, till my cock plops out of her mouth.

She stands up, her fingers coming out of her pussy. She lifts them to my mouth. I lick them clean while she tells me, "Couldn't waste that now, could we?" She winks at me, turning to bend over and grab her shorts.

The view is too much to pass on, so my hand comes down to meet her perfect ass, hard enough to leave a light pink mark. I don't know what I expect, maybe for her to stand up, turn her head. What I'm not expecting is for her to just wiggle her ass in the air again, her legs spread even more, her hands landing in front of her. I reach behind me, grabbing my wallet from my pocket, taking the condom out, and ripping it with my teeth. I sheath myself, my cock harder than it was before. I smack her ass again, then rub it slowly. I repeat it with the other side. This time a moan comes out of her. I bend a little to align my cock with her. I rub it through her folds, the heat of her pussy coming through the condom when I line up with her. I enter her in one hard thrust, sending her forward, my hands on her hips squeezing her and keeping her in place. The way she feels on my cock makes me throw my head back and bask in it. Buried to the hilt, I almost don't want to move, but her pussy squeezes me tight. So I pull out and slam back in so hard my balls hit her wet pussy. She meets my thrust, smashing her ass back into me. I pull out and slam back in, this time my palm hitting her ass. The sting makes her pussy squeeze me tight.

"Fuck," I say, repeating the action five times till her ass is bright pink. I start on the other ass cheek and it's too much because she comes with a loud moan, her head falling forward. I ride out her orgasm before I close my eyes and empty myself in the condom, groaning out the whole way.

I slowly pull out of her, turning to walk to the kitchen and throw out the condom. By the time I walk back to the door, she is pulling her shorts back up. "What the fuck do you think you're doing?" I ask her, my voice higher than it should be.

"Um, I thought we were done." She smiles at me. "Weren't we?"

"Baby, I just scratched the surface." My cock is semi hard now. "It's time you rode the horse, don't you think?"

She drops the shorts to the floor, also taking the top from around her waist. "I would really love nothing more than to ride your horse. The only question is, will I be a regular cowgirl or shall I reverse it?" She winks at me as she starts to stroke my cock, which is now ready to join the party.

We spend the rest of the night doing it on the couch, on my kitchen counter, walking up the stairs, sitting on the stairs, in my shower, on my counter. We finally fall into bed when the birds start chirping outside. She falls asleep face down in a starfish position. I don't even know when I fall asleep, but I definitely know that when I wake up she isn't here.

"Son of a bitch," I say, getting up and dragging my shorts on. "I swear to God I'm going to get a fucking shock collar for her."

CHAPTER EIGHTEEN

Kaleigh

My eyes blink open slowly, the light from outside being semi blocked out by the shades. I stretch and have this tender pain between my legs. I smile as I think back to last night. We are definitely past the point of being friends. I look over at Noah in all his naked glory. His body is a work of art. He lies with the sheet at his waist, one hand on his stomach while the other is thrown over his head. His cock is outlined perfectly. Fuck, did he ever give me a workout last night. And his cock was always ready for action. Never once did he need to stop and take a break. I challenged him and he didn't disappoint and neither did his cock.

I slide off the bed, trying not to disrupt him as I make my way into his bathroom. I open the water, going to the linen closet to grab a towel. I find boxers on a shelf and grab a pair, throwing them on. Once I clean my face, I make my way downstairs. I pick up my clothes that are in a pile at the front door along with his button-down shirt. I put on his shirt, take out my phone from my purse, and order an Uber. My eyes go from my phone screen to the stair leading upstairs.

Why am I leaving? Why don't I just go upstairs and tell him I want coffee? Why don't I go and make him breakfast and serve him in bed? Why don't I wake him by sucking his cock? The answer to this is I have no fucking clue. My first instinct is to run. I open the door when the app tells me that my driver is waiting outside. I pick up my shoes, carrying them in my hands along with my outfit from last night. I make it home without my phone buzzing. Maybe he is going to wake up and think I had something to do. Maybe I should have left him a note, I say to myself, while the devil on my shoulder puts in her two cents, 'Maybe you shouldn't have left.'

I get out of the Uber and try to sneak into the house, but I hear voices. I tiptoe into the kitchen, clothes in my hand, purse hanging from my wrist.

"Look what the slut dragged in," Lauren says, leaning against the counter next to Austin.

His arms go around her. She glances up at him with a 'your penis is so good' kind of look.

"Funny, funny, ha-ha. I take it the cobwebs have been cleared out?" I fire back.

"Oh, there are definitely no cobwebs in there," Austin murmurs with a little smirk. "Isn't that Noah's shirt?" he asks.

"I hope you told him you were leaving, Kaleigh." She looks at Austin. "She isn't exactly known for sticking around the morning after. She, um, likes to leave before it can get awkward."

I glare at her while she tells Austin this.

"He's going to lose his shit," Austin states.

"Did you use my almond milk?" I ask while he continues to drink his coffee and shakes his head. "Oh. So, you used the breast milk, then?"

Austin spits his coffee out of his mouth all over the counter. I smile wide, crossing my arms over my chest on the island.

"What?" he questions, looking into his cup and then looking at Lauren.

"She's just messing with you." Lauren laughs. "You are going to clean up that mess." She points to the counter that now has his coffee splattered all over it.

"I'm not messing with him. I ordered frozen breast milk this week and switched it out," I inform her, while she looks inside her coffee cup. "You put butter in my potatoes, remember?" I raise my hand up in fists, hitting them together.

"You let me drink someone's breast milk?" She throws the coffee down the drain along with the rest of the milk. "That's sick, Kay."

"Where the fuck do you even order breast milk from?" Austin is looking under the sink for cleaning products. "Do we need to get, like, a hepatitis shot or something?" he asks, coming up with some Windex in his hand.

"I ordered it online." I shrug my shoulder. "I switched it yesterday morning after the kids left," I say as I study my nails, while Austin and Lauren start to freak out. I giggle to myself.

"What if the woman has a disease? Jesus! Could we catch it?" Austin turns to Lauren. "I feel a little funny." He puts his hand to his stomach, making us both roll our eyes.

"Relax, it was from a reputable website for mothers who can't produce enough milk." I try to reassure them right before someone starts banging on the front door.

"Kaleigh! Are you in there?" Noah yells from outside.

I open my eyes wide, my mouth opening and nothing is coming out. It's like I am caught eating candy before dinner.

Austin smirks at me and walks to the door to open it. "Hey, man."

I hear from the front door. I'm about to get up and rush out the back door. I eye the house, looking for an exit plan.

"Come in. Can I get you some coffee? With or without breast milk?" Austin asks as Noah follows him, looking at him like he's crazy.

"What are you doing here?" Noah walks into the kitchen and eyes Lauren dressed in Austin's now buttoned-up shirt before shifting his gaze to me.

"You took my shirt? And then you just fucking left?" He puts his hands to his waist. He looks like he just rushed out of the house, which he probably did. His T-shirt fits him so snug I want to rake my hands up his shirt and fall to my knees.

"She's not good with the whole morning-after thing," Lauren adds, trying to be helpful, while I shoot her a glare and then up it with the middle finger.

Noah walks toward me. No, that isn't a good word for it. He pounces on me like I am his prey. He turns me around on the stool as he cages me in between his arms with his hands braced against the counter. "I thought we said we were doing yoga this morning?" He leans into me.

Austin laughs from beside Lauren. "You couldn't do yoga if you tried." He continues laughing while Noah glares at him.

"Plus, you said we could do the downward dog thing," he whispers to me. Coming close to my ear, he adds, "I want to make friends with you." He kisses my ear then licks it, giving my body goose bumps. I shiver under his touch.

"What's the downward dog?" Austin asks in a whisper that is not at all quiet. Lauren just shushes him.

"Don't you two have to be somewhere?" I look back at them.

"Nope," they both answer at the same time and then look at each other and smile.

"Come back home with me," Noah asks me, leaning in and tracing my jaw with the tip of his nose. "Please."

I'm melting. My insides are totally caving for this man who I said I would never sleep with again, this man who I left twice now. This man who knows how to play my body like a violin. His blue eyes say words that we are both not ready to say out loud.

"Okay," I reply, and Lauren gasps from her side of the kitchen. She knows I never let my guard down with men, *ever.* "Besides, I think Austin is going to kill me for making him drink breast milk."

Noah looks at Austin as he stands back, making room for me to get up and gather my stuff. "You drank breast milk, dude? Can you die from that?" He slips his hands in his shorts pockets.

Austin stills, while Lauren says, "No, you can't. Now, go away before he goes nuts," before turning to Austin. "You can't die from drinking breast milk. Well, unless the mother had like HIV or something."

Noah bursts out laughing, grabbing my hand and dragging me back out the door.

He doesn't say a word before bringing me to the car, opening the door, and pushing me inside. Once he gets behind the wheel, he locks the door. "Just in case you want to jump out."

I take my hand and toss my hair behind me. "Oh, please, you were sleeping. I didn't want to wake you," I say, grabbing the seat belt.

"Your nose is growing there, Pinocchio," he says, starting the car. "Going to wake me my ass. You hightailed it so fast I think I still smell the rubber from the tires."

I open my mouth to say something, anything, but nothing comes out except, "I want coffee, please."

He pulls away from the curb, making his way back to his house but stopping at Starbucks first. Once we get to his house, he rounds the car to grab my hand as I'm getting out. "You know, just in case you bolt."

"Okay, I get it, you don't like it," I huff out. "It's just." I start saying and drift off.

"Oh, we will get to all that the minute we get inside," he says, almost dragging me into the house. "So where do you want to do this?" he asks.

"We've done it almost everywhere." I smile at him, sipping my Americano with soy milk. "I mean, I think we missed the coffee table, so maybe we can start there." I point to the middle of his living room.

"Let's go outside. We can sit by the pool," he says, still holding my hand, dragging me there. He makes his way over to the outdoor lounger bed that we sat on before. He flips over the lid so we are blocked from the sun. I crawl inside and sit up with my back to the throw pillows. He follows me and does the same, holding his ice coffee in his hand. "So. We are going to get some things straight right now."

I don't say anything because his voice is curt and I have trouble swallowing, so I just nod while he continues.

"Number one. We do not *ever*, ever leave when the other person is sleeping or not aware." He side eyes me.

I roll my eyes at him, taking a sip of my coffee again. "Okay, I get it. No leaving without telling you. Jeez."

"You did it twice, Kaleigh, not once, twice. It might get my feelings hurt." He looks at me now. "Why?" he asks the question that gets my heart going. It's beating so fast I'm sure he can tell. He grabs my hand and kisses the inside of my wrist where he can feel my heartbeat. "This is me and you, Kay. You can tell me anything and I promise to never ever use it against you."

"It's nothing really. I just…" I shake my head, moving my eyes away from him and staring at the pool, watching the water move. "I fell in love with a man who never ever spent the night, ever. We actually only dated a couple of months, but it was my first real 'love' if you know what I mean."

He nods his head.

I swallow while he squeezes my hand. "We would date and go out and always come back to my place because, well, he 'lived' with roommates. I guess that should have been the first red flag. I would wake up every single day hoping he'd be there, but would always find the sheets cold.

I tried to not get my hopes up, tried to not make a case out of it. I mean, he was there when we went to bed, he had clothes in my closet, yet he would never stay." I sip my coffee, gearing up the confidence. "Then one day I went home and all his things were gone, with a note that said 'later'." I take a deep breath. "It's almost as bad as Carrie getting dumped by a Post-it. Anyway, his phone was shut off or cancelled, who knows, and then one night I slept over at Stephanie's apartment. We fell asleep after watching *The Goonies*." I shake my head. "So the next day we got up and decided to hit up this new coffee place that had just opened and there in the middle of the store looking like he just woke up was Alex with his arms around the neck of a woman who was clearly wearing his wedding ring, something else he didn't wear around me. He saw me, his eyes opened with shock, and instead of going up to him and telling him what an asshole he was I turned and walked away. My heart was broken for what might have been, but it was broken more because I trusted him and in the end, he played me for a fool. So, I've made it my motto to never ever get involved from then on. I was more like an in and out kind of person. But I would never lie. I would never promise things." I watch his eyes go soft. "Happy now you know my deepest and darkest secret?" I smile, trying to get the topic back to fun. "Well, at least one of them."

He takes the cup from my hand, putting them both on the floor, then grabs me, pulling me onto his lap. My legs straddle his waist. His hands push the hair away from my face while he grabs my cheeks. "I don't know where this thing is going. Hell, I'm not even sure I know what the fuck the right thing to do is, but"—he smiles at me and his blue eyes light up—"what I can do is promise to never lead you on or lie to you. I will probably fuck up, but the good news is that I can learn." He brings my face to his. "So what do you say, want to do this not leave me in the middle of the night thing?" He kisses me gently. "Either that or I'm buying you a shock collar and it'll just zap you when you try to leave. I mean, that's my last straw." He smiles and I kiss him with a smile of my own.

We spend the rest of the afternoon really going into downward dog position. And that night when I go to bed it's with him with no plans of sneaking out.

CHAPTER NINETEEN

Noah

I swear there is a swing in my step, or it's the fact that my balls are always empty now. I mean, this whole having a girlfriend is the best thing I think I've done. She hasn't even tried to sneak out and it's been a whole three days. Score one for me.

"Noah," Hannah says from the door way. She walks in, swaying her hips. The normal Noah would try to see if she has panty lines in the white skirt she is wearing. This Noah is hoping she hurries up.

"Hannah." I lean back. "To what do I owe the pleasure?"

"Just giving you a heads-up. Leonard will be arriving on Monday, so Norma is going to have to go back and work with him. He is meeting with the new lawyer. So as of Monday, you are either on your own or I have to send you a temp."

I throw my head back, moaning. "Fine. I will see what I can do from my end."

"That's it?" Hannah asks, eyeing me. "No make sure she looks good bending over? No make sure to get her Facebook picture? No she must be under twenty-five?"

I laugh and throw my hands up, and then place them on my chest. "I would never."

"Yeah, right," she says, walking out, and I still forget to check and see if she is wearing a thong or not.

I pick up my phone, calling Kaleigh, who responds right away, her voice scratchy.

"Hello."

"Jesus, what is wrong?" I ask her, sitting up straight, worried.

"I have no idea. I have a fever and my body hurts." She sniffles. "And I'm freezing. I'm going to see the doctor in thirty minutes. I can't even swallow."

"Where are you?" I ask, already on my way out of the office, getting in my car.

"I'm at home. I'm waiting for Lauren to come home so the kids aren't alone."

"I'll be there in ten and then I'll bring you to the doctor."

"No!" she shouts then coughs. "It's contagious."

"We made out this morning, thoroughly. Plus, I'm immune. I never get sick," I reassure her and continue talking to her till I pull up and ring the bell.

"You're so annoying," she says, hanging up and answering the door. She's wearing baggy sweats that swallow her and a pink fuzzy robe while she coughs into her hand. "You shouldn't be here."

I have to be honest. I don't know how to touch her, so I go in then back up when she starts hacking. Rachel and Gabe are waiting for her on the stairs with masks on. "Hey, guys." I raise my hand in greeting.

They both wave back but don't have any time to say anything because Lauren's bus comes barreling into the driveway.

She gets out, rushing to the front door, taking in Kaleigh. Her hand goes directly on her mouth. "Hey, Noah," she says to me then back at Kaleigh. "I called Mom and Dad and they are expecting you tonight. Mom is making up the spare room."

Kaleigh nods, grabbing her bag and walking out toward her car.

"What are you doing?" I ask her when she gets to her car, opening the door. "You can't drive," I say, ushering her to my car. "Um, I need your doctor's address," I say, opening the door for her. "And, um, is it normal you have no shoes on? Should I go in and get a pair for you?"

Kaleigh just groans as she opens her bag and gets some flip-flops. "There." She groans as she fastens her seat belt and puts the seat down, closing her eyes. I close the door and make my way to my side. Opening the door, Kaleigh opens her eyes and hands me her phone with the doctor's address already loaded in the maps. I put it on my lap as I follow the instructions to her doctor's office. Once I turn the car off I rub her leg, waking her up. "Let's go get you some meds."

She nods her head, getting out of the car and walking almost hunched over into the doctor's office. She hands the nurse all her papers, coming to sit down next to me. I pick up a magazine, flipping through the pages, when the nurse comes out and calls Kaleigh's name. I watch her get up while I continue flipping through the magazine as she stops near the door. "Aren't you coming?" she asks me, her face so pale.

I put the magazine down and get up and follow her in.

She sits on the doctor's table while I sit in the chair.

The nurse asks her questions while I look around till she asks something that makes my ears perk up. "Date of your last period?" she asks and Kaleigh's eyes fly to mine right away.

"Last week," she responds, looking at the nurse again.

"And you're still on birth control right?"

I roll my lips in to not laugh while she squirms on the table.

"Yup," she says before the nurse gets up and tells us the doctor will soon be in.

"So, you're on birth control?" I ask, tapping my index fingers together. "This is great news." I wink at her.

"Yes, just what I want to hear when I'm sick as a dog and dying is how good it's going to feel without a condom," she says, groaning while she shivers.

The doctor comes in and smiles as he sees Kaleigh. I hate him already. What is he, twelve? His slicked back hair, perfect clothes, fake veneer teeth. I sit up right when he starts talking.

"Kaleigh, it's been a while. How have you been?" he asks her, reading her chart.

"She's sick, so," I say, stating the obvious.

He smiles at me. "I'll take good care of her."

He takes the thermometer out and asks her to open wide and I swear I want to throat punch this fucking tool. "You are running a fever," he says, tossing the top of the thermometer cover into the garbage. He goes to feel under her neck while she whimpers out. I'm about to get up and take her somewhere else.

"Oh, that doesn't feel good." He grabs a wooden stick, asking her to stick her tongue out. "Ouch, that must hurt. Looks like you have strep throat," he says, walking to the desk, writing something on his prescription pad. "Here you go. You should be feeling better in about two days. If not, you have to come back." He smiles and puts his hand on her knee.

What kind of doctor is this clown?

I get up, clearing my throat while Kaleigh whispers at him, "Thank you so much, Todd."

He leans in and kisses her cheek. "Take care." And walks out.

"What the fuck is that all about? He just kissed you. Isn't there like an oath or something that says thou shall not come on to my patients sexually?" I huff out while Kaleigh jumps down, coming up to me and tapping my chest.

"Relax there, Tarzan. Let's just say that between the two of us, you are the one with the right equipment for him." She winks at me, turning to walk out. We pass his office on the way out and Kaleigh leans in and says, "Please say hi to Troy for me and tell him that I owe him one."

"Will do." He smiles at us as we walk out.

Fifteen minutes later, we have a whole bag of medicine and we are pulling up to her parents' house. "Should I come in?" I ask her and all she does is shrug her shoulders and grunt. "Are your parents expecting you?" I ask after I get out of the car and jog over to her as she is unlocking the front door.

We walk in and all you hear is "Me Tarzan, you Jane." And her father jumps out from behind the couch, showing us he is in nothing but his loincloth and white safari hat.

My eyes open huge while Kaleigh shrieks next to me. "Dad." She throws the bag of meds down and he shields his pecker with his hands, his eyes as wide as saucers, just as her mother comes around the corner into the living room.

"Oh, Tarzan, I hope you have your rope for me to swing on."

I take in her outfit and throw my head back and let out the biggest laugh of my life. This woman is wearing a leopard bikini top and a leopard print wrap around her waist. Her hands go up and she shrieks out at the top of her lungs. "Oh my God."

"Hey," I say, raising my hand. "Dede, you look great."

She shoos me with her hand. "Oh, stop it, Noah." She then looks at

Kaleigh. "Oh, dear, you look horrible," she says, coming to her.

"Mom, please tell me you're wearing something under that loin scarf," she says, taking in her mother's outfit. Meanwhile her father has put the couch throw blanket around his waist, his hat still sitting on his head.

"No, dear, it didn't come with panties," she says softly. "Are you sick?"

"Yes, Mother, I'm sick. I called you and left you a voice mail," she says, raising her hands.

"I don't even know where my phone is," she says as she turns around and shows us that she is in fact not wearing anything because you can see the bottom of her ass peeking out from the scarf.

Kaleigh puts her hands to her face. "I can't do this. You need to take me to a hotel." She pushes me out while I nod to her father and blink at her mother.

An hour later, I have her tucked into my bed. She fought me the whole way home. She took her meds and spoke to her mom on the phone right until she knocked out. I smile as I put the water bottle that she asked me to go get her next to the bed. Making my way downstairs, I grab my phone to call Austin. He answers right away, his frustration coming through the minute he picks up with a snarl.

"Jesus, you would think once you dip your dick in the honey you'd be less fucking high-strung," I say, walking to the fridge. "Oh my God, unless you didn't finish? Did you get dick shy?"

"Why are we friends?" he hisses out.

"Because I've seen your dick and I have a picture of your testicles. Besides, no one would put up with your mood swings. Jesus, you're worse than my mother and she is way into menopause."

"Fuck off, what do you want?"

"Kaleigh is sick, so I need to order her soup, but she is vegan, who doesn't eat meat."

"So order her vegetable soup. And what do you mean she's sick? Where is she?"

"She has strep throat. She is upstairs in my bed."

"Wait a minute. You actually have a girl in your bed and you're not sticking your dick in honey?"

"Well, she's my girlfriend. I don't have the boyfriend manual on hand, but I'm pretty sure there is something in there with take care of your girl." I open a beer. "How's your girlfriend? Last I saw, she was running into a house."

"She's not my girlfriend," he hisses. "She showed up to work on Monday and we decided that we should not work and sleep together."

"We?" I ask him. "Or you and that stupid rule?"

"It's not a stupid rule!" he yells. "I can't sleep with my assistant."

"Oh, this all makes sense," I say, sitting down on the stool. "You're not just cranky, you're dick cranky. Your dick can't get into the honey, so now your bumblebee is going nuts." I laugh out at him. "Dude, just break the rule. Who knows, you might actually like smiling."

"Have you hit your head? Maybe you have a brain tumor. This might explain all the shit you're spewing."

I breathe out. "I gotta go and make sure Kaleigh is okay."

I laugh out, knowing it's killing him right now, but he just disconnects. I get up, going to the drawer with the take-out menus. After going on Google and finding an actual vegan restaurant, I order a shit-ton of soup along with some cookies and by the time I'm done I have spent two hundred dollars and it didn't include one fucking steak. I pour some soup in a bowl and walk upstairs with it. All her clothes are on the floor in a heap and my cock thinks it's time to come out and play.

"Simmer down there, boy." I see Kaleigh's head come out from under the covers.

"I might be dying," she says, her voice all scratchy. "And your sheets need to be changed. I sweat a pool."

I look down at my cock to see if maybe he will be grossed out by a girl sweating in my bed, and not because of sex, but because she is sick. Nope, he says there alert. Ready for combat. "I brought you soup," I say to her as she sits up and shivers.

"I need a shower, and can you show me where the sheets are so I can change them?" she says, getting out of bed and walking to the bathroom with her hands in front of her while she shakes.

"Go shower. I'll take care of this," I tell her while she goes into the bathroom and I hear the shower turn on. I put the bowl down and peel the sheets off. She wasn't kidding. They are soaked. I toss them in the basket as I get a whole new set out. After doing the bed with the fresh sheets, I walk to my closet and take out my terry cloth robe. I walk out as soon as Kaleigh walks out of the bathroom with her hair wrapped in a towel and one around her body. "Hey, gorgeous," I say, placing the robe over her shoulders.

"You made the bed?" she asks, her eyes closing halfway. She puts her arms into the robe and takes the towel off her head. "I just took two Tylenol to help with the fever."

I bring her to me and hug her, just fucking because, which is a crazy fucking notion.

"Come eat some soup and you can go back to bed. You need to stay hydrated," I tell her, leading her to the bed.

She gets underneath the fresh covers. She sits up with her back to the headboard and the four pillows piled behind her.

"I ordered every single soup they had, four servings each. So you have twenty soups." I sit next to her and hand her the bowl of soup.

She grabs the spoon and slurps it. "Is this homemade chicken soup?" she asks, her eyes going wide. "I'm vegan."

"I know. I ordered it from the vegan restaurant. It even looks like chicken soup," I say, watching her continue eating.

"You ordered vegan soup for me? You changed the sweaty sheets for me?" She puts the empty soup bowl down. "If I wasn't sick, you'd so be getting a blow job right now," she says as she sneezes all over me.

My head shoots back to avoid getting sprayed, but it lands all over my hand.

"Sorry," she says, trying to wipe it, but I walk to the bathroom where I try not to be grossed out that all her germs are over me.

When I make it back into the room she is lying down on her side in a fetal position, her wet hair spread out on the pillow.

"I'm just going to take a little nap," she says, her eyes already closed as she speaks.

I get in bed next to her, turning on the television on low and watching her sleep. I don't know how long I watch it for. I turn it off and get under the covers, my body finding her, and we fall asleep as I hold her.

The next morning she wakes up still with a fever. After she takes her meds and some more Tylenol, she crashes out on the couch while I watch CNN. Her feet are in my lap, my arm lying on her leg. I had already taken off work, knowing I couldn't leave her alone, when her phone next to her buzzes once. It's a text from Lauren, so I open it up.

Hope you're feeling better and that Mom isn't making you want to commit suicide.

Should I wake her or should I just tell Lauren that she is with me? I go with plan B.

It's Noah. She's with me. I'll take good care of her.

She answers right away.

I thought she was staying with my parents?

She was until she walked in on them playing Tarzan and Jane. Your mom looks hot in a loincloth, BTW.

Ewwww! You're a sick man. Off to the arena with Austin. Tell her to text me later.

He finally got over that 'don't shit where you eat' bullshit?

No. Know anyone hiring?

You can come work for me. I definitely won't want to have sex with you. I shoot out without even thinking about it. This can either be really good since I need a decent PA, but Austin will be shitting a nut when he finds out she will be working with me. I laugh thinking about it.

Funny guy. Okay, well, if you have a real suggestion, let me know.

I'm serious. I need a PA to keep my shit in order, and I heard you're the best. Think about it. Let me know. That way, Austin's balls won't get swollen again. BTW, I will never ask you to get me coffee or food.

She doesn't answer me back, so I put the phone down and continue watching mindless television while I hold on to my girl. I smile. My girl. Fuck yeah.

CHAPTER TWENTY

Kaleigh

It's been two days since I thought I was dying. I knew I was getting sick. The pain in my bones started first, then it spread to the chills and by the time noon came around I was full-blown lethargic. What I wasn't expecting was for Noah to come in on a white horse, full knight in shining armor, but with a kilt, with nothing on underneath it.

He made soup for me, called in sick, changed my sweaty sheets, and never once did he try to have sex with me. I mean, don't get me wrong, his penis was alert and ready every time I moved next to him or even when he saw me showering and sneezing on myself.

Now I just got up from a nap, another one. Jesus, I feel like I've slept for a week straight. Noah is napping also. We have done nothing but watch television and given new meaning to Netflix and chill. I grab my phone when it buzzes on the table next to the bed. I make sure the noise didn't wake him. He is wearing a pair of sweats and nothing else. One thing I've learned about Noah is that if he's home he's without a shirt. I've also noticed he's almost OCD with having dirty dishes in the sink. I had my ass on his counter but God forbid I put a dish in the sink and not rinse and put it in the dishwasher. The world has to stop. Yesterday I did it just to see him freak out. It was quite entertaining till he realized what I was doing and threw me over his shoulder, slapping my ass so hard it stung. The phone buzzes again in my hand.

Tell Noah to call me after nine to discuss his proposition.

I really hope your proposition isn't about sex.

Are you still high?

No. Maybe. Yes. I'm so sick. I hope you catch it.

Gee, thanks.

He said the job is yours and to tell him when you want to start.

When I woke from my nap, he mentioned that he and Lauren texted and that he may have offered her a job. I was surprised that he would do that, but the way he said it made sense. "He wants to bang her so bad he's making everyone miserable. I will just take one for the team. Besides, I heard that Lauren puts your email in alphabetical order." It was as if she hung the moon.

How does next Monday sound? She asks and I know it works perfectly because he mentioned losing his latest PA starting Monday, so it doesn't leave her much time since it's already Wednesday.

It sounds like I need to have sex with him. He's so hot taking care of me. I should give him a blow job.

With a throat infection? He might catch it!!!

In his dick?

No, dumbass, in his throat. Gotta go.

I laugh at her and then put my phone back, looking over at him with his hands crossed and resting on his stomach. My body starts perking up for him. I slowly rise to my knees and take off the robe I'm wearing, leaving me naked. I lick my lips, crawling to him, the bed dipping a bit, but not enough to wake him. My hands go to the elastic of his pants. I pull them down a touch. I don't have that much space since he's lying on his back, but just enough to get his cock out. It's semi hard already. I cup him in my hand softly, looking up at him to see if he will stir. His eyes don't even flicker, so I go a step further, leaning down and taking him in my mouth a bit, just the tip. When my hand cups the base that is now fully erect I throw my leg over his hip and lean back down, taking him all the way in my mouth. I repeat it three times before I feel his hands in my hair and a groan slips out of him. Letting his cock go, I look up.

"Sorry. I couldn't wait any longer," I tell him, going back down on him again.

"You can wake me each and every single time like that." He lifts his hips, pushing his pants down his hips and giving me full access to his cock.

I twist my hand down his base, my mouth following. My nipples rub against his sweats, making them pebble from the friction. It also makes them ache to be touched.

"Fuck," he says when I take him all the way in.

"So," I say, letting him pop out of my mouth, then lick down the base, "when was the last time you got tested?" My tongue twirls around his balls.

His hips thrust up into my hand. "Last month," he says, fucking my hand, and I switch from the left ball to the right one. "At my yearly." His eyes try to stay open, but I suck one of his balls into my mouth gently.

"Me, too." I wink at him. "Must be a sign," I say, crawling back up to take him back into my mouth. His hands find their way into my hair. His cock starts to get bigger in my mouth and I know he's almost there because his hips start thrusting to meet my mouth each time. Letting his cock go, he groans out his frustration but slowly stops when I move up. "So if I sat my pussy on your cock right now without a condom, would that be okay?" I ask him as I squat over his cock. My feet are placed beside his hips and my knees off the bed.

"I would be more than okay with that," he says, grabbing onto my hips.

I grab his cock, squatting on top of him. I rub his head from my clit to my entrance. Once he is there, I use my legs to lower myself on him. My thighs shake since I'm going so slow. He slides in me, one centimeter at a time. It is so slow I feel every single ridge of his cock. We both throw our heads back when he is planted all the way inside me. Using my legs again, I rise up and when I'm going back down he thrusts up, hard.

"I want to do all the work," I tell him breathlessly. "You rest," I say, riding him, my thighs starting to burn a bit.

His hands leave my hips and go up to cup my breasts. He twirls my nipples with his fingers while I ride him. Slowly at first, then my body takes over. The need for him takes over. The need to cum takes over. My pants fill the silence of the room.

"I love your cock," I say and move one hand to his stomach and another to my mouth, sucking a finger in, then bringing it to my clit. I start rubbing my clit in little circles. My pussy gets tight, my pace a little bit more frenzied. I look at Noah to see that he is watching his cock enter my pussy. "Like what you see?" I ask him, almost panting.

One hand leaves my breast as he comes down to my clit. He follows my finger, throwing me off at times. It's a battle of who is going to play with my clit. A battle that I will let him win.

"This little pink clit peeking out," he says, his teeth almost clenched. "If I pinch it, you think you can come harder?" he asks and I'm almost past the point of understanding.

I moan out my answer, my hands now coming up to play with my nipples. I roll them the same time he pinches my clit. It's too much. My stomach clenches, my toes curl, and my pussy pulses around his cock.

"That's it," he says, hissing out. As I pound down on him, my juices run down his cock, dripping on his balls. "Fuck." He lets go of my clit and I cum on him again.

My legs start to shake as I ride out my orgasm, to the point that now the burning increases. I'm almost to the end of the orgasm when he grabs hold of my hips, his fingertips digging in, and plants me down on his cock. My knees fall forward. His hips come off the bed, trying to get deeper and deeper in me as he cums in me with a roar. I collapse on top of him. Our breathing starts coming back to normal.

"If you want to wake me up like that every single day, I will not say no. Ever," he says, pushing the hair off my face, leaning down to kiss the top of my head.

"I'll keep that in mind," I say. "I'm really glad we did this on your side of the bed. I hate napping in a wet spot." I giggle then sit back up, his cock still in me. I peel myself from him and walk to the bathroom. "I need a shower." I look over my shoulder at him. "You coming?" I don't have to ask him twice as he is already stumbling out of the bed and his legs are trying to get out of his sweats.

We stay in the shower till our hands look like prunes and the water turns to ice. By the time night comes around and we are both sitting downstairs at the island enjoying the last of the soup, I feel almost human.

"I have two meetings tomorrow morning," he says, putting his plate in the dishwasher. "You think you'll be okay?" he asks, his hair all tossed around. He stands at the sink with just his boxers on. His white Calvin Klein boxers, which mold him everywhere. "Um, hello?" he says loudly.

I blink my eyes, finally coming out of my cock dream. "Yeah, I'll be fine. I think I'm okay to go back home. I don't think I'm contagious."

He comes to me, picking me up under my armpits, and my legs wrap around his waist.

"Want to see me put my legs behind my head?" I wiggle my eyebrows at him as he starts to walk toward the stairs, stopping mid-step near the stairs.

"Is this enough space for you to show me and for me to ram my cock into you?" he asks with fire in his blue eyes.

I swallow a big gulp. "Yup, this is perfect." And then I show him exactly how a pretzel looks. Naked. By the time I peel myself away from him the next morning at six a.m. I'm counting the hours till I see him again.

I unlock the door just as Lauren is coming downstairs for coffee. "You look so much better," she says, walking to the machine, taking out two cups for us.

"I feel a hundred and fifty times better. Jesus, I thought I would die," I say, grabbing the cup of coffee she just poured for me. I get up, going to the fridge, and getting my coconut milk. "Did you fuck with my milk?" I ask her, watching her bring the cup to her lips and then smile behind it.

"Who, me? No, I didn't." She takes a sip. "But I can't confirm that Austin didn't."

I groan out, pouring it out in the sink.

"Asshole," I say under my breath, sitting down on the stool, drinking my coffee black.

"He drank someone's breast milk." She tries to plead his case. "Someone we don't know."

I shoo her off with my hand, rolling my eyes. "Blah, blah, blah, how are my monkeys?" I ask about the kids.

She starts telling me a story about Rachel and her yoga poses.

"I'm so bloated," I cut her off.

"When is your period?" she asks, leaning on the counter.

"I just finished it," I tell her, pushing down on my little pot that is there. "You know what, I think it is air."

Lauren looks over at me, confused.

"I've had so much sex these last couple of days he probably pushed air into me." I watch her stand up. "You know, from pumping in and out."

"Are you insane? You don't get bloated from having air pushed into you from sex." She folds her arms over her chest.

"Well, his dick is huge." I shrug.

"Kaleigh, that is the craziest shit you have ever said, and trust me, I know you say some pretty crazy shit. You are not bloated because his dick is big and he pushed air into you. It can't happen." She turns to put her cup in the sink.

"You don't understand," I say, fisting my hand and slapping it with the other, making the motion of air being pushed in. "See, it's being pushed in."

"I don't have time to go over this with you. I have kids to get ready," she says, walking away.

"That's because I'm right," I say to her back. Lifting up the cup, I bring it to my lips. "You can totally get bloated by air being shoved inside by a big dick."

CHAPTER TWENTY-ONE

Noah

I kiss her goodbye just as she walks out and I get ready to go for my run. I watch her ass walk away, thinking maybe tonight we should try something else. I smile, thinking about it. I start my run, making lists in my head about things I need to do. The first thing I need to do is meet Sal and make sure everything is okay with the contract. I have to make sure Lauren is actually coming to work with me. Then I make a note to pick up some more vegan stuff for Kaleigh.

The office is flowing without any issues when I get ready to leave for the meeting. The meeting with Sal is so fast I'm out before the hour is up.

I decide to visit Austin. I smile at Carmen when I get off the elevator and make my way down the hallway. When I walk into the room, John is sitting on the couch already talking to Austin.

"Jesus, did this week go slow or what? I didn't think it would ever end." I slap John on the back and sit next to him on the couch. I look over at Austin. "Are you sick?"

"He isn't sick. Lauren is holding her vagina hostage till he lets go of this whole 'I don't shit where I eat' bullshit," John explains.

"It's not bullshit," he snaps at both of us. "What if we have a good run and then she gets mad at me, we break up, and she sues me for sexual harassment?"

"What if you spend the rest of your life banging the best pussy of your life?" I finally fire back. "Listen, if you want, she can come work for me." I try to get a feel about how he feels.

He sits up in his chair right away. Oh, fuck, this isn't good. "Not a fucking chance in hell. You've fucked every PA you've ever had."

"That was before. I'm a changed man. I went to the strip club to meet a client, and my dick didn't even twitch. In fact, he was bored. I think he might have even yawned." I look down at my crotch.

John studies me. "No shit, you got the bug?"

I just shake my head. "I did. By the way, I'm bringing her tomorrow." I lean back. Fuck, I have to tell her that we are going out tomorrow to a club opening. "She's so fucking hot. She can put her legs behind her head, man."

"I don't want to know that shit!" Austin yells. "That's Lauren's sister."

"She's not your sister." I turn to look back at John. "And she can hold them there." I raise my hand for a high five. John smacks it.

"Is Lauren bringing a date tomorrow?" John asks Austin.

And I leave my hand in the air, turning my head to hear his answer.

"No." But he picks up the phone to text her something.

I don't know what she says, but he throws his phone down, "Jesus, she's making my life impossible."

"Poor baby. Just fucking get over it. Have sex with her, work with her, and then I'll have a lot fewer complaints in my email." John gets up. "Now, if you bozos will excuse me, I'm going home to have sex with my wife. On the couch, because we can."

"You liar," I say. "Married people only fuck in a bed. Google it." I wink at John as he walks out.

"I bet they don't even fuck in the shower," I continue while Austin keeps looking at the phone.

"Let's go to the gym. You can work out your frustration there." I get up. We spend the next three hours beating the shit out of a punching bag.

I get into the car, tossing my gym bag in the back. Once I'm on the road, I call Kaleigh.

"Hey," she answers softly.

"Hey, are you sleeping?" I ask her.

"Yeah, I just climbed into bed," she says as I hear the sheets rustle in the background.

"Did you get my text about tomorrow? Is it okay?" I ask, wishing I could go over to her place.

"Yup, I even have an outfit planned and everything. What time will you pick me up?" she asks, yawning at the end.

"I'll call you tomorrow and we will hash out all the details," I tell her, turning on my street.

"Okay, sleep tight," she says, laughing and then telling me goodbye.

I hang up, pulling into the garage and closing it behind me. Walking into the house, I toss my bag in the laundry room, going upstairs. Once I get into my room, I stop in my tracks. There in the middle of the bed is Kaleigh, who gets up on her elbow, looking at me.

"I hope you don't mind I made myself at home." She smiles at me and I walk to her, the smile growing so big on my face I feel my eyes crease.

"This is the best surprise ever, but how did you get in?" I ask her, peeling my T-shirt from my body.

"The garage pad." She now turns to sit up, holding the sheet to her chest, showing me her naked shoulders.

"Who told you the code?" I ask, unbuttoning my jeans and having them fall to my ankles and stepping out of them.

"Noah, you really should be more original than 6-9-6-9. Rachel could have broken that code."

"If it gets you in my bed, I would go with 1-2-3-4," I tell her, getting under the cover, grabbing hold of her waist. "And naked to boot. I must have done something really good today to come home to you."

"Well," she says, shimmying against me, "we can make sure you do something really, really good now." She drapes her arms around my shoulders, her hands running through my hair.

"I think I want to eat cookies," I tell her, kissing her cheek, then her jaw, then her neck, then her nipple, and then I make my way down to her cookie and I show exactly how happy I am that she surprised me.

The next day we have breakfast together outside by the pool. After we clean up the dishes, Kaleigh grabs a yoga mat from her car and goes outside to do yoga by the pool while I watch television inside. She comes in, grabs a water bottle, and comes to sit next to me. "What time do I need to be ready?" she asks, curling her feet under her.

"We need to be there around eight or so." I look over at her. "I've never had a woman get ready with me. Do you need like a separate room or something?" I ask, not sure what it's going to look like in my bathroom. Will it look like an explosion of makeup or is she a 'locking myself in the bathroom for five hours' kind of girl.

"Aww, are you popping your girlfriend cherry, Noah?" She smiles at me, leaning in, brushing her nose against my jaw. "You'll be happy to know I'm not that much of a makeup fan and it takes me about thirty minutes to get ready after I shower."

"You're a natural beauty, so I didn't think it would take you long, but I just had to make sure." I drag her on my lap.

"Is that a banana in your pocket or are you just happy to see me?" She laughs, her ass wiggling on my cock. "We should shower together to save water."

"Is that so?" I ask her, my hand snaking up her shirt while my other hand finds her tit.

"It's for the environment." She giggles when my face buries itself into her neck.

I carry her upstairs where we save water for the environment, and now here I am in my closet, deciding what to wear. "Should we go matching or is that too much?" I yell over my shoulder and she walks into the room wearing a cream-colored bra and what looks like full underwear. "Are those granny panties?" I ask, seeing how much of her is covered.

"Yup, full-on granny panties. And I'm wearing a cream lace dress, so you can go with whatever color you want." She turns around, walking back into the bathroom.

Fuck, I never thought about granny panties being so sexy, but now I'm tempted to make her wear them more often.

I grab my blue suit and my baby blue button-down shirt. I am sliding my arms through the jacket and putting on my brown shoes when she comes out of the bathroom.

Her blond hair is tied on top of her head in a ponytail, her hair wavy in that ponytail, but what stops me is her outfit or lack thereof. Her dress is lace all right, long sleeves, all with embroidered flowers. You can see right through it, which is why she chose that underwear. The hem falls mid-thigh and it's not just straight. It zigzags across. And on her feet are the sexiest shoes I've ever seen in my life, what looks like rose gold transparent barely there heels with a lace up ankle tie wrapping around her ankles. A champagne color purse hangs from her wrist.

"I'm done," she says. All she has on is mascara and pink lip gloss. I know for a fact that her lip gloss tastes like cherry. "So do I look okay?" she says, twirling around and then my mouth drops because it ties at the neck and her whole back is bare. There isn't even her bra strap. My cock fights his restraint to get out.

"Um," I stammer out, my eyes blinking, my palms sweating, my collar not even tied but feeling like it's strangling me.

"You look so hot right now. If we didn't have to leave, I would be down on my knees." She winks at me, walking out of the room where all I can do is watch her.

I cup my cock in my hand. "I'm so sorry, buddy, but I promise you'll have lots of play time after."

Once we get downstairs, I don't walk into the garage. Instead, I go to the second garage door and press in the code, the door opening up to reveal my Aston Martin DB11 Coupe. I'm about to walk forward when Kaleigh knocks into me.

"Is that yours?" she asks, looking at it with blinking eyes.

"It is," I say, taking the keys out of my pocket and pressing the unlock button, hearing the beep. I walk to the passenger side of the door, opening it for her. "After you, babycakes."

She stops in front of me. "Have you had sex in this car before?" she asks, tilting her head back.

"No," I say, bringing my hand up to her jaw, rubbing it with my thumb.

"Interesting," she says, getting on her tippy toes and kissing under my chin and then climbing into the car. Her skirt rises up, showing her long, perfect legs. Legs that were wrapped around my waist not too long ago, legs that intertwine with mine at night. I close her door and get into the driver's seat. Her legs are crossed at the ankle while she places her hands on her lap.

I start up the car, the purring noise music to my ears. "I love this car," I say, backing out and making my way down the street.

"It's really pretty inside," Kaleigh says from her side of the car, her fingers running up the stitching in the middle console. "And the seat is so comfy." She moves her ass in the seat. My cock rises like a beast trying to get out. "Does your seat recline all the way back?" she asks. "I wonder if I could fit on that seat with you."

I look ahead then back at her, merging into the middle lane on the highway and then going back into the left lane, putting my blinker on to get off the highway.

"I would have to sit on you, of course." She now leans over, her finger trailing up my thigh. "But would I have to sit facing you or facing the steering wheel?" she asks, leaning more and more in while I maneuver the car through the streets, searching for a parking spot, when I turn right and hit the industrial side of the town.

All businesses are closed for the weekend. Pulling into an empty parking lot, I don't even put it in park before our seat belts fly off and we dive for each other. My hands grab her face while her hands grab my neck. Our mouths find each other in the frenzy, my lips on hers, our tongues sliding with each other's. I hold her cheek in my hand as the other moves to her neck, moving her closer. Our lips part, our breaths panting heavily as she climbs over the console. Her knees go to the sides of my hips. My hands move up her dress while she unties the buttons on my shirt. Her lips go to my neck where she inhales deeply, right before sucking in and then twirling her tongue.

"Fuck," I say, my hands cupping her ass, squeezing it. Her hand goes to my belt where she unties it and the button. The sound of my zipper being pulled down echoes so loud in the small confines of the car. My cock springs free while she cups me.

"Move my panties to the side," she says breathlessly, rubbing her hot covered pussy on my cock.

"You want my cock?" I ask her, grabbing her ponytail in one hand, pulling it back, giving me all access to her neck. "Go get it," I tell her.

She gets up on her knees a little and moves one hand to her panties, pushing them to the side. I'm expecting her to grab my cock and sink down on it. What I'm not expecting is for her to plant two fingers inside of herself and moan out. Her back arches as she fingers herself twice and I watch her eyes get hazed. I watch her pleasure herself till she takes her fingers out and puts them in my mouth.

"You want my pussy?" she asks while my tongue licks her fingers clean.

She finally grabs my cock in her hand, rubbing the head through her wet slit. She aligns me to her and then sinks down slowly, too slowly, so I thrust up hard, making her gasp out as I fill her hungry pussy with my cock. I grab her hips, guiding her up and down. My heart beats faster, my chest heaving like I'm running a marathon. I'm trying not to think that her pussy is soft like silk, warm like the sun. Her hands go to my shoulders as she rides me, her face coming close to mine, her lips lingering in front of mine. Her breath blows on my lips. I lick my lips, knowing I want to taste her, knowing that the taste of her pussy is still lingering on my tongue. I lean closer to her, my tongue now coming out to lick her lips, her tongue coming out to follow mine, till she leans in and her chest is flush with mine. Her hands move from my shoulders to around my neck as she rises and falls all the while holding on to the kiss that we are now in the middle of.

My hands rub up and down her bare back and our lips connect and my cock fills her. My hips meet her each time she comes back down. Her hands never leave my neck, except now when she is going to come. I can feel it, her pussy convulsing around me, and her moan comes out as she throws her head back while still pulling me closer. My hands lift her hips up and down while I let her ride out her orgasm. When I know she's almost at the end, I watch her head bend back down as she looks at me, her eyes dilated, her cheeks pink and flushed, and while looking in her eyes I come deep inside of her. I slam her down on my cock and shoot over and over and over again. When I finish, my hands roam up from her hips to her back, her skin getting goose bumps from my fingers.

"From now on, we take this car at least once a week." I smirk at her and she just giggles and looks down shyly.

"I don't think I can move," she says and places her head in the crook of my neck.

"Then don't." I cross my hands across her back and kiss her head while we sit here in the middle of a deserted parking lot, our clothes almost all on, and I just made love to her.

CHAPTER TWENTY-TWO

Kaleigh

I put my hand almost under my chest as I rest my head in the crook of Noah's neck. I don't know what just happened but that was unlike anything I have ever done. I mean, I've had sex before, but this was more. It was so much more. I could see it in his eyes and feel it in my body and not just the big cock that he had planted inside me. I don't know how long we just stay in this dark parking lot, but when I finally peel myself up, Noah has his eyes closed. I lean in, kissing his cheek while he opens his eyes.

"Babycakes," he says as I smile and go about setting my clothes back to their original order.

I button his shirt and get up, trying to gracefully get back over the console. "Why was it so easy to get over but getting back requires me to hit things?" I ask as I stumble into the seat onto my ass. My feet are still over the console while I pull them back to me. I see him tucking his cock into his pants and zipping up. He opens the door, getting out to make sure his pants are fastened properly.

When he gets back inside he says, "Going out, take two." And slowly pulls out and gets back on the road.

By the time we get to the club, it already has a line in front. The valet has six men running to get everyone inside. A valet opens my door, putting his hand out to help me out. I grab it and place one leg out and then another, putting my purse in front of my crotch to make sure there is no vagina sighting. Noah meets me at the back of the car, grabbing my hand in his.

"Ready?" he asks and I nod and let him lead me inside. We walk the red carpet, past the photographers that are snapping away and yelling out Noah's name. I put my head down, smiling till he stops at the end of the carpet right before the door. "Smile," he says as he grabs me around the waist and tucks me into his side.

The doors open and we make our way inside. The music is loud compared to the silence outside. The floor thumps from the bass and all the people dancing and moving around. I look around and see that it's dimly lit with candles. It's almost impossible to move through the throngs of people, but Noah somehow makes his way over to the stairs where we walk upstairs to meet everyone. I search for familiar faces when I hear Noah say, "This place is insane." He shakes Austin's hand. "Congrats, man."

"Your shirt isn't even buttoned properly." Austin points out to him while we both look at the shirt that is indeed one button up.

I smile and shrug my shoulders. "I can't help it if he dresses like a guy on GQ. Where is Lauren?" I look over his head and around to see if I can see Lauren, but instead I find Jake. Fuck.

"Oh, shit. Is that Jake and the home-wrecker?" I motion toward the bar.

"Fuck," Austin says right before he makes his way toward Lauren and now an angry looking Jake. I see the two of them start talking and then, Jake turning around and walking away.

"Let me introduce you to everyone," Noah says, moving into the booth that his friends are now sitting in. "John," he says, pointing to a guy who has his hands stretched across the couch he is sitting on, "this is Kaleigh, my girl."

John leans forward and puts his hand out to shake mine. "Finally the one who broke his penis," he says, laughing while he looks over at the woman who is sitting on his right. "This is my wife, Dani."

It is me who now leans in to shake her hand.

"I never thought I would see the day that someone could tame him," she says, sipping her drink.

"You guys are going to scare her off," Noah says, leaning down to grab a bottle of water while he makes me a vodka cranberry. "You didn't break my penis, I promise." He kisses me on the nose while he continues introducing me to Cooper, who is an ex NHL player and smoking hot, and his equally hot wife, Parker.

"You guys just missed Matthew and Karrie," John says.

"Oh, shit, sorry we were otherwise"—he looks around, trying to think of a word—"entertained."

Dani bursts out laughing. "Since when are you shy about telling us about your banging adventures?" She nods at me. "I like you already."

"I don't kiss and tell," Noah says, sitting next to them while pulling me down next to him.

His arm goes to the back of the couch around my shoulders while the Cooper guy laughs out loud, inputting, "Dude, you kiss and brag."

John leans forward to say, "Fuck, once he showed me a picture of his dick. I almost threw up."

I lean back into the crook of his arm, laughing.

"That's because you found out your dick was small and you knew you had no chance left in life," he says, pointing at him with his water bottle.

John just laughs at him while Dani leans in. "Your cock is just fine. Don't let him get to you."

We all laugh now.

It's then that I see Lauren walking up the stairs with Austin following right behind her.

"Hey," I say when she is close enough. "Where have you been?" I ask, leaning over Noah to look at her, while we slide over in the booth, giving them space to sit down.

Austin sits first and then pulls Lauren down on his lap. I take in my sister, hair a little disheveled, cheeks pink.

I open my mouth and lean in. "You totally just had sex!"

She gasps loudly and looks at me, trying to deny it by shaking her head.

"Oh, yes, you did. You are glowing and have the 'I've just been fucked' face. Trust me, I know that look." I point to myself with both fingers.

Lauren looks around to see that everyone is talking amongst themselves and the music is loud so no one is really paying attention to our conversation. "You're crazy," she tells me and then changes the subject.

"I'm starving," I say loudly, and everyone agrees.

"Pizza?" Dani suggests, standing up. "Let's go."

We all get up to make our way outside.

We follow the gang outside while I look around the club that is getting even more busy. Walking outside, Noah makes his way to the valet, giving him his ticket and arranging to have the car delivered to him at home. I pull Lauren aside. "What did Jake want?"

She shakes her head. "Just to let me know he's now engaged, and that I shouldn't be dating my boss or at least that is what I got from it. After I saw the engagement ring, I zoned out."

Some fans have spotted Cooper, and he goes over to them to take some pictures. While he's doing that, the rest of us climb into a huge black party bus that Scarlett, the party planner, has ordered for guests who drink and don't want to drive home.

"I can't wait to take off these shoes," Parker whines, propping her feet up in Cooper's lap.

"You can wear flip-flops tomorrow when we go skating with Austin," he tells her.

"Skating?" Lauren asks.

"Oh, yeah. I was telling them about Gabe, and since Matthew is in town and wants to run drills with Cooper, we are all meeting at the rink at noon."

"Oh, that sounds like fun. Can I come?" John asks from his side of the bus.

"Can you skate?" Austin asks.

"Well, not like you guys, but I can keep up," he states as Dani laughs out loud.

"Honey, I love you dearly, but you can't skate." Dani leans over and kisses his cheek.

"I'm coming," Noah announces from his seat.

"You skate?" I ask him, suddenly getting hot again.

"Yeah, I played in college," Noah says.

"He was pretty good, could have actually done it professionally if he didn't follow in his family's footsteps," Cooper says.

"He was okay," Austin puts in. "No need to get his head bigger than is possible."

"Okay my ass, I was the second leading scorer of the teams. I had the most minutes on the defensive line."

"I was top scorer," Cooper says. "In case anyone is asking." He laughs while Parker laughs at him.

We spend two hours at the pizza place, laughing over their stories from the 'old days.'

Austin asks Lauren, "Your place or mine?"

I guess that settles the question if they are together or not.

"I'm going to Noah's. So you can go home and have loud monkey sex without me hearing it." I run up behind Noah, who has already flagged down a cab.

"Let's swing by my house and grab some clothes for tomorrow," Austin suggests, yelling at Noah to wait for them.

We wave goodbye to everyone as we cram into the cab. "You live near each other?" Lauren asks.

"I couldn't leave my boo," Noah jokes.

We pull up on their street, a chic, modern neighborhood, where all the houses are three stories high.

"I had no idea that you guys were neighbors," I say to them when we get out of the cab. "There goes skinny dipping." I blink at them while Austin fakes throwing up.

"Close the windows, you two," Noah jokes as we walk up his steps. Once inside the house, I throw my purse on the table and he grabs my hips from behind, kissing my neck. "I think we have sex with just the shoes on this time." His hands come up, cupping my breasts. "Besides, I believe you promised me a taste," he says, leading me to the couch where he pushes me down and shows me exactly what he wants to taste.

When the sun comes up, we are just winding down. We are both covered in a light sweat, our chests both heaving as he falls down next to me, his cock slipping out of me,

"Fuck, it never gets old." His hand lies on my stomach.

"I need a shower and we need to light a candle. It legit smells like sex in the room."

"I don't smell anything," he says, pulling me close to his side. "Let's rest a couple of minutes and then we can shower."

I close my eyes. "Just a couple of minutes," I say as I slowly listen to his soft snores filling the room. I don't know how long I sleep for but when I try to move I'm pinned down by Noah's leg that is thrown across my own legs.

"Move," I say, sliding out from under him as he moans out and falls to his stomach. We never did take that shower. I pick up our clothes and pile them on the table as I go into the kitchen and start the coffee. I grab our clothes and head upstairs to the bathroom. It's only been a couple of weeks, but half of my stuff is here. It almost looks as if I live here. I mean, I don't. I turn the water on, trying to think about when the last time I slept at my house was. My legs are sorer than normal. I put my head under the water while it cascades around my body. I relax under the warm water, rolling my shoulders when I feel his body behind me.

"You showered without me?" he says as he kisses the back of my neck. "We are supposed to be conserving water." His cock now pokes me in the back.

"I'm on a sex break for the next day," I say while his hands come up, cupping my tits and rolling my nipples. "Well, at least till tonight." I feel his lips on my neck now smiling while his hand goes to my pussy and two fingers slip through my folds. "Okay, at least for an hour." I push myself away from him, turning around to take him in.

His hair is half wet from the water, his chest on point with drops of water on him, some drops leading all the way down to his cock, which is ready for more. His arms shoot out, trying to get to me, but I move out of his way.

"No, vagina break!" I say to him, grabbing my soap and loofah. "Can you not get cock cramps from using it too much?" I ask him as he reaches for his own body wash.

"I don't think that's really a thing." He shrugs and starts washing himself. "I mean, we have used it a lot, more than I've ever used it before."

I rinse myself off and step out of his way so he can step under the water. I walk out of the shower, grabbing myself a big, fluffy towel that he has on the rack. Wrapping one around my body and another around my hair, I go to brush my teeth. I watch him as he finishes his shower, coming out and grabbing a towel, wrapping it around his waist. He walks over to the counter, going to his own sink, and does his stuff. He grabs his toothbrush while watching I watch him.

"See something you like?" he asks, winking at me and proceeding to brush his teeth.

I shake my head and head into the bedroom. I dig through the clothes I have on the chair in the room. Seeing nothing I want to wear, I walk to his closet and snag a white T-shirt, throwing it on. It fits me mid-thigh. I go downstairs with the towel still wrapped around my hair. I open the blinds around the house, letting some light come in as well as some candles. The smell of sex from last night is gone. I go to the kitchen, making us coffee. I sit on the stool, grab his iPad, and scroll throw my Facebook. I see a couple of pictures from last night that John posted. There is a picture that he caught of us at the pizza parlor. I'm laughing at something that Noah just said about his dick while he leans in and his nose touches my temple while my head hides the smile that you know is on his face from the way his eyes crinkle. His jacket is around my shoulders because I was chilly. A simple picture yet something so intimate. I save the picture and send it to myself.

"I like that picture," he says from over my shoulder. "Save it as my screensaver," he says, going to get his coffee, then opening the fridge to grab some orange juice.

"And cancel Austin's balls. Are you sure?" I say, smiling at the iPad.

He grabs some cereal out of the pantry and pours himself a bowl.

"I can't believe it's almost eleven," I say, closing the iPad. "My body is stiff from sleeping on the couch. I'm going to go stretch," I tell him as I get off the stool and put my cup in the sink.

"Dishwasher," he says with his mouth full of cereal.

I roll my eyes at him and put it in the dishwasher. Shaking my head, I go to the living room, unrolling the towel from my hair, my damp hair falling down. I take my hair and braid it to the side. I start with my hands on the side, putting one arm in front of me and the other on my shoulder. I repeat with the other arm. I then bend forward with my legs together, grabbing my ankles, bringing my head to my shins, and stretching my legs. I breathe in and out when I feel his hand move my shirt up over my ass.

"We should do this naked," he says, dropping his shorts that he is wearing.

I laugh at him as I stand up, having the shirt cover me back up.

"This is too much clothing," he says as he pulls my shirt over my head. "Now this is so much better, don't you think?"

I shake my head and turn around. He wants to play with fire, I'm going to burn him. So, I start my stretching again left to right. I look over my shoulder as he mimics my moves. I bend over in front of him, grabbing my ankles again. He bends his knees a little, aligning his cock with me. He bends over me.

"Is this couples' yoga?" he asks as he starts to move his hips. "Like should I thrust into you for you to be centered?"

"Where did you learn that from?" I laugh as I'm trying not to focus on his hardness.

"I saw it in a movie once," he says and then starts going again. "Boom." Thrust. "Boom." Thrust. "Boom." Thrust. "Boom." I'm about to open my legs and give him access when I hear a woman's voice shrieking.

"What on earth is going on here?"

My head snaps up and I'm staring at a blond woman wearing a linen skirt and matching jacket.

My mouth opens, sending out a shriek as I jump up and cover myself with my hands. I bend over to grab the T-shirt that Noah just took off me, putting it in front of me.

"Really, Noah?" this woman asks again as I take her in. Her hair is perfectly coifed, a Chanel bag in one hand.

"Mother," he says and my head snaps back as I take in Noah bending over to grab his shorts and placing them in front of him. He also gets in front of me, blocking me from his mother, who is not even trying to cover her eyes. "Have you ever heard of knocking? Or, I don't know, ringing?" he says as I hold the shirt to my chest and lean into his back as I close my eyes and wish for the floor to swallow me whole.

"I did. I knocked and nothing, so I used my key," she says, going to the couch sitting down, looking around sniffing. "What is that smell?" she says. "Aren't you going to dismiss her?" she says, getting comfortable.

"Mother, if anyone is going to be dismissed it's you. You can't just barge in here." He stops mid-sentence because her hand goes up.

"Seriously, Noah, did you not have enough last night and this morning?" She shakes her head, doing a tsking sound. "And no condom. I thought you knew better. She's probably trying to trap you into a child or"—she looks over—"give you something."

My back snaps and so does my head.

"Leave." I hear Noah shout.

"No," I say from behind him, putting my shirt on, then stepping in front of him. "For your information, I don't want anything from him besides, well, besides all of him," I stutter out. Nice time to get blocked for words. "You don't even know me and yet you come in here, unannounced, and assume you know the type of person I am. Wow. I see he didn't get that from you." I'm about to walk away, but Noah's hand comes out to grab mine.

"I think you need to go, Mother, and how about next time you call and not use your key. You never know how you will catch us. And there will be a next time," he says, his hand moving around my shoulder while his shorts still cover his penis.

She eyes us both, getting up, grabbing her purse. "I would say hope to see you again, but let's be honest, you'll be a funny story we will tell at Christmas." She turns and walks out of the house.

"I need to go," I whisper, walking upstairs.

CHAPTER TWENTY-THREE

Noah

"I need to go," she whispers, walking upstairs. How did the best two days of my life turn to shit so fast? I throw my head back, rubbing my hands over my face. Not waiting another second, I run up the stairs, taking them two at a time. Once I get to the bedroom door I see her scurrying around the room, packing not just what she wore last night, but everything that she has here.

"What the hell is going on right now?" I ask her, walking into the room.

"Um, I think we should have a little space," she says to the bag, going into the bathroom to get more stuff.

Walking over to the bag, I start unpacking it and putting things back where they belong. She comes out of the bathroom, her hands full of her shit, and let me say I love her shit, stopping mid-step.

"What are you doing?"

I don't bother looking at her. I just put her clothes back on the chair in a heaping mess, some falling sideways. "I think it's pretty self-explanatory," I say, walking back to her, grabbing her stuff out of her hand. "There is no little fucking space." I walk back, dumping the stuff on the counter, turning and watching her at the door of the bathroom while I lean back on the counter. "My mother is a bitch. It's a known fact. Fuck, even my father doesn't like her. He tolerates her, but…" I stop when I see the questions in her eyes. "My parents had me because it was the thing to do. Two hotshot lawyers creating life. It took them into a new level, but once I was here it was a level that my mother didn't want, so I was brought up by nannies."

Her eyes turn soft.

"My parents aren't loving like your parents, babycakes." I walk to her, grabbing her face in mine. "My mother will be a bitch till she closes her eyes and even then she might come back just to fuck with me. Don't define me or us because of my mother."

She puts her hands on mine. "She really is a bitch. It's a good thing my parents taught me manners because—" And I stop her there by bringing my lips to hers while I squeeze her cheeks in my hands.

"Now, can we go back down and do naked yoga, please?"

Her smile shines bright, her eyes light, and her giggle shoots straight to my heart, then my cock. Whoa, did I just say heart? Fuck. This is what it feels like. I kind of like it. Could be worse.

"We are not doing naked yoga till the locks are changed on your front door," she says and I let her go, walking over to my night table where I pick up the phone. "What are you doing?"

"Calling a locksmith." I turn and sit on the bed and forty-five minutes later I have new locks on the door and forty-seven minutes later I'm buried balls deep in her while we do naked yoga.

The next day I kiss her goodbye when we both leave for the day and I'm strolling into the office and stop as soon as I see Lauren walking in also.

"Look at you being early and shit." I smile, holding the door open for her.

"We start at nine, right?" she asks, looking down at her watch.

"Yeah ish, give or take," I say to her, nodding to the security guards in the entrance.

"Ish, what is ish?" she asks, pressing the elevator button, going up.

"Lauren, I'm not Austin. I won't freak out if you're ten minutes late. Shit happens. Now I have Norma coming to just show you the ins and outs. You have her for two hours because Leonard is coming back this afternoon," I say, getting out of the elevator and showing her to Norma's office. "I hope you're a fast learner." I wink at her as she takes a notebook out of her bag. I smile to both of them and then go to my office, checking my emails. Two hours later when I look up, Lauren is sitting at her desk with four, first-year associates. I don't know what she is telling them, but it looks like she she's telling them a super-hot dirty sex story. I grab my phone, snapping a picture and sending it to Austin.

My PA is better than yours!

Fuck off! He replies, making me laugh.

Dude, she is the shit. These chumps are eating her up.

I look back at her as she points to something on the computer screen.

All jokes aside, she just cleared my schedule in ten minutes.

He doesn't answer me anymore. Instead, flowers arrive. Lots of them. I laugh, thinking well played. I pick up the phone, calling my girl. She answers breathless after the second ring.

I smile and lower my voice. "Are you playing with yourself?"

She laughs. "Most def. How did you know?"

"My cock has a radar for when you're in the mood. He stands at attention ready for war."

"That is a picture. Your cock dressed up ready for war with a little helmet."

"Hey," I snap, "there is nothing little about my cock. You never put little and cock in the same sentence."

"Okay," she says, giggling, "your head is so big they don't have a helmet to fit."

"Better, so much better." I turn my chair, looking outside. "Now what are we doing for dinner?"

"I have to watch Rachel and Gabriel so Lauren can go get her car fixed."

"Oh, okay, so I'll come there. How about I grab some pizza? Do kids eat that?"

"Yes, Noah, kids love pizza. Can you get me a vegan one?" she says softly. "There may be a surprise tonight if you do."

"I'll make the pizza myself if they don't have one."

She laughs. "Okay, come by at five ish."

"See, you get ish. Why doesn't your sister get ish?"

"She will never get ish. Ever," she sighs. "See you at five."

"Later, babycakes," I say, disconnecting.

The afternoon goes by uneventful. Lauren has everything organized and I don't know what I did before her. The pizza is now sitting on the passenger seat. Not knowing what the kids like, I think I went overboard. Because now there are six pizzas. One just cheese, one pepperoni, one meat lovers, one veggies, one Hawaiian, and one vegan. Pulling into the driveway, I see they are all outside. Gabe is with a hockey stick, doing some stick handling while Kaleigh is doing some poses with Rachel. When I turn off the car, they all run to the car.

"Hey there," I say, getting out, kissing Kaleigh hello and then bending to kiss Rachel.

"Did you get me epperoni?" Rachel puts her hands on her hips.

"I did," I say, slapping Gabe on the shoulder. "Who is going to help me carry these in?" I say when I open the door and raise the boxes up.

"How many people were you expecting?" Gabe asks, laughing.

I shrug my shoulders, following them inside, carrying all the boxes. When I place them on the counter, we open them and Rachel scrunches her nose up when she sees the vegetable one. "I no want that one."

Kaleigh goes to get plates, coming back and handing me and Gabe one. Then she grabs a slice of pepperoni for Rachel. We sit down at the table where I listen to stories of all the kids in Rachel's class. Each and every one of them.

When it's time to clean up, I tell Kaleigh I'll take care of it so she can give Rachel a bath. I roll up my sleeves while Gabe goes to do his homework and I go about placing things in the dishwasher. I open it to see that it's not even organized. I shake my head and start rearranging everything. By the time I finish, Rachel comes bouncing down.

"Aunt Kay said she is taking a shower and to not go show her your toy. What toy do you have?" she asks and I take in the little girl with fresh pjs and her wet hair combed and braided.

"Um." I start to think of something.

"Can I paint your nails?" she asks.

"Sure," I say if it's going to get her to not think about what toy I have for her aunt.

She squeals with delight, clapping her hands and jumping up and down.

"I go get my spa tings," she says, running back to the dining room corner, bringing up a bright pink square makeup case. She walks to the living room and puts it on the table. "Come sit, Noah," she says and I go sit down. She opens this pink case, showing me that she has about ten nail colors. "What color you want?" she asks and I bend in, looking at the colors. Green, yellow, blue, orange, red, pink, brown, white, gray, and black.

"I don't know," I say, grabbing a bottle out of the case. "What color do you think I should do?" I ask her, picking another bottle.

"I love the orange," she says, grabbing the bright orange out of the bag. "It means social butterfly."

I pinch my eyebrows together. "Does it really?" I ask her.

"Yes, Google it," she says, making Gabe laugh from the dining room where he is still doing homework.

I pull out my phone, searching for the information, and what do you know, she is right.

"Look at that. How about we do orange on my feet and pink on my nails?" I tell her, reading the description for pink.

She nods and goes to get a small stool to sit on while she paints my nails, or actually paints the skin around my nails, with my nails. One finger has polish all the way to the knuckles.

"Don't move your hands or you'll smudge it," she tells me to put up my feet on the table.

Luckily I had taken off my socks when we started this adventure.

"You have big feet," she says, painting my big toe. "Aunt Kay says big feet mean big—"

"Rachel," Lauren shouts from the entrance of the living room.

"Mamma, you're home. Look, I'm painting Noah's nails. He doesn't want anyone to know he's a social butterfly, so I put it on his feet."

She walks in, taking in the paint job. "Oh, isn't that nice, you are doing a wonderful job." She kisses her cheek while Rachel misses my whole toenail altogether and paints the top of my foot. Lauren comes in eating and talking to Gabe as I wait for my nails to dry. When Kaleigh finally comes down, I see that she is wearing her pjs and her hair is piled on top of her head.

"I guess you're staying here?" I ask her as she sits next to me.

"Aren't you sick of me yet?" She tilts her head to the side.

"Yet? Why, are you sick of me?" I mimic her move with my head and the question.

"Not even a little."

"Good, so leave your car here and I'll drive you back tomorrow. I have to be in court at nine. So it will work out," I say, leaning in. "Plus, you owe me a surprise and I want to show you my toy."

"Oh, yeah, is your toy a big toy?" She leans into me.

"Can you guys not talk about toys on my couch, please?" Lauren shouts from the kitchen.

"I didn't see any toys," Rachel says from somewhere else.

"Okay, let's go," I say, getting up and saying bye to everyone.

When I walk out of court the next day I drive straight to Austin's to see how the bastard is doing.

"Hey there, stranger." I go to his couch, unbuttoning my jacket and sitting down. I look at Austin. "Well, at least you won't try to bang your new PA, right?" I laugh, brushing my hands into my hair.

"That really isn't your color." He points to my hand.

"Rachel painted my nails yesterday." I inspect my nails. "You should see what she did to my feet."

He throws his pen down and sits up straighter. "You saw Rachel yesterday?"

"Well, we had to babysit Rachel and Gabe so Lauren could bring her car in to get the radio fixed," I say and then notice a change in his facial expression.

"What?" he yells.

"A CD of *Frozen* was jammed in her player and was stuck on repeat, so it played it all the time. You know this." Surely he remembers he kept bitching about it for a month.

"I know what you mean. What I don't understand is why you were babysitting."

"She needed help." I open my hands.

"Why didn't she ask me?"

"I don't know, maybe because you hightailed it right out of there the minute family shit started happening on Sunday night?" I stand up, now remembering the story Kaleigh told me in bed last night.

"Fuck off!" he yells back at me. Austin sits up in his chair a little straighter. "She was busy, so I left."

I glare at him now. "You left or you took off, it's the same thing."

"Is that what she said?" He waits for an answer.

"She didn't say anything. I just found it weird that she would ask us and not you. Kaleigh said to drop it, so I figured you didn't want to."

"I wasn't asked. I didn't even know."

He gets up, grabbing his jacket, ready to run out of the office, when I grab his arm. "Where the fuck do you think you're going?"

"I'm going to tell her that I'm not scared of her kids."

"Think about what you're doing. You are planning to barge into her workplace to profess this to her. Dude." I shake my head and grab my phone to call Kaleigh. "Babycakes, are you home?" I smile and nod.

"Yup," she answers. "Why? Are you going to come and feed me your toy for lunch?"

I look at Austin to make sure he didn't hear.

"Okay. Austin needs to come over and do something. Can you go to my place? Pack a bag, or better yet, just bring everything with you."

"Funny, if you're asking me to move in this isn't exactly the way to do it. I'll leave the door open for him and make arrangements with our parents for the kids."

I smile and then hang up. "Okay, Kaleigh is leaving the door open for you. Go woo your girl."

"Woo?" he asks me.

How he has even gotten laid is beyond me.

"A meal, rose petals, champagne, lingerie, vibrators, cuffs. You know, romance."

"This, I can do." He taps his chin, thinking. "I'm going to woo the fuck out of her."

He rushes out of the office while I laugh and follow him, stopping in front of his assistant's desk. "Don't make plans for him. He is going to woo." I wink and walk away.

CHAPTER TWENTY-FOUR

Kaleigh

The alarm buzzes and my eyes slowly open, taking in the light coming in from outside. "Noah." I slap his arm while he mumbles in his sleep. It's been over two weeks since he said bring everything. I haven't actually brought everything, but I might as well. I never go home anymore. I mean, I go home to get the kids off the bus, but come dinner time I'm out and here. I keep waiting for him to get over us. But it is just the opposite. We've gotten into this routine and it's not even an effort. It's just natural. Like we have always been doing it.

"Noah." I slap him again as he lifts his head from the pillow, then slams his hand down on the phone to stop the alarm. He then rolls into me, spooning me, his morning wood wishing me good morning also.

His hand comes up to cup my breast.

"They are so sore," I say as he rolls my nipples, making me arch my back. "I think it was all the nibbling you were doing on them."

"It's not my fault you put them in my face," he says into my neck, giving me soft kisses.

"I was watching television. How were they in your face?" I smile as I place my hand on his.

"But then you straddled me, putting them in my face."

"You yanked me onto you and said ride 'em, cowgirl."

"Which you did, putting them in my face," he says, moving a little bit so his cock can squeeze into me. "Let me put just the tip in."

I laugh, opening my legs and giving him access. "Just the tip my ass," I say as he puts in the tip, then the shaft, and then he's buried completely. We both moan out, not saying a word as he fucks me from behind slowly, his hands playing with my nipples as I play with my clit.

"Hmm," he moans from behind me. "Fuck, you're so wet."

My eyes close as I take in the feeling of him all in me, around me. My senses are on overload this morning. "I'm going to cum," I say as I feel it in my tits, my stomach, and my clit. It's all too much, so I let go, pulsing around him, once, twice, three time till he plants himself in me to the hilt and I feel him cum in me.

"Well, that was a great good morning," he says after a couple of minutes when I move away, having him slip out of me. "What time do we have to be at your sister's?" he asks me as I walk to the bathroom.

"She said lunch, so noonish." I stop walking. "Fuck, I feel queasy this morning."

"Again?" Noah says, getting out of bed, coming to me. "It's that bug you had."

I look at myself in the mirror. "I'm so pale."

"You're beautiful," he says, wrapping his arms around my waist, smiling. "So beautiful."

"Yeah, yeah, yeah," I say and start to get ready for lunch.

When we pull up to the house a couple of hours later, my stomach is rumbling again. "I think I'm going to yak," I say, getting out and walking into the house.

"Well, you threw up most of the night, so I don't think there is anything left inside you," Noah says, getting out of the car and walking with me.

"Are you okay?" Lauren asks me as soon as I walk in. She is busy preparing the roast and the sight of raw meat makes me even more sick.

"I just feel tired, and I think I caught a bug." I sit on the stool at the counter.

I take in the change in Lauren, the happiness in her eyes, the freshly fucked cheeks.

"She was up all night barfing. You know it's love when you get someone water while they are yacking," Noah says, grabbing a coffee cup and filling it up.

"That is really nice of you, pal," Austin comments from his side of the counter while he looks at us. Both Austin and Noah are dressed down in jeans and button-up shirts.

"I can do a lot of things. I just can't do the whole vomit thing. But I was proud of myself." He reaches over and rubs my head.

We don't have a chance to say anything before we hear my mother. "Knock, knock, knock!" she calls out before walking into the house.

"Mom, it defeats the purpose if you just walk in," I say. "What if we were all naked?"

My mother gasps. "It's noon, why would you be naked at noon?"

"Oh, dear God," Lauren says under her breath.

The kids come barreling downstairs, yelling for grandma and grandpa.

"Hey, Austin," my father greets him, hitting him on the back. "How are you, son? Should we be expecting any penises today?" He laughs as he comes to me to give me a side hug. "Hey, beautiful girl," he whispers.

"Kaleigh, you look like death," my mother remarks while she comes to hug me and then Lauren. "Austin, it's good to see you, without, you know." She motions her hands into the shape of a penis in the air.

"That was a fun time," Noah says into his cup, smiling, while Austin and Lauren just glare at him.

"I don't feel good," I say as I get up to go to the bathroom.

I go upstairs to the bathroom in my room. When I walk in it looks so empty, no clothes thrown around, no empty glasses by the bed, just still air. I look at the nightstand and see a box of tampons there. I walk over to the box, taking one out. "When was my last period?" I say to myself and the walls. I start counting down in my head and my eyes open wide. "Oh no, no, no, no, no, no, no," I say, running to my desk and opening the drawer. I grab the pregnancy test that I got as a gag gift for my last birthday. It was in the basket of single girl's survival basket along with condoms that are long gone.

"This is not happening right now. It can't be happening," I say as I walk out and go to the bathroom, hiding the test under my shirt. I open the box and take out the instructions. Opening the test, I get it ready to pee on. I pull down my pants and grab the test while I sit down. I sit here with my hand between my legs, waiting for pee to come out. "Great, I get a shy bladder now, today of all days."

I sit here, thinking of lakes, and water, and waves and still nothing. I get up a bit, leaning over, and open the water tap. Maybe if I hear the water running my bladder might work. I don't know how long I'm actually here for. It feels like forever, an hour, maybe two but actually a couple of minutes when finally pee starts to come out and I miss the test completely, wetting all over my hand. I stop and look through my legs and aim it for the stream of pee.

Getting up, I put the test on the counter and clean myself up and wash my hands. I grab the pee stick, wetting my hands again and watch it while I say a prayer. I watch one line turn a bright blue, so I grab the box, reading to see what that means. "Not pregnant." I smile and look down again and see that another line is coming through, faint at first, almost like it isn't there and then turning bright blue. "Oh, fuck," I say. Maybe it's broken. Maybe this one is broken. I take another test out. Thank fuck they got me the combo pack, and I start the thing again. This time I pee in a matter of seconds. I put it down and watch it, the first line appearing right away and then the second line coming brighter this time. "Oh my God." I pick them both up and stare down at them. I wrap them both in toilet paper and I'm putting them in the box when Rachel knocks on the door, scaring me so much I drop the box right into the garbage.

"Auntie Kay, I got to tinkle," she says softly.

So I open the door and let her come in. I look at myself in the mirror, seeing if maybe you can tell what is going on. Will people be able to tell I'm pregnant by looking at me?

I walk into the kitchen right when I hear my mother saying, "Maybe you caught Kaleigh's bug." My head snaps to Lauren as I see frustration on her face.

"I think lunch is ready." Austin heads to the stove. "Kaleigh, we made you some tofu stuff that Lauren found in the freezer. I made sure to put it in another pan."

"Awww, so you forgive me for tricking you into drinking breast milk?" I ask him with a smile, trying to act normal when all I want to do is go back upstairs and stare at the tests again.

Lauren grabs the side dishes that have been warming in the oven with the roast, while Austin grabs the roast. My father grabs drinks from the fridge, and my mother calls the kids. Noah walks over to the wine fridge, grabbing two bottles.

We make our way to the dining room. Gabe runs in, while Austin puts the roast down. Rachel comes into the room, banging two white things together. "Tap, tap, tap!" she shouts. "Click, click, click."

"What is that?" Lauren looks at the white sticks in her hand.

And I think this is what it feels like to have a heart attack. I have a numbness in my arm. I think it's numbness I don't really know since I can't really hear anything over the pounding going on in my ears.

"They're drum sticks. I found them in the bathroom." She is still tapping them together. "Like a wand. Bippity boppity bo."

"Oh my God," I say in a whisper as my mother grabs one of the sticks from Rachel's hand.

"Oh my God." She looks at Lauren. "You're pregnant!" She sits down at the table.

Lauren's head snaps back and she grabs the other stick from Rachel. Sure enough, it's another positive pregnancy test.

She looks at Austin, who has gone paler than a ghost.

"Lauren?" he questions, holding the table with one hand, while he looks like he is going to fall over.

"You have to marry her," my mother announces with tears in her eyes. "A child out of wedlock is a no-no." She shakes her head no over and over again

"Lauren." We hear Austin again, this time his voice quivering.

She looks around the faces at the table. Her eyes searching mine, she knows I know she knows just by looking at me.

"It's mine," I say, then I look at Noah. "I'm pregnant."

Noah places the bottles of wine on the table. "What do you mean?"

"I mean, I'm pregnant," I repeat, throwing my hands in the air.

"But...but...but," Noah stutters.

"This is worse than Lauren being pregnant," my mother groans with tears running down her face.

"Mom," Lauren snaps at her, walking over to me and hugging me tight, whispering in my ear, "It's going to be okay." The tears now run down my cheeks. What if he doesn't want a baby? What if I have to have a baby by myself? What if my baby hates me for not giving him or her a father?

"Holy shit," Austin breathes, finally sitting down.

Noah walks over to us, grabbing my face in both his hands. "I love you. So, so much. More than I love me." He smiles at me and rubs away the tears that are rolling down my cheeks. "Marry me? Be my wife?"

"Are you sure?" I ask him while I put my hands on his.

He just declared his love for me in front of my whole family the same time he found out he is going to be a father.

"More sure than anything I've ever done in my whole life." He pulls me close to him.

"Yes," I say right before I throw myself at him, kissing him.

"This is wonderful," my mother squeals. "Frank, we are planning a wedding."

"Great!" My father looks at Austin. "Open that wine."

"I'm getting married!" I turn, shouting to everyone in the room.

"Um," Noah murmurs as we all turn to look at him. "I just need to get divorced first."

"You need to get divorced?" my sister, Lauren, yells from the other side of the room.

Lunch at my sister's is usually eventful but not this eventful. Five minutes ago I found out I was pregnant. Four minutes ago everyone else did also. Three minutes ago I agreed to marry Noah, who is my baby daddy. Two minutes ago I found out he's married and needs a divorce. What the heck just happened?

"Oh my God," my mother shouts from her chair that she fell into when I declared I was pregnant. "She's an adulterer." Her hand goes to her chest. "I think I'm having a heart attack." She looks at my father.

My father goes to her side, tapping her hand. "Now, now, dear, let's not get ahead of ourselves. I'm sure there is a logical explanation to all of this, right, Noah?" My father looks over at my soon-to-be fiancé, who just looks back at me, his mouth opening to say something, but my mother cutting him off.

"She will be branded the other woman. We might as well mark her with the red A on her shirt." My mother continues grabbing hold of my father's hand with tears in her eyes. She is almost hyperventilating at this point.

"Okay, everyone needs to calm down for a second." My sister tries to be the reasonable one.

"You're married?" I turn to Noah, pulling my hand from his. "How did you not tell me this?" I blink away the tears forming. Okay, fine, when we were together we were like rabbits trying to hump each other, but still I think 'I'm married' might have come out before now.

"He can explain." Austin turns to Noah. "Tell them." He motions to Noah with his hand. "Tell them it's all a mistake."

"I'm not really married, married. Per say." Noah's voice is soft while he grabs my hand.

"You're either married or you're not married." Lauren glares at him, folding her arms over her chest. I'm sure she is planning her revenge as we speak.

"I'm married, but not." He speaks with his hands.

"Are you fucking married or not?" I yell, getting up. How can this be happening to me?

"Dear, the stress isn't good for the baby," my father speaks quietly.

"I got married to help a friend out." Noah gets up, coming to me, his hands rubbing my arms up and down. "She was Canadian and needed a green card."

"Idiot," Austin says from behind my sister, shaking his head.

"It was Sabrina." Noah looks at Austin like the name should ring a bell.

"Sabrina, college Sabrina? The Sabrina you chased for nine months? The one you tried to have sex with? But then found out she was a lesbian Sabrina?" Austin asks.

"I didn't try to have sex with her or chase her for nine months. It was more like nine weeks," Noah says, shaking his head.

"You snuck into her dorm room and lay on her bed naked with a can of whipped cream," Austin reminds him. "You asked her if she wanted cream in her coffee while lathering yourself with said whipped cream."

"Okay, fine, I tried to sleep with her once." Noah finally looks over at him.

"Didn't she try to get a restraining order against you?" Austin asks, slamming his hand on his pants, laughing. "You sent her a dick pic and she sent you a picture of a knife with a carrot cut in two."

"Okay, that's enough." Noah points to him. "She needed help, so she came to me because she knew I would help her."

"How would you help a lesbian Canadian?" Lauren asks the question everyone is dying to ask.

"Sabrina and her girlfriend, Tonya, came to me and asked for help. You see, Sabrina's student visa was running out and the only way for her to stay in the country was to get a green card. Well, back then, lesbian weddings were not legal, so they came to me." Noah tells us his side of the story.

"So you just helped them out, no strings attached?" Lauren asks him with her eyes going into slits.

"Well, not really." Noah looks down and then up. "I had to watch them have sex." He puts his hands up when my mother gasps and my father closes his lips together to stop from laughing.

"You had to?" Austin tries to hide his smirk.

"It was one time and I wasn't allowed to join in. They tied me to a chair. I couldn't even." He motions to his hand moving up and down. "You know."

"He has lost his mind." Austin looks at him, then at me.

"It's okay. It'll be okay. I'll just get the papers drawn up, and then we can get it signed. We can be married right away." He pushes my hair behind my ears. "I just have to find her."

I look up into the eyes of the man who is going to be the father of my child. Into the blue eyes of the man who literally swept me off my feet. Only for me to find out that he's married. "You're married." I pull away from him, looking at everyone in the room. "Are you fucking kidding me right now?" I go into the kitchen to get a knife.

Dad jumps into action, coming to me while Austin pushes Lauren behind him and Mom shouts in horror.

"You son of a bitch, I'm going to cut off your small ass pecker." I lash out with the knife, but Dad takes it from me. "After everything that I told you, after I poured my heart out to you, you would think this would have been brought up. Like 'hey, funny story, I got married,' or 'I'm a fucking moron and did something so stupid' but nothing, not a fucking word." My hands go up and I slap them down. "You're an asshole and you're just like them." My voice gets quiet. "I need some alone time." I start walking out of the room, feeling all eyes on me, and feeling Noah's body heat right behind me. I turn to face him and he almost crashes into me. "That means from you, too." I turn to walk up the stairs, zoning out the arguing that is coming from the living room. Closing the door behind me, I turn the lock closed. I fall onto my bed, making some of the throw pillows fall on the floor.

CHAPTER TWENTY-FIVE

Noah

"I know you fucked up before, but this is the biggest fuck up of your life," Austin says to the room.

I just watched the love of my life—that is right, the love of my fucking life—walk away from me with our child. I turn, watching everyone watching me. "I'm going to fix this and then we are going to get married and we are going to be married forever," I tell her mother, who looks at me with half murder in her eyes while Lauren is straight out planning my death and from the look on her face it's going to be painful.

"Everyone needs to simmer down now," Frank says from behind Dede, where he has one hand on her shoulder. "He was helping a friend, so now he finds that friend and gets divorced. No one has to know anything." He nods at me, giving me the moral support a father should give.

"Exactly. No one has to know anything. Tomorrow morning we go in there and we get the cavalry ready and we find Sabrina and by the end of the week we could be divorced." I look back up the stairs, the need to run upstairs itching my legs. I feel a hand on my arm and look down to see Lauren.

"I'll go and check on her."

I nod to her and watch her walk up the stairs to my girl and child.

My family.

She comes down right away. "She's sleeping, so I didn't bother waking her. Why don't we eat? She'll come down later," she says as we sit down and eat. I barely touch anything. My feet bounce up and down as I wait for Kaleigh to come back downstairs.

When all of the plates are washed and put away I sit on the couch, the whole time watching the stairs, waiting to see her bounce downstairs. "How is she still sleeping?" I ask Lauren, who is sitting with Rachel doing homework.

"Her body is going through changes," Lauren says. "It is normal, trust me."

I nod at her then look back at the stairs.

"I should go," I say, getting up. "I don't want to go, but I want her to feel safe." I look at them both. "Can you just text me after to tell me she is okay?"

They both nod at me as I walk out.

"And tell her that I love her."

I make my way home. Walking into the house without her seems strange. There are all little things everywhere that shows you she lives here. Her yoga mat in the corner rolled up with her weights in a basket. Her yoga magazines are on the coffee table. Her empty glass of water is beside it. Her flip-flops are in the kitchen. Every time I turn around I see something of hers. I close off the lights, going upstairs into our room, because it isn't mine anymore. It's ours. I collapse on the bed, her smell all around me. I grab her pillow, bringing it to my face. I turn, looking out the window. I get up, bringing the pillow with me, going downstairs to the couch. I look up at the ceiling, making a list of everything I have to do. When I hear something at the door, I turn my head, wondering if maybe it was all in my head when all of a sudden I see her walking in.

She sees me on the couch and comes over. "What are you doing on the couch?" she asks, sitting on the table in front of me.

"The bed felt empty without you," I say, sitting up, facing her.

"So you came down with my pillow?" She points to the pillow still in my arms.

"It smelled like you," I say, putting it aside, leaning forward to grab her hands in mine. "Babycakes, you have to know I honestly didn't think about Sabrina till I was in the moment and, well, then I had no choice but to tell you."

"I know," she says softly, looking down at our hands. "I didn't do this on purpose." She again stops talking. "I know people will say I did." She shrugs her shoulders. "But I didn't. It must have been the medication when I had strep."

"I don't give a shit when it was or who says what. The fact is I know and you know and that is all that matters," I reassure her. "Now how are you feeling? Are you okay?" I ask her, putting her hair behind her ear.

"Yeah, I slept like a baby actually and when I woke all I wanted was you, so I got up and came here. But this is the last straw. If there is anything that you are hiding and I find out, I will slit off you penis the next time."

I get up, picking her up in my arms. "I have no doubt. Now let's go to bed. I have a busy day tomorrow. I need to get myself divorced."

The next day I jump out of bed and put on my power suit. A suit I know I'm going to kick ass with. I walk out of the elevator. "Round up the cavalry. We have a big client. Board room in ten," I tell the receptionist, who picks up her phone and places an intercom announcement. Walking to my desk, I see that Lauren is already in.

"Hey, good, you're here," she says, getting up. "We need to get working," she says with her no nonsense bullshit. "I will not let my niece or nephew down."

"It's a boy," I say to her as we walk down the hall to the conference room.

"How do you know?" She looks over with a smirk.

"Because according to an article online, the sex is determined on who the dominant one in bed is. So therefore we are having a boy. Now don't get me wrong, your sister can ride the shit out of me, but—"

She puts her hand up. "Can we not discuss my sister and your sex life?" She shakes her head, opening the door, going in and seeing the whole room full.

I nod to Harvey, who looks at me funny. "Okay, people, we have a code red."

"What the fuck is a code red?" Harvey asks, confused.

"So as some of you know I'm off the market." I look around to see everyone staring at me. "As in I'm in love with one person and one person only."

"This is what this meeting is for?" says Fred, another criminal case lawyer. "I mean, I'm happy for you, but—"

I put my hand up to stop him from talking. "I need to find my wife and get divorced before I can marry the one I really, really love."

"You're married?"

I hear someone shriek out. I look up and see that it was a third year associate who kept bringing me doughnuts last year.

"I am, but now we need to find my fake wife and get a divorce. Her name is Sabrina Collins. Last I heard she was somewhere on the east coast. She was majoring in pediatrics. She is also a lesbian."

"Why is that an issue?" someone asks.

I look over and see a new face. "Who are you?"

"Oh, I'm sorry, my name is Luca. I'm the new associate who just graduated Harvard," he says, his voice sure of himself.

I look him over, perfect suit, perfect hair, pretty face. I like him.

"It's important because if you find her on Facebook she will probably be in a relationship with a woman."

"Now I want everyone on this. I would like for this to be over by Friday," I say, looking at everyone as they all nod their heads. "Let's go, people."

Everyone gets up to leave except Harvey, who sits back in his chair.

Once everyone is gone but Harvey, Lauren, and me he finally talks, "You committed fraud." He throws his pen down. "Seriously, Noah. You're a lawyer."

"It wasn't fraud." I look at Lauren, who crosses her arms. "Per se." When Lauren pffts I continue, "Okay, fine, I knew she was a lesbian, but you never know, people can change."

"I agree," he says, now sitting up, crossing his arms in front of him. "People change all the time, but sexual orientation doesn't change. Did she make you think she would change?"

"She sent him a knife picture when he sent her a dick pic," Lauren buts in, earning her a glare from me.

"It wasn't my finest moment, okay, but I need to get that divorce. I'm going to be a father," I say. I don't think I have ever been more proud in my life to say those words. "I'm going to be a dad," I say again. This time my chest puffs out more. "Me a father." I get up, smiling. "Lauren, order Kaleigh flowers and fruit baskets and some vegan shit she eats."

I turn, walking out of the office and then turning back around. "A dad. Me. I have super sperm," I say, walking out to my office to start my own search.

By the end of the day, Harvey, Luca, and I are in the boardroom going through all the notes the associates have given us. The boardroom is full of notes, leftover lunch boxes, empty Starbucks cups.

"How is this girl not traceable?" I say, running my hands through my hair, pulling at it.

"It's like she's a ghost," Harvey says. "Um, Noah, take no offense, but are you sure this woman exists?" Harvey says to me.

Luca raises his eyebrows, waiting for the answer.

"Trust me. She was real. Even Austin met her," I say to them.

"Well, we know that she had a driver's license when you guys were together, but that was never renewed," Luca says, looking at the white board with all the writings. "So she probably doesn't drive anymore." He sits up, snapping his fingers. "We need to look in the states that have public transport faster than driving."

Harvey slams his hand on the table. "Yes, New York, Chicago maybe? L.A."

Luca shakes his head. "No, everyone in L.A. drives. It's why you're stuck in traffic for hours."

Harvey looks at his watch, getting up. "I have to go. My son has his soccer game tonight."

"That's amazing," I say.

"Well, considering he's five and picks daisies because he hates the fucking sport, yeah, should be a fun time for everyone." I laugh as he leaves.

"Okay, Luca, let's take a breather and start fresh tomorrow," I say, gathering the papers.

"It's okay, you go ahead. I'm new in town. I don't know anyone, so I don't mind staying."

"You have anyone that you're dating?" I ask him as I put my papers away.

"Nope," he says. "Law school was my only focus." He shrugs. "Besides, I have my whole life for that."

I smile, walking out, wishing him a good night. I take my phone out, calling Austin. "Hey, I think I need to buy a ring for Kaleigh."

"You think?" he asks, laughing. "Isn't that supposed to be done before the whole marry me stuff?"

I laugh. "I like to do this unconventionally."

"So I've heard. I also heard word on the street and by street I mean my parents called me to ask if the rumors are true. It seems your parents got a memo that their son is having a baby."

I curse out, "Fuck."

"Yeah, well, I thought I'd give you the heads-up. Your mother is flying on her broom stick and I just hope someone has water nearby to throw on her."

"If you see the cops at my house when you get home, you'll know why."

I disconnect the phone and then try to call Kaleigh and it goes straight to voice mail. Fuck. I say, now jogging to my car. I contemplate calling my mother, but first I have to make sure I get to Kaleigh before my mother does.

CHAPTER TWENTY-SIX

Kaleigh

My whole body hurts. Why does my body hurt so much? I blink my eyes open. And why is it that all I want to do is curl up in a ball and sleep? I went into work today and took a two-hour nap in the relaxation room. Then I got up, came home, and then napped again till the kids came home. I got to Noah's at five-thirty and drifted off while watching *House Hunters*.

I pick up my phone, noticing that Noah called me four times in the last five minutes. I'm about to call him back when the doorbell rings. I walk to the door, opening it and coming face to face with his mother.

If I thought she was well dressed when she was here the last time, it's nothing compared to now. She is wearing a charcoal knee-length skirt with the matching jacket tied at the waist and flaring off at the hips. A cream-colored Hermes bag finishes the well-polished look. Her hair is once again styled flawlessly.

"Well, look at this," she says, walking past me into the house.

I close my eyes and say a prayer that Noah gets here before I kill her. "Please come in," I say to no one really.

"Where is my son?" she asks, looking around the living room.

"He is at work or on his way home."

"I see. Well, then this is even better. We can have a conversation woman to woman," she says, holding her purse handle in two hands now. "So tell me how much is it going to cost me to make you go away?"

My head snaps back and I stop. I can't swallow because my mouth is suddenly dry. "What?" I ask in almost a whisper.

"I got a call today. It seems you've got yourself in a situation and I need to know how much it will take to make you and the situation go away."

My hand goes straight to my stomach in protection mode.

"We both know that you saw Noah and found out who he was and then starting hatching a plan to get your claws into him. So, I'll ask you again, how much will it cost me to have you be a bad memory?"

"I'm going to be as polite as I possibly can because my parents taught me that. But get the fuck out," I say, pointing to the door. "There is not a price that you can pay me to as you put it 'go away.' And this situation you are talking about is your grandchild."

"Can we really be sure?" she says and I gasp in shock.

"Get the fuck out." Is roared behind me.

I turn to come face to face with Noah. Actually it's not Noah. I have never met this person before. Gone are the clear blue eyes. In their place are dark blue cloudy ones. His hands are clenched at his sides while the vein is in forehead is ticking. "Take your bullshit and your vile words and get the fuck out of my house, Mother."

She actually rolls her eyes at him. "Noah, you can't honestly tell me that it didn't cross your mind that the child might not be yours."

"I may be a lot of things. I may be flighty. I may be nonchalant, and I may show up later most of the times. But one thing you can never say about me is that I'm a liar." My hands now clench at my sides while I feel Noah come to me, putting his arm around my shoulders, giving me strength.

"I've seen you pull a lot of stunts in my life, Mother, but this right here is the straw that is breaking the camel's back. My whole childhood, all I wanted was for you to give a shit about me for two fucking seconds, but the only time you actually paid attention to me was when you were parading me around like a show dog. I graduated top of my class and you didn't show up because you had to prepare for a case."

I slip my hand around his waist, bringing me closer now.

"You aren't a mother, you're a name that they put on a birth certificate. But Kaleigh, she is everything that I want my children to have. She is beautiful, she is kind, and most of all she's fucking loyal."

"That was quite a declaration, but it doesn't answer my question. When are you going to have a paternity test?"

Noah shakes his head. "Go put on your shoes, babycakes," he tells me as I turn to slip on the flip-flops that I took off near the couch. "Since you can't get it into your head to get the fuck out, we will." He grabs my hand, turning around. "Oh and, Mother, just so we're clear, you'll never set eyes on my children."

The door closes behind us with a big thud. I look up at Noah, seeing the tears in his eyes as he blinks them away.

"Fuck this," I say, turning back around and storming back in the door.

"You are…" I start saying, watching her blink her eyes at me. "Your son is kind. He is so kind. He's loving. He took care of me and bought vegan food just because I was sick. He's caring. He held my hair while I threw up. He's selfless. He let my niece paint his nails and toenails just to keep her busy. He is everything that you could ever wish your child to grow up to be and more. And instead of welcoming it into your life, you push it away because you're an egotistical bitch."

Her mouth opens wide.

"Yeah, that's right, I said it. You're a bitch. A high-class, nose so high in the air, I'm surprised you can see all the little things." My hands fly up in frustration. "You know that throne you sit up on that is high, well, let me tell you when you fall it's going to be a bumpy fucking fall and you'll have no one there to help you, no one." I turn now, walking out of the room and turning my head over my shoulder. "And all because you're a bitch." I turn back around and walk out to see that Noah and Austin are now there watching me.

"That was some speech," Noah says to me.

"Yeah, well, she poked the bear," I say, walking past them. "Now can someone please feed me? All this has gotten me hungry."

"I'll leave you two be. Just making sure I didn't need to get the go-to bag out to bury a body." Austin winks at me and then slaps Noah on the shoulder.

"Can we go eat, please?" I say, walking to his car, getting in as he gets in and buckles himself in.

"Can I just say I got so hot watching you stick up for me?" He leans over, giving me a kiss on the lips. "So hot I'm going to make sure I show you exactly how hot."

I roll my eyes. "Like I could stop you from showing me."

We pull out of the driveway and make our way back to our favorite Italian restaurant when he gets a call on his Bluetooth.

"Hello," he answers. "You're on speaker."

"Hey, Noah, it's Luca." A male's voice fills the car. "Guess what?"

"I have no idea," he answers.

"I found her," he says. "She lives in New York and works at Lennox hospital in the NICU."

"Shut the fuck up," he says, his voice booming out.

"Yes, sir, lives in Brooklyn, which is why she doesn't need a car. She has two kids and lives with her partner, Ruthie."

"Holy shit. I owe you one, man," he says, hanging up. He looks over at me. "Want to spend the weekend in New York?"

"You want me to come with you?" I ask him, not sure how I'm going to feel meeting his actual wife.

"Of course I want you to come with me. We can make a mini vacation out of it. Stroll through Central Park, take pictures in Times Square, have vacation sex."

I laugh at him. "I would love to go on vacation with you and have vacation sex."

He pumps his fist in the air and dials Lauren's number.

She answers on the third ring. "Hey."

"I need you to book two tickets first-class to New York. For Thursday to Sunday. I also need a swanky hotel to take your sister to."

"I'll do it tomorrow morning first thing. So I take it you found her?" she asks.

"Yes, we did," Noah says and then makes plans to see her tomorrow morning bright and early, and by bright he said he will be in by ten.

"I love you," I say, turning my back to the door.

His head whips around to look at me.

"I never got a chance to tell you when you declared your love for me and I wanted to say it back." I smile at him as he pulls over to the side of the street. "This thing with us started off as just me wanting to have really good sex.

"Great sex," he interjects. "With my huge cock. Proceed."

"Yes, great sex with the biggest cock I have ever seen in my life." I giggle.

"That's more like it."

"I ran away after the first night," I tell him, getting on my knees in the middle of the seat.

"And the second." He points out.

"And the second, but you chased me and never took no for an answer. You ate my food, which I forgot to tell you I burnt a pan and buried it in the back." I laugh when I see his eyes open wide. "You were there and you made me see that love isn't hard, it's work, but it's a work I want to do. So, let's go to New York and get you divorced so I can put a ring on it."

CHAPTER TWENTY-SEVEN

Noah

"Ladies and gentlemen, please fasten your seat belts, we will be landing shortly." The captain comes on and tells us. In the last three days it has been a rush of things. All papers have been filed and the divorce decree is in my pocket. I have someone waiting for me in New York who will accompany me to be the witness when we both sign it. I replay the conversation I had with Sabrina in my mind.

"Hello," she answered on the fourth ring, breathing as if she was running.

"Hey, is this Sabrina?" I asked her just in case it was her partner.

"This is she."

"Hey, it's me, Noah, Noah King. Your, um, husband of sorts," I said in one long breath.

"Holy shit, Noah," she said and I heard people in the background and the sound of horns in the distance. Definitely New York City. "How the heck are you?"

"I'm good," I said. "Actually, I'm great. I'm engaged and I'm going to be a father."

"That's wonderful," she said. "Congratulations."

"Thank you, thank you." I stopped and paused. "So about that, I would need an annulment."

"Is that so?" she asked and I could tell that she was smiling.

"Well, at first I wanted to ask for a divorce but then my future mother-in-law had a semi heart attack when I mentioned city hall. So divorce got thrown out and annulment was put on the table. I mean, since we never really consummated the wedding."

She then laughed out loud. "I get it. Actually my partner has been trying to drag me to the altar for years, but I always stalled. I guess this means I just may be a bride also."

I smiled as I leaned back in my chair. "That's wonderful. Listen, I'm flying into New York this Thursday. How about we meet Friday and sign the papers?"

"That sounds great. I'll text you my home address since I'm not working and I will be home with the kids."

"Great. Nice talking to you," I said, hanging up.

Now I look over at Kaleigh, who is passed out. She fell asleep as soon as we sat down. All she does is sleep and eat. I was worried at first, but after speaking with a doctor we found out it's perfectly normal. Once the wheels touch down she opens her eyes. "Are we here already?" she asks groggily, sitting up and looking out her window.

"Just landed." I watch her look out the window. "How did you sleep?"

"Great. I must have knocked out as soon as I sat down."

"Just about. How's your stomach? Are you still feeling queasy?" Another thing that is normal is that she is always queasy. She eats so many saltines I may have to buy stock in it.

"It feels a little bit better," she says, slipping her ballerina shoes on. She leans into me, kissing my lips.

Something else that has changed. I mean, we were pretty active in the sex department before, but now I have to make some nooners to quench her appetite. Her hormones are through the roof. At one point, I actually thought my cock would chafe. But nope, didn't happen. We walk off the plane first since we are in first class while I hold her hand, walking to get our bags. She's wearing her yoga pants and an oversized T-shirt and knitted sweater and she is the most gorgeous thing ever. Also you can start seeing the changes in her body. Her breasts are fuller and so fucking sensitive I made her cum yesterday just by rolling them.

"What are you thinking about over there?" she asks, laughing.

"Um."

"It better be because of me that you're sporting a boner. Here." She hands me her purse. "Cover that up."

I take it from her, holding it in front of me. When we get into the car, I give the cab driver the hotel's address.

"Swanky," she says, watching the city coming into sight. "I've actually never been here," she says, looking out at the Brooklyn Bridge. "Do you think we will have time to go to the Statue of Liberty?"

My hand reaches out to grab hers. "We can make it happen. What do you want to do first?"

"I think that is a given. I want to go and do yoga in Central Park." When we check in, her eyes open even more when we walk into our penthouse suite, overlooking Central Park. The floor-to-ceiling windows give you a panoramic view. She stands in the corner as the doorman deposits our luggage in the bedroom.

I walk to her, pulling her shoulders back to me. "It looks so busy," she says, watching the little yellow cabs zoom down the street. "Look over there." She points down to the park where we see all green and little dots that have to be people. "I want to go there."

"Then let's get changed and go," I tell her.

"It must be really cool here at night with the light and everything," she says, walking away from the window. "I wonder if we turned the lights on and you pressed me to the window and fucked me if people would see." She smiles at me like the little minx that she is.

"I may or may not have brought some lingerie with me, some that don't require you taking anything off." She runs her hands down my chest and cups my dick. "Some that give you easy access. You know, like if I would bend over and open my legs there would be nothing blocking you from pounding into me."

"Okay, first sex then yoga," I tell her, picking her up and placing her on the dining room table in the room.

"I think I need stretching. You might have to throw my legs over your shoulders." Her hands comes out to rip off my T-shirt while I pull her shirt over her head. The white lace bra, showing you her nipples that are pebbled and waiting for me. My hands go straight to her as I lean down and take one in my mouth, lace bra and all. I bite down on it, making her throw her head back as she grinds her hot covered pussy against my raging hard on. The next thing I know is I'm buried balls deep in her while she leans back a bit on the table and has both legs wrapped around my neck.

When we finally make it to the park, we see that we aren't the only ones with this idea and there is actually a couple that stops next to us, copying Kaleigh as she goes through different positions. She makes friends with about fifteen people as I lie on my yoga mat perfecting the corpse pose.

"Do I look okay?" Kaleigh asks as she comes out of the bathroom. It's finally annulment day and Kaleigh has been a nervous wreck the whole time. She has changed her outfit four times already. Now she is wearing tight blue jeans with a loose peach sweater. "You look amazing, just like you did in the skirt, and the shorts, and the other jeans. Stop, it's going to be okay."

"What if she doesn't sign it?" she asks quietly while she wrings her hands. "What if she decides she still wants to be married to you?"

I walk to her, grabbing her face in my hands. "Babycakes, it's going to be okay. Now let's go before you need to change again," I say, grabbing her hand and leading her downstairs where the car is waiting to take us to my wife.

We pull up to her address and we both take in the apartment building. Walking up the six flights of stairs, I'm almost starting to sweat till we finally make it to the door. Kaleigh squeezes my hand, smiling up at me. I knock once on the door and a deep voice says, "One minute."

I don't know what I'm expecting or who that is, but the woman answering the door is almost like she's from the Amazon. She must be easily over six foot four, her shoulders are almost wider than mine, and I'm pretty sure she can snap my neck like a twig between her legs. Her hair is wrapped in a bun on top of her head. "Yeah." Her voice comes out harsh.

"Um, I'm here for Sabrina," I finally mutter out while I try to stand in front of Kaleigh to have her blocked in case she snaps.

"So," she says, folding her arms over her chest. "You're the husband."

I don't know what to say because my eyes are on her bulging biceps. "Um," I stutter right when I see Sabrina in the background walking toward the door. She puts her small dainty hand on her bicep and laughs. "Relax there, Zena." She pushes in front of her when 'Zena' puts her hand on her shoulder and tucks her in front of her, one arm going around her neck.

"Noah," Sabrina says, smiling. "You haven't changed a bit. Come on in. Your friend just got here," she says, turning and pushing Zena away.

"I see you met my partner, Ruthie," she says to us both. "Her bark is worse than her bite." I smile and look back up and can kind of guarantee that her bite might take chunk out of me.

"Hi," Kaleigh says from beside me. "I'm Kaleigh, the baby momma." She reaches her hand out to shake Sabrina's hand and Ruthie's. It's in that moment two boys run into the room, both of them running around their mothers.

"Mom," one says.

"Momma," the other one says while chasing each other. "Bryan hit me."

While the other one says, "Dominic hit me first."

"You two, we have company," Ruthie says, stopping them both. "Now behave or I might have to put the smack down on you."

I look at her, then Sabrina and then the boys laugh out loud.

"Yeah right, Momma, we would just tickle you till you yelled mercy."

"Go watch a movie while Mom and I sign a couple of papers." She ushers them down the hall to wherever they watch television.

"Come on. I had him set up in the kitchen if that is okay," Sabrina says, walking down another tiny hallway. Till we make it back to the kitchen, which is no bigger than my walk-in closet. Will, who is going to be our witness, gets up, coming over to me.

"Hey, man, how you doing? Long time no see."

I shake his hand, nodding. "Shall we get to it?" I say, eager to have these papers signed.

Once Will sits down, I pull out the papers for him to look over. I had forwarded a copy to Sabrina the day after we spoke. She takes her copy and reads just to make sure nothing is changed and grabs the pen from Will and signs on the dotted line. I almost sigh in relief, but till I sign and Will signs, this thing is still legal. When she finishes, she hands me the pen and I hurriedly sign my name, handing the pen to Will.

Once he finishes I throw my hand in the air and yell, "Mazel Tov."

Which earns me a glare from Ruthie, a smile from Sabrina, a shake of the head from Will, and a kiss from my girl.

We leave soon after, holding hands, swinging them as we walk. "I have a surprise for tonight," I tell her, watching her eyes light up.

"Do you now?" She smiles. "Is it your dick in a box, because I gotta say I already got that surprise. In fact, twice today." She puts up her hand with two fingers. It would have been three if I had enough time to recover after she rode me this morning at breakfast.

"No, but it's a great idea for next time," I tell her as she rolls her eyes.

"What should I wear?" she asks me. "I don't think I packed anything fancy."

I throw my hand up to flag down a cab, opening the door and watching her climb in. "I have that all taken care of. All you have to do is sit down and be pampered."

"Really?"

I look at my watch. Right on time. "When we get back to the hotel, there will be two women there waiting for us."

"A threesome? Really, that's my surprise? And why two girls and not two guys?" She angrily hits my leg.

"Um, two women who will be massaging you and then doing your hair and makeup. But let's discuss this threesome, would you?"

She folds her arms over her chest. "Would you watch me fuck another guy?"

"Fuck no." I don't even take a second to think about it.

"Then I guess that answers your threesome question," she says.

"All I want for you today is for you to relax and be pampered. And be ready at ten."

"At ten?" She gasps out. "I'm going to have to take a nap before we go out."

"Already planned that," I say, knowing full well she would be half asleep by the time we walked out of the hotel room.

When we walk in the hotel room, the massage table is already set up, as well as the candles and roses. "Aww," she says, walking in. "Isn't this romantic." She leans up and kisses me. "So getting laid tonight."

I pull my eyebrows together and laugh, like that wasn't a given.

I leave her to her massage and go about planning the biggest surprise of my life and hopefully by the end of the night she'll be saying yes to forever.

When it's five minutes to ten I hear her yell, "Okay, I'm coming out."

I'm looking at the city lights as I sip some whiskey, my tux bowtie almost choking me. I turn to watch her walk out of the room and my heart stops.

She's stunning. Her hair is tied in the back and curled under. A few loose strands fall out, but I don't see anything else but her dress. A dress I entrusted Lauren to pick out. It's a champagne covered lace dress. Sweetheart neckline with little lace sleeves. There are crystals all down the dress, as well as on the little sleeves. It falls right to the floor, the bottom loose and sways as she walks over.

"You look beautiful," I tell her as she walks to me.

"And you have never looked more handsome."

I put my whiskey down and take her in my arms. "Shall we?" I lean down, kissing her lips lightly. We turn heads as we walk through the marble lobby, the sound of her heels on the floor. The limo driver waits for us to open his door.

"Oh, a limo." She claps her hands together with glee. "Best night ever."

"I hope so," I mumble, getting in after her.

"Where are we going?" she asks as soon as the door closes behind me.

"All in due time," I say as my palms start to sweat and my heart starts to pound fast. I use my finger to pull the collar away from my neck, giving me room to breathe.

We pull up to an underground parking garage. I step out first when the driver opens the door and hold my hand out for her to come out. "Oh, this is very secret service." She laughs as I guide her to the unmarked elevator.

I press the button and then turn to her. "You trust me?" I ask her as she nods. "Good, now close your eyes." And as soon as she does the elevator door pings open.

I hold her hand, escorting her inside and pressing the top button. When it comes to a stop and the door opens I guide her outside. It's perfect, as I look around and take in the tea candle lights hanging everywhere. The little table in the middle of the roof is filled with food and a bottle of non-alcoholic champagne chilling. A group of string quartets wait to play. I see the man who arranged it all. Marshall, Barbara's brother, also known as Empire State Building security honcho.

I guide her to the middle of the Empire State Building where you can see the whole city. Stopping her, I take both her hands in mine, kissing them and then dropping on one knee. "Open your eyes," I say and watch her, only her, as she takes in the whole thing.

Champagne rose bouquets are placed all over the roof top. The tea lights twinkle. She looks at the quartets that are now playing "Can't Help Falling in Love with You." Her hand goes to her mouth and she looks down and sees me on my knees. The whole thing finally dawns on her.

"From the moment I laid eyes on you, I knew you would change my life," I say to her, swallowing the lump that is forming in my throat now, a tear escaping her eye. "I sat next to you and I was drawn to you like a magnet. Did you know that when I got home that night I stalked you on Instagram?" I say, laughing, as I remember what seems like forever ago, while she shakes her head. "Then I texted you and you blew me off. Killed me, especially my ego."

She now laughs.

"That day I came to your work and watched you through the bushes."

"What?" she asks, smiling, wiping another tear.

"John, Austin, and I went on a stake-out. That's why I had black under my eyes. I used shoe polish. I had to see if you were with someone else. I had to scope out the competition."

"There was no one else," she says, shaking her head.

"Then I pretended that I wanted to be your friend when all I wanted was to spend time with you. You see, for the first time in my life, I didn't have to pretend to be interested. I was. I didn't have to pretend that I was happy, because I was generally happy to be wherever you were. Well, except that goat yoga shit. I just felt violated, but I would do it again if you asked me to. When you left me the second time, I thought I was going to turn green like the hulk and bust out of my clothing. But then I came to you and I looked in your beautiful blue eyes and I saw that you were just as unsure of what was going on as I was, but more importantly I saw that you wanted to be with me."

She rolls her eyes at that one.

"I never thought I wanted kids, but the minute you told me you were carrying my child the only thought was when can we have another one. The only thing I could think of was to make sure you stayed with me forever." I smile as a tear falls on our hands. "So I know we do things a little bit backward, and I know I drive you crazy," I say, reaching inside my suit jacket to grab the blue ring box that has been burning a hole in my pocket the second she told me she was pregnant. Okay, not the second but two days after. Opening the ring, I see her gasp. I know they say size matters, but not with Kaleigh. Instead of your perfect round diamond, I went with a blush pink oval one in rose gold. "Kaleigh Harrison, will you do me the honor of being my wife? Of growing old with me, of driving me crazy with your empty cups all around the house? Of being the best mother that I know our children will have?"

The tears are now flowing freely as she nods and whispers out, "Yes." I get up now, placing the ring on her finger, grabbing her up, and kissing her while I twirl her around.

"You guys can come out now," I yell while she looks around in shock as her whole family comes out all dressed to the nines. The men all sporting tuxes and the women have ball gowns on. Lauren and Austin are there with Rachel and Gabe. Her mother and father come out both with smiles on their faces. John, Dani, Harvey, and his wife along with Stephanie all come up to us to congratulate us. She looks around. "What is everyone doing here?"

"Well, you see, I know I promised your mother a big catholic wedding, yada, yada, yada, but I knew I didn't want another minute to pass without you being my wife, so we are going to get married here. Tonight."

Her hand flies to her mouth as I walk her around the table and she sees the aisle I had set up for her. There is a red carpet down the middle with white chairs on each side. An overhead canopy of champagne roses sit in the middle with someone waiting in the middle to marry us. Lauren comes over and hands her the bouquet. She reaches out to hold on to her while they whisper something in each other's ears with Lauren nodding and saying, "Where else would I be?"

So we take our places, me in the front of the altar with Austin by my side as Lauren walks down first and then Kaleigh, her face radiating with the biggest smile I have ever seen, her arm tucked in her father's arm.

On a beautiful night in New York City, on the top of the Empire State Building, I finally get to kiss my bride as she tells everyone that she finally tempted the playboy.

CHAPTER TWENTY-EIGHT

Kaleigh

Three ish months later

I'm sitting here on the couch with tears running down my face. My body almost looks the same, except my tits are bigger and I have a basketball in my belly, or better yet, I have Noah's son.

That's right. A month ago we went for an ultrasound. Well, there was no mistaking that.

As soon as they placed the wand on my stomach, there was my little man's legs open, penis floating. Noah lifted his hands in the air as if he'd just won the lottery. "I need a picture of that. My kid is packing," he said to the unamused doctor. "Actually make it ten. I need to send them to my friends."

I was just mesmerized that a human was actually growing inside me.

Now here I am sitting down, waiting for Noah to come home. I don't have to wait long before he rushes into the house, worry and panic on his face. "Oh my God, are you okay? Is the baby okay?" He sits in front of me, putting his hand on my stomach, the baby kicking as soon as he knows his father is near. He wipes my cheek with the tears that are staining it.

"Look," I say to him, pointing to a McDonald's bag. "Look at what your son made me buy." I sob out while he leans in and opens the bag, showing him that there are eight cheeseburgers in there. Not one, not two, but fucking eight.

"What?" He looks at the bag with a smirk and then asks with a smile on his face. "Did you eat any?"

"NO, not yet. But I want to." I grab the bag from him, bringing it to my nose. I reach in, taking one out and opening it. "I hate meat, I hate dairy," I say, biting in, moaning, "but your child wants it. My only craving is meat. Can't this kid crave, I don't know, Brussel sprouts? Or, I don't know, spinach since he's like in the ninety-fifth percentile." I take another bite, then another till I'm on my third one. "Why is this so good?" I say between chewing. My mouth is full of the cheeseburger.

"Babycakes, you know this is normal. The doctor said so." He looks at me while he holds my knee in his hand and puts one hand on my belly. "You made me eat five Philly cheese sandwiches last week just so you could smell it," he says and the baby kicks his hand, so he leans in, kissing my belly and saying, "Hey there, slugger, can you give your mom a break, please?"

The baby kicks and kicks and punches. I glare at him. "I bet he's going to like you better than me," I say and my eyes start to burn. So I blink them faster. "I'm the mom. They are supposed to love the mom more. I mean, look at me," I say, looking down at my belly. "He's in me. He should love me more."

"Kaleigh," he says, sitting down next to me and then dragging me on him. "He is going to worship the ground you walk on. You will be the reason he smiles and his eyes light up. You will be his whole world."

I swallow down my tears. "You think so?" I ask him while the baby plays gymnastics in my stomach.

"No, I know so." He leans in to kiss my lips softly. "Now how about I take you upstairs and run a bath for you?" He kisses my cheek and then my jaw.

"Will you join me?" I ask him. I thought that once we got married and once we got into the hang of things that the sex would stop. I was wrong. We have it more than ever. The only thing we worry about is what positions we can do it in. Missionary is pretty much out of the question since my stomach gets in the way, but we always keep things interesting.

"Is that even a question?" he asks me, getting up and starting to walk to the stairs.

"Wait!" I yell before he gets any farther. "The burgers," I say, reaching my hand out to the air while he turns around to come back to the table.

"You're going to bring the burgers in the bath with us?" he asks, walking upstairs.

I tilt my head to the side. "No, silly, that will get them wet. I'm going to eat them after."

"Whatever you want, babycakes." And just like that I feel more in love with him. "We can't fill the tub too much. We almost flooded the kitchen last time."

"That was all your fault. You teased me to no end." I smile, thinking of when he came into the tub and decided to 'wash me.'

"I wanted to make sure that pussy was extra clean. It's not my fault the soap got all slippery and I had to rub places." He leans in, licking my ear. "You loved every second of it." His hot words in my ear make my body shiver. "You want that again, me washing your pussy, my fingers going in and out of you while you have your feet on each side of the tub, open for me, your clit." And that is the last of what he has to say because I turn around and attack his mouth with mine. And I make him wash me till I turn around and ride him so hard, we actually do flood the kitchen this time.

I'm sitting in the middle of the bed when he finally comes upstairs after having a guy come out and check out the mess. "Jesus, did you finish it all?" he says while seeing the empty pizza box in front of me.

"It's not me, it's the baby." I start to feel tears come. "I didn't want to eat it. I told him it wasn't good." I rub my full belly, feeling my boy do cartwheels.

"Honey," he says, coming closer to me. "It doesn't matter. Just next time I'll have to order two meat lovers instead of one," he says, opening the veggie one, finding it all in one piece. "The things you do for your kids," he says while eating the veggie pizza.

"Do you think we should have a baby shower?" I turn on my side, watching him eat. "I mean, it's a normal thing to have."

"Who wants to throw you a baby shower?" he asks while taking another piece.

"Well, Lauren did actually." I look at him. "It's tradition."

"Oh, I wonder if we can get the same girl Austin got when he ordered the penis balloons."

"We are not getting penis balloons," I say, sitting up, my stomach blocking me, having my shoulders slouch.

"Why? He has a penis," he says, throwing the veggie pizza back into the box. "We have to have some penis decorations."

I sit here as I scratch my stomach round and round. "I'm leaving everything to Lauren. We need to go and make a register."

I hear him groan as he rolls to his back. "We barely survived crib shopping."

"That's because you asked them if you could get in and see if it was sturdy enough." I point at him.

"If my son is going to sleep in it we need to know it's top of the line." He gets up, grabbing the pizza boxes. "Anyway, let's do this whole registry thing and see what happens." He winks at me and walks away.

"Bring up some of those disgusting pepperoni sticks!" I yell and then send a text to Lauren with the go ahead for the baby shower.

With the amount of meat I am eating, I'm surprised I don't moo when I walk down the street. "Noah," I yell from the bathroom. I am now almost nine months. Thirty-seven weeks, to be exact. Noah comes running upstairs, his body slick with sweat from just running.

"What happened?" he asks, coming in, panic in his eyes.

"I'm so fat," I cry, my hands coming out to my sides. "I don't even know if my vagina is swollen or not." I try looking down and see nothing. "See, nothing. I can't see anything. It's just stomach. I miss my toes."

"Babycakes, you look like a goddess." He comes to rub my huge stomach. "You're a goddess for my kid." He kisses my stomach. "And more to come."

"I don't think I want another child. I mean, I want more than one, but I'm not sure my body can handle it. I mean, look at me." I point up and down my body.

"It will be okay. You have a pretty new dress. You will put it on and smile and laugh and eat lots of hot dogs and hamburgers."

"My whole body looks swollen." I look down and although I have gained almost forty pounds it is all in my tits, ass, and belly. "You put this baby in me. You need to have sex with me to take it out."

He looks at me, confused.

"Lauren said if I play with my nipples and we have sex, I might dilate or something."

"Wow, I don't think I've ever felt more like a piece of meat than now, and I like it," he says, walking into the shower. "But Lauren just called and she said if we are late she will skin us both alive. Me first, you after you have the baby."

I waddle—yes, you read right—I fucking waddle over to the bed where I sit down, my stomach feeling like it's in my throat. I lean back while I pick up the bra that I'm using today. This is one place that went from zero to hero. My nice B cup is now a solid D if not closing in on DD. Putting on my bra and thong, I walk over to the closet we both share now. I grab the blue full-length lace dress with slits all around the legs. Noah comes into the closet with a towel wrapped around his waist. Little drops of water linger on his chest. I lean in, kissing his chest, then step into my dress, turning to have him zip me up. The zip goes up and he kisses my neck after I lean into his chest, turning my head so he can kiss me. His hand goes to my stomach while he kisses me softly on the lips.

"Love you, wife," he says with a smile on his face.

"Love you, husband."

He holds my hand gently, softly, securely while we walk into Lauren's backyard. I stop when I take in the scene. There are more penis balloons than I thought would be possible to have in one sitting. It makes the anniversary party look like child's play.

"What the hell is all this?" I look around, seeing Lauren with a scowl on her face.

She comes storming over, her eyes shooting daggers at my husband. "I said you can have a couple of balloons. I didn't say over five hundred." She looks around as the helium penis floats high.

"Actually there are six hundred and fifty." He looks at his work with a smile on his face. "The suppliers ran out," he says, grabbing a drink from the waiter passing by, in the shape of a penis, topped with a penis straw.

"Oh, honey, you're here." My mother comes to me as she is wearing glasses with a penis point up in the middle. "These glasses are so funny. Look, I have a penis on my face."

I take in my mother dressed in a floral dress, with pink sunglasses and penis but what gets me is a wide brimmed hat in a black paper braid material featuring a wired 'shapeable' brim, hatband, and bow in a wide, white-on-black polka dot ribbon, white 'pearl' accents and an extra-large white rose. "Mom, what is with the hat?" I ask her, confused.

"Oh, this, it's a derby hat," she says, throwing her hands in the air. "I didn't want Noah's friends to think we didn't have class, so."

"I love it." Noah puts his two cents in as my father walks outside from inside.

"Would you look at this," he says, watching his feet at he comes down the stairs.

He's coming to us with something strapped to his chest. "It's called 'nurse me tender.' It's for Noah so he can see what breastfeeding looks like." The thing is tied around his waist and over his shoulder, a bottle placed where the breast would go. He grabs a baby doll and puts it to the bottle. "Look, I'm almost a woman."

"Holy shit," Austin says as he comes into the backyard. He goes to Lauren and wraps his arm around her waist, bending to whisper in her ear.

Her hard face goes from kill him to it's going to be okay. She nods her head at him while he walks to us, looking at my father and him trying to breastfeed the baby and then my mother and her ridiculous hat.

"You're lucky that you're giving her a nephew." Austin points at Noah while he smiles.

My stomach gets tight for a second as I rub my hands over it in a circle. "Oh," I say out loud. "That was a big kick," I say as I get another tightness around my belly and this time it leads to my back. "Ouch," I say while Noah looks at me and then the unthinkable happens. My water breaks, gushing out and onto Austin's shoes.

"What the fuck?" Austin says while I look at Noah.

"I think my water just broke."

CHAPTER TWENTY-NINE

Noah

"Heee hhheee hoooo hooo heee heee hooo hooo. That's it, just breathe through your nose, out through your mouth," the nurse tells Kaleigh while her eyes are closed and she is focusing on the pain.

She is sitting in the middle of the hospital bed with her legs crossed, wearing a hospital gown. The contractions are every four minutes. I am kneeling behind her, rubbing her shoulders and her back when the contractions come again.

We are in the hospital finally after her water broke all over Austin's shoes and he turned and almost yacked. We all got her into the car where I got us to the hospital. We went through lots of arguments over where to have the baby. Kaleigh wanted to have it in our bedroom, in a tub. I was almost in agreement when she took us to go watch another room do it. One look at the tub and I vetoed that. So we compromised. We'll have it in the hospital if I bring all her Zen stuff. The room lights are dim, to almost off, the sound of the ocean and waves in the background softly playing along with some flutes and bells.

"Knock. Knock. Knock," Dede says as she walks in with her balloons in one hand and flowers in the other hand, her hat still on her head. "What is that noise?" She scrunches up her nose.

"It's Zen music, Mother." Lauren walks into the room, pushing herself forward. Sneezing once, twice, three times. "Is that sage?" she asks and Kaleigh just grunts.

"Okay, time to do a check," the nurse says as she gets off the bed. "Lie back, feet up," she says, getting up and going to the side and grabbing a pair of gloves. "Okay," she says, lifting up the gown. As soon as she does that Austin walks right in, his eyes going straight to Kaleigh on the bed. "Oh my God," he says and looks to the side and then at the floor and then puts his hand to his mouth. "I'm going to be sick," he says, looking pale.

Lauren goes to him, grabbing his face.

"Why does it look like that?" He looks like he is going to cry. "Why is it puffy?"

I put my head back and laugh. "Dude, the baby is almost crowning. You should come watch."

"Are you fucking insane?" Austin says and walks out of the room while Lauren grins.

"He gets queasy."

I look down to see that the nurse has her hand all inside Kaleigh.

"You're at nine centimeters. This one is coming in fast."

"It's 'cause she played with her nipples and we had sex before the shower." I look at Lauren. "Sorry about that. I just couldn't resist. She needed the sperm."

The nurse gets up, throws her gloves in the trash, and calls someone on the phone. "Okay, the doctor is on his way up. We are going to get everything ready," she says, going to the corner of the room and turning a light on in one of those glass cases. She grabs some blankets and opens them up. She rolls it close to the bed.

"Something is happening," Kaleigh says while her face is now covered with sweat. "I feel so much pressure. It hurts so much now." Her head goes from left and right and she tries to breathe, but that is out the window and now she is howling in pain.

My hands go to my head, pulling my hair while Lauren holds her hands and tells her that everything will be okay.

I'm holding her other hand now as I move the hair away from her face.

"Okay, Kaleigh, how about we try some pushing?" the nurse says as she stands in front of her. "Bear down and push." Kaleigh grabs my hand, puts her chin to her chest, and groans out as she pushes.

"One, two, three, you're doing great. Seven, eight, nine, ten. Okay," she says, grabbing another pair of gloves. "Okay, that was great. The baby is crowning," she says, looking down at Kaleigh.

The doctor comes in with another nurse, who puts on the doctor's scrubs jacket. "Hey there, Kaleigh, Noah," she greets us as she sits on the stool in front of Kaleigh as she takes in the baby's head.

"Okay, looks good. How about we push one more time?" Dr. Noelle says as she puts some gloves on and the nurse starts counting.

I look down at the head coming out and put my hand over my mouth. It's not a normal size head. "Holy shit, is he going to have a small head? Did my penis knock him in the head? Is that why it's so small?"

Dr. Noelle looks at me and laughs. "Noah, she's crowning, which means the head is coming down. It'll show more soon. Now, Kaleigh, stop pushing for a second," she says and puts her finger inside, turning it around the baby's head. "Now let's push again, okay?" she says and as Kaleigh bears down I take my phone out and tape my son's head popping out of his mother. "Okay, stop pushing. The head is out." I look up to see Lauren and Dede with tears running down their cheeks. I look down and see the doctor grab onto his head and watch as his shoulders come out and his whole body slides out like a snake and she suctions his mouth while she holds him upside down and tears run down my face. I look down at Kaleigh, who has a red face and her chest is going up and down while she pants and cries as the doctor places our son on her chest.

"Oh my God." She sobs out and her hand cradles our child as he cries out his first sound. "My baby." She sobs as I lean down and kiss his wet head and then kiss the mother of my child, the wife I'm so lucky to have and the warrior in our family.

"I love you so much. You are so brave, baby, so, so brave." I kiss her face while the nurse takes the baby from us and the doctor asks me to cut the umbilical cord.

She hands me the scissors and I cut between the white plugs. The nurse takes him to the bed, where she weighs him, cleans him, puts a diaper on him, and then brings him back to us. "Here he is, a whopping ten pounds, two ounces." She smiles as the doctor finishes with Kaleigh and pushes back.

Lauren and Dede have given us time to ourselves by going to tell everyone about him.

"Hey there, it's me, your dad," I tell him while he blinks at us, just looking. "This is your mom. She's the best. She is going to make you try some crazy stuff with her food. Just go with it, okay? She is going to make us do things we don't want to do, but we will do it only because we love her and want to see her smile. You probably fell in love with her the second you looked at her, didn't you? I should know, it happened to me also. She was the one who finally tempted the playboy." And with that, I kiss him and my wife and thank whatever lucky star out there that made me fall into her life.

EPILOGUE

One year later

"Daddy's home," I say as I walk into our new house we just bought on the water. It has a huge amount of property and a barn in the back that Kaleigh has converted into a yoga studio.

I look around and don't see or hear anyone, so I walk through the house that now holds every single child's toy known to mankind. My mother, even though she is a bitch, has taken a liking to her grandson. Some even say she likes him a lot. Sometimes she sends him packages twice in a day. I think it's overboard and our relationship is still strained, but Kaleigh says as long as my mother gives him love she will hold her tongue.

With curly blond hair and sky blue eyes, his chubby face is always smiling, except when his mother walks out of the room or you don't give him meat fast enough. Walking over to the back door, I open it and see my boy walking with his hands in the air, trying to balance himself while Kaleigh runs after him. I watch the two of them with a big smile on my face. Love, it's a great fucking feeling. "I'm going to get you," she says while my son squeals with delight, his chubby legs going as fast as they can.

"No, mama, no."

I make my way to them and they both don't see me till I grab my wife around the waist, throwing her over my shoulder. The baby weight is long gone from her long and her frame is lean. Her bare tanned legs kick up a storm as she laughs.

"Matteo, look, I've got mommy," I tell him as he turns around and comes to us. He falls on his bum and then bends over to get up on his feet again, walking to me. "Dada, Dada, Dada." He comes to me, pulling on my pants to pick him up. I drop Kaleigh while I bend down to grab him. Picking him up, he grabs my face while he comes to give me an open-mouth slobbering kiss. "Hey, handsome. Were you a good boy for mommy?" I ask him as he points to himself and says, "Boy".

I smile at him and look down at his mother. "Hey, you." I lean down and kiss her lips, and it always gets me like it was our first time. I still get hard every single time I'm near her.

"Jesus, do you two ever keep your hands off each other?" I hear from Austin who is coming into the backyard, followed by Rachel, Gabe, who I swear grew a foot in a month, and a waddling Lauren.

"As long as she's near me, my hands will be all over her."

"Yeah, remember when I slept over and you and Uncle Noah had a naked sleepover? That was gross," Rachel says while Austin glares at us.

"She's exaggerating. I wasn't naked; Kaleigh was covering all my parts," I whisper. "I was hiding in her vagina." I laugh while Austin groans. "What are you guys doing here?" I ask them.

"We came to get Matteo for a sleepover at our house," Rachel says, putting her hands out for Matteo, who flies down to join his favorite cousin.

"What, why?" I turn, looking at Kaleigh.

"Well, I wanted to have adult time. Besides, it's our dateaversary." She wraps her hands around my waist.

"Okay, I've got his bag already. Let's go," Lauren says. "It's so hot outside that I'm sweating rivers."

I look at Austin. "If you think that is a lot of water, wait till it's gushed when she gives birth." I laugh as his face pales. "Remember when I came out into the waiting room after Matteo was born and showed you the video, you fainted." I throw my head back, laughing at him turning pale and slumping in the chair.

"Okay, give mama kisses." Kaleigh picks up Matteo and kisses him on the mouth. "You be good for Auntie Lolo and Uncle Austin."

"Lolo," Matteo mumbles while he reaches out to her.

"There is my little boy. Auntie Lolo brought you a ball. You want the ball?"

I watch as they carry my son out of the backyard while I look at my wife. "So what do you have planned for our dateaversary? By any chance are we naked during this thing?"

"I'm sure we can work that out," she says as she grabs my hand and walks into the house with me holding onto her hand. "I was thinking a massage. With oil." She wiggles her eyes at me. "Some pizza in bed and," she turns and whispers, "Netflix and chill."

I stop on the stairs and put my hand to my chest. "Jesus, I think I just fell more in love with you. What type of pizza?"

"Meat lovers. Is there any other choice?" She smiles at me, turning to wrap her hands around my neck and kissing my lips. "Come on, playboy. Let me tempt you with some meat." She throws her head back and laughs with her whole heart. And, in that moment, there is no place I would rather be than here in this spot.

COMING 2018
TEMPT THE NEIGHBOR

Luca

A weekend of fun, a weekend to let go and be wild. Booze cruise that is what they called it and they were not lying. For that weekend, I was just Luca. Not Luca the one with the highest IQ, or Luca that will graduate Harvard Law first in his class. Just plain old Luca.

Attending a welcome back party for my boss's daughter isn't how I want to spend my Sunday. But walking in and seeing her turn and look at me knocks me on my ass. but not as much as seeing my eyes looking right back at me in the form of my son.

For five years she haunted my dreams, now she's my next door neighbor and the mother of my child.

For five years, I've looked into my son's face and seen his father smiling back at me. Now I'm home and he's there every time I walk outside.

Only one thing left to do. I have to tempt my neighbor.

BOOKS BY NATASHA MADISON

Something Series
Something So Right
Something So Perfect
Something So Irresistible – January 2018
Tempt Series
Tempt The Boss
Tempt The Playboy
Tempt The Ex – December 2017
Tempt The Neighbor – 2018
Heaven & Hell Series
Hell and Back
Pieces of Heaven
Novellas
Cheeky
Madison Rose Books
Only His

ACKNOWLEDGMENTS

Every single time I keep thinking it's going to be easy. It takes a village to help and I don't want to leave anyone out.

My Husband: Thank you for holding my hand and being there with every step that I take. Thank you for understanding how much this means to me and for supporting me/ I love you!

My Kids: Matteo, Michael, and Erica, Thank you for letting me do this. . Thank you for going on this journey with me.

Crystal: My hooker and bestie. What don't you do for me? Everyone needs someone like you in their corner and I am so blessed than you chose to be in mine. I can't begin to thank you for the support, love and encouragement along the way.

Rachel: You are my blurb bitch. Each time you do it without even reading this book and you rocked it. I'm so happy that I ddin't give up when you ignored my many messages.

Lori: I don't know what I would do without you in my life. You take over and I don't even have to ask or worry because I know everything will be fine, because you're a rock star!

Beta girls: Teressa, Natasha M, Lori, Sian, Yolanda, and Carmen, Yamina. You girls made me not give up. You loved each and every single word and wrote and begged and pleaded for more.

Madison Maniacs: This group is my go to, my safe place. You push me and get excited for me and I can't wait to watch us grow even bigger!

Mia: I'm so happy that Nanny threw out Archer's Voice and I needed to tell you because that snowballed to a friendship that is without a doubt the best ever!

Neda: You answer my question no matter how stupid they sound. Thank you for being you, thank you for everything!

Emily: Thank you for holding my hand and not giving up.

BLOGGERS. THANK YOU FOR TAKING A CHANCE ON ME. You give so much of yourself effortlessly and you are the voice that we can't do this without.

My Girls: Sabrina, Melanie, Marie-Eve, Lydia, Shelly, Stephanie, Marisa. Your support during this whole ride has been amazing. I can honestly say without a doubt that I have the best Squad of life!!!!

And Lastly and most importantly to YOU the reader, Without you none of this would be real. So thank you for reading!

Made in the USA
Middletown, DE
04 June 2020